This book is for anyone who
wearing a mask than bei
I see you.

You are beautiful the way you are.

feels more comfortable

in their own skin.

One

The Dead Boys were Kirsty's favorite band. They'd gotten her through every tough time in her life—breakups, book rejections, moving into her own place...even if it was approximately five minutes from her mom.

Yeah, sure, she was thirty and still talked to her mom every day. But she liked her mom.

Anyway. What mattered was that she turned to the Dead Boys when things were hard. And tonight was one of those times.

She was away from home on a book tour, so the last thing she was doing was normal Kirsty stuff. Tonight she wasn't the hometown girl that everyone knew too much about. She was here to blow off some steam. Be normal. Whatever that was.

The Zombies Music Hall hosting the event reminded her of House of Blues but slightly seedier, which was totally her jam.

Hardwood floors were peppered with dark patches from too many feet trotting over them. Thick velvet curtains blocked the stage from view with the Zombies logo burned into it. A sea of bodies covered in black, ripped jeans and Dead Boys tees filled the standing room area. Looking around the room, the last of Kirsty's tension melted away. These were her people.

She'd downed two local IPAs and had a nice buzz going. It was her last night to get wild. Indulge herself and be this Kirsty before she headed back to her real life. The way things were going, she was totally hoping to hook up tonight. It had become sort of a habit to have a one-night stand when she was on tour for a new book.

The bar was packed. The Dead Boys had been popular when she was in college. Though not as popular now, they still did gigs like this one in smaller venues and stages across the country. The Dead Boys were made up of three women who dressed all in black. They had a dark academia vibe that was right up her alley.

The lead singer, who was also the guitar player, wore a long Victorian-style skirt with a slit up one leg. Her hair was always up and she wore dark round glasses with black lenses. Totally giving Mina Harker vibes. The bass player was a goth Britney from her "Baby One More Time" era but with Doc Martens instead of sneakers. The drummer gave Velma from *Scooby-Doo* if Velma was a salacious, all-black-wearing badass.

Their songs had been the soundtrack to her latest book and the chance to see them live on her book tour was too good to pass up.

Even if it was way too people-y here.

Instead of her normal author garb—which was a basic black with subtle goth makeup framed by her thick fall of black bangs—she was wearing blue jeans and a band tee she'd ordered off the internet. She'd been traveling all day so hadn't had time to straighten her hair. Instead it was up in a messy bun. And her contacts had made her eyes itchy and red, so she wore her backup glasses. The big, red-framed pair that she liked to use when she was writing. They made it easier to see the monitors on her desk.

Some guy bumped her, spilling some of his beer on her arm. Because of course he would. But this was a concert, and she expected to leave smelling of stale beer and weed. Just not so soon.

"Sorry. God, it's packed tonight."

"Yeah," she said. Trying to make it clear that she wasn't here to chat. But then she took in his shaggy black hair with long bangs that fell over his forehead. High cheekbones and a mouth that was wide and lush. He even had on the same Dead Boys tee she did. The band's name and two skeletons with large fluorescent sunglasses wearing sombreros.

This man was sexy and a fan, just like her. So she changed her mind. "Good for the band that more people are into their music again, but sucks for fans like us."

"Indeed."

There was a sparkle in his eyes as he clocked her tee. A slow smile lit his face.

"Can I get you a drink instead of just spilling one on you?" he asked.

"I'm not sure we should leave this spot," she said, glancing around the crowded floor in front of the stage.

"I've got a table in the VIP section near the stage," he said.

VIP seats. There was more to hot T-shirt than met the eyes. She was a fan but hadn't thought to get the VIP package.

"Nice for you."

"You too. Want to join?"

"Duh."

He nodded and turned toward the bar. The rear view was just as nice as the front, she thought. His black jeans were skintight, hugging a cute firm ass. His shoulders were broad and his arms were muscly. Not that she normally went for the jock type.

Not that he was a jock. With the dark hair, eyeliner and black clothing he was dressed like the goth guy type that she was usually attracted to. He had to be broken in some way— we all are.

Did he grow up with too little money? Or too much? He had VIP tickets and that look of ease that said he'd been comfortable growing up. Surely there was more than a bit of envy as she observed him. *Stop analyzing it.*

Her problem was that after spending so much time at her keyboard writing, she tended to break every person she interacted with down like they were a character in her book, or worse, a puzzle she had to solve.

He stopped at the bar. "What do you want?"

She ordered the same craft beer he was drinking and then followed him to the table. The VIP section was literally two tables with four chairs each jammed around them. They were separated from the general admission section with a very tatty-looking velvet rope.

He gestured for her to sit at the lone table with a reserved sign. She sat down just as the house lights dimmed, the velvet curtains opened and the band started playing. The lonely sound of the acoustic guitar of her favorite of their songs... "Death is Just a Pit Stop."

She sang along with the opening, realizing the guy next to her was singing too. Their eyes met in that way that only happens at concerts where time almost stops as you enter the band's world. They both nodded and stood up to sing and dance. Getting lost in the music.

They had an intermission after "Hunting in a Killer Moon," so they sat down and ordered shots. "What's your name?"

His voice was low and raspy like hers from singing along with the band.

"Kirsty. You?"

"Jasper."

"Nice. I bet you were the only kid with that name in school," she said.

He flushed. "It was my dad's name."

"Everyone always calls me Kristy even though it's Kirsty."

"Annoying," he said.

"Yeah," she said. Growing up it had hurt. Why couldn't teachers and other kids remember her name. As if she were invisible. Which had led to the one lie she couldn't shake. In those moments, it made her feel better to pretend a voice from the other side was calling to her and create an excuse to leave. No one forgot her name after that, even if it did make her weird in a different way.

Tonight though, she enjoyed just being a girl who liked the Dead Boys.

Six shots of tequila were delivered to their table and after the waitress left, Jasper leaned back in his chair crossing his big arms over his chest. "Favorite song from the Dead Boys."

"'Death.' I mean, that one got me through my first breakup," she said. True, though that the breakup was with her first literary agent—one that totally didn't get her voice. It made her so angry that she started writing her odd little cozy mystery series about a woman who could talk to the dead and used their help to solve crimes. Funny that as soon as she stopped trying to write to please her big agent, she found her voice and a story that publishers actually wanted to buy.

"Nice. I found them after a breakup too. Same song. I blasted it in my room every day for two weeks. My roommate hated it and would pound on my door telling me to use headphones."

"You can't listen to 'Death' with headphones," she said as she licked salt from her hand, glancing up to see him watching her. She dropped some salt onto his hand and arched her eyebrow at him. His pupils dilated.

He licked his hand slowly…sensually. It took all her willpower not to imagine his tongue on her hand. Then they raised their shot glasses, downing their shots and then biting into their slices of lime.

"What was your major in college?" she asked. It was hard to guess. At school she'd been able to peg everyone's archetypes at a glance, but out in the real world it was harder.

She suspected most people struggled to know who they were. How to define themselves away from the roles they'd fallen into in school. Popular, jock, geek, misfit. The adult world blurred those lines.

Personally she was still struggling to become who she wanted to be. She had her author persona, a serious woman with a gothic edge who theoretically spoke to ghosts. And then she had regular Kirsty who still wore anime T-shirts and jeans and wanted to live close to her mom.

"Film and Television production. I'm a broadcast journalist. You?"

"Wait what?" she asked.

He shrugged. "Not as glam as you might be thinking. I'm a segment producer on a morning chat show. Basically I make sure things run smoothly."

"That sounds cool," she said.

"Yeah?" A surprised smile lit up his face. "What about you?"

"Medieval French literature and philosophy."

He started laughing. "Something practical."

"Don't start. That's what everyone says." His hand was lying on the table between them. She wanted to thread her fingers through his—anything to touch him and make sure this guy she was vibing with was real. Time to act first and think later. She lifted his hand, gently licking the back of it, and shook some salt on it.

He took her hand and did the same. A shiver of awareness spread up her arm at the touch of his tongue against her bare skin, tightening her nipples in a way that had her squirming in her seat.

They did another shot. As the tart lime wedge drowned the aftertaste of cheap tequila, she realized that she actually *liked* this guy. He was fun. Just what she needed more of in her life.

Normally she hooked up with a guy in the hotel bar while on a book tour. An average bloke she'd never regret not seeing again. Jasper was fresh—a nice guy that she had more than off-the-charts chemistry with. Plus she was leaving in a day, so there was no way this could get complicated.

Three hours later the show was over and they were standing outside of the bar. She was drenched with sweat, slightly buzzed from a third round of shots, and feeling good in a way she hadn't in a long time.

His blue eyes looked bright and fascinating as she stared up at him under the umbrella that he'd offered to share with her. It was September; she should have anticipated rain when she left her hotel, but really had just wanted to get to the concert so she'd have a good spot to see the band.

They were so close; his body heat kept her warm against the chill of the rain. Glancing up she couldn't tear her eyes from his jaw and his full mouth. That lower lip of his caught her attention and there was no way she could look away. She licked her own lips without even thinking about it.

He groaned.

Going up on her tiptoes, she sucked his lip into her mouth as she'd been wanting to do for hours.

He groaned again. The sound reverberated through her body.

His free hand gripped her butt, pulling her closer, more fully into contact with him. He was warm and tasted of beer and tequila. Her ears were buzzing with the drums' beat and lyrics from the Dead Boys' last song, "Find Joy."

Joy was one thing she didn't really give much time to. There was writing and worrying about royalties and if she'd be paid on time. There was adulthood and figuring out what would happen next. And there was the anxiety that someday her fans would discover that she, unlike her famous heroine, couldn't actually speak to ghosts.

But as Jasper's tongue rubbed over hers…joy exploded through her fuzzy brain.

Her body buzzed with need. Desire consumed her as a car pulled up next to them. Jasper broke off the kiss and lifted his head.

"This one's ours," he said.

She got into the back seat, sliding all the way across. Once Jasper had the umbrella closed he draped one arm along the back of the seat, his fingers playing with a tendril of her hair that had come free, wrapping one of her curls around his finger while he cupped the back of her neck.

Then his mouth was on hers again. Jasper was tequila, joy and freedom. No responsibility or consequences.

Delicious.

They got out in front of a building that wasn't her hotel.

"Where are we?"

"My place. I didn't know your address," he said, his arms around her waist. The rain had lightened up as they stood outside. "That okay?"

For a minute she hesitated. He was a stranger. A cute, racy one, granted. But a stranger all the same.

"I'm a decent dude. If you want to go somewhere else, the Uber will take you," he said. "My mom raised me right."

She wasn't really worried about going with him. Her gut said this guy was okay, and frankly her body didn't really care. It had been a long time since she'd been laid. And this hookup felt right.

"I'm good," she said, kissing him again.

He let the Uber driver go and then took her hand, leading her into his building. It was a blur as they climbed up two flights of stairs. And then he opened his door.

The music of the night still floated through Jasper's mind, but really, he couldn't think of anything else but Kirsty. It had been too long since he'd brought a woman home. He didn't dwell on the fact that there was still a chance things could go wrong tonight.

Instead the energy and primal need that had been coursing through him since they first locked eyes was in charge.

His apartment was neat-ish. There were dishes in the sink, but he wasn't planning on taking her to the kitchen. His apartment was a mix of furniture his mom had given him and IKEA stuff. He wouldn't say it had any style except for the corner where his record player, vinyl albums and an old recliner that had been his dad's sat.

His dad had worked at a local hotel while he'd been studying to become a high school physics teacher, but his dream had been to be a science fiction writer. He'd been working part-time at a local hotel to try to pay his way through college, then when he graduated he'd pursue writing full-time. According to Jasper's mom these albums were the soundtrack of that project he'd been working on when he died.

Thankfully from the outside the collection just made him look like a hipster—broadcasting his membership in the dead dad's club wasn't exactly foreplay.

He led her into the living room, noticing how quiet it was after the thrilling noise of the concert. The couch was one of those big overstuffed ones. Glancing at the physics book on the coffee table, he was tempted to toss it into the other room.

It could invite some questions he really didn't want to get into. But as soon as he sat down, Kirsty straddled his lap, brushing his hair back from his forehead.

"Comfy?"

She wrapped her arms around his neck, pulling him closer to her. Her breath was warm, smelling slightly of booze which turned him on. He'd tried to be cool and not let things drift too far into the sexy zone. But the entire time they'd been doing shots he'd wanted to feel her tongue on his skin and his on hers. "Getting there."

The television flickered on. Shit.

"*Don't spit on my cupcake and tell me it's frosting.*" Of course it was on *Judge Judy* and she was coming in hot with her tough love.

"What was that?"

"Uh, sorry. I think I must have sat on the remote," he said, knowing full well he hadn't.

"Was that *Judge Judy*?"

"Yeah. Must have come on after whatever I was watching," he said. Honestly he should just shut it and stop trying to overexplain.

"She's a hoot."

"Sure," he said. Maybe if he hadn't heard her advice, wisdom and wisecracks too often, he'd think so too.

He shifted her to the couch and got up to try to find the remote and turn off the TV. Of course the remote was nowhere to be found. He was tempted to unplug it but the plug was behind the big wall unit that housed his *Star Wars* Legos.

The lights flickered in the kitchen but Kirsty didn't seem to notice as he finally found the off button on the TV. Kirsty danced around as she sang "Find Joy."

Glaring at the kitchen, he turned back to Kirsty. Her eyes were closed behind those red framed glasses and her hair was a halo of curls around her head. She opened her eyes and smiled at him. "Dance with me."

He pulled her back into his arms, singing softly along with her. A few furtive glances confirmed that the television and the lights were all back off.

Picking Kirsty up he walked backward to the couch, sitting down with her once again straddling his lap. "Where were we?"

"About here," she said, her hand snaking up under his T-shirt. Her fingers were long and slender and cold against his hot skin. As she scraped her nail down his stomach he felt his erection grow.

"I think you have too many clothes on."

"You too," he said, stripping his tee up and over his head, tossing it on the floor. Then the lights in the kitchen flickered on and off three more times.

For fuck's sake.

Kirsty turned her head. "What's going on?"

The confusion was the only thing saving him. If he gave her a moment to think she'd probably freak and run from his apartment. Jasper brought his mouth down hard on hers to distract her.

Her tongue tangled with his, her arms snaking around his waist, pulling them closer. He forgot about everything going on around him, losing himself in her.

He wasn't ripped or anything, but she didn't seem to notice or mind as she kneaded her fingers into his pecs. A trail of fire followed her touch as she undid his jeans.

Removing her glasses, he tugged her T-shirt off. The blender started whirring, a loud jarring sound that had him biting back a curse. Picking up a pillow he tossed it toward the kitchen.

The blender stopped. Glancing down at Kirsty he saw her head resting on his shoulder, soft exhalations brushing against his neck. She'd fallen asleep.

"Thanks a lot, Paul," he muttered.

He held her for a few more minutes. The light in the kitchen was out again. No need to worry about that right now. Instead he carried her down the hall to his bedroom.

He set her on the bed as she rubbed her eyes sleepily. Grabbing a T-shirt from his clean laundry basket, he handed it to her. She pulled it on before she snuggled under his sheets and curled on her side.

Standing in the doorway he watched her sleeping. His head was fuzzy from the shots and the music and the fun. God it had been a while since he'd just forgotten about all the crap in his life and let loose.

Bringing her back here…he couldn't regret it. He folded her clothes into a neat pile and placed them along with her glasses on the chair next to her side of the bed.

In the living room, he picked the physics book up off the coffee table. One stupid book had so much control over his life. That ended tomorrow. He tucked it in his work backpack, hoping that would keep things calm in the morning.

Buzzed she might not comment on flickering lights and the TV, but sober she was bound to notice.

Going back in the bedroom, he gazed down at the woman, already fast asleep. He initially figured he could sleep with her, but somehow that seemed more intimate than the almost-sex they'd had. Instead he returned to the living room and, grabbing the blanket his mom insisted he'd need, he tried to get comfortable on the couch.

His feet hung off the edge, but the aftermath of almost-sex and the drinks combined to help him drift off to sleep. The soundtrack to his dreams was made up of Dead Boys songs, and his mind drifted off full of images of Kirsty.

The sound of *Judge Judy* in Spanish blasting from the TV brought him bolting upright at 6:00 a.m. Sitting up and frantically searching, he found the remote, but hitting the off button did no good. He was finally able to mute it after a few seconds of fumbling around.

"What the fuck?"

He glanced to the hall where Kirsty stood in one of his old T-shirts, tousled hair looking adorably messy. Her mascara had smudged, creating black lines under her eyes, and she looked aggravated and seductive as hell.

"Sorry. Must have hit the remote," he said.

"Judge Judy…wasn't she on last night?"

"Uh…"

It was hard to come up with a reason on the fly, she looked tousled, he had a boner, his mind wasn't on excusing the TV.

He pulled the blanket up to his chest. She furrowed her brow at him. After last night, the modesty might have been a little much. But the fact was they were essentially strangers. Last night's energy was gone.

"Thanks for letting me have the bed," she said.

Nodding, he got up, wrapping the blanket around his waist. "Do you want coffee? You're welcome to use the shower."

"I'll get both back at mine." She turned to go back to his bedroom.

Should he offer to order her some breakfast? Was anything even open at this time of the day? After last night he should have expected that this TV shit would happen…though it wasn't usually this early.

She returned a few minutes later dressed in yesterday's clothes. "My Uber should be here in a few minutes."

"Uh, I'll go down with you," he said.

She shook her head. "No need. Thanks for last night."

Just like that, she walked out his front door. He should have gotten her socials so they could keep in touch, but last night hadn't felt like the start of anything more than a hookup.

Their almost hookup was merely an extension of the fun they'd had at the concert. She'd been looking for a one-night man and honestly that was all he had the emotional bandwidth for. Best to leave it at that.

He walked to the window. Responded to his mom's good-morning text. And watched until she got into her Uber. He took a photo of the license plate just in case. As he walked into his bedroom his phone started playing "Nobody" by Hozier.

"You fucker. You couldn't let me have a nice morning with her?"

The music kept playing, so Jasper just went and took a shower.

This was the final straw. Today was the day he got rid of Paul. *For real.*

His dead college roommate had been haunting him since he died junior year. Jasper had moved four times before he determined that Paul's spirit was tied to an old physics book. One that Jasper had no remembrance of ever packing or bringing with him.

He'd thrown that damned book out more times than he wanted to count, and it always showed back up. Blasting *Judge Judy* at all hours, and it was always *Judge Judy.* Making his phone play random songs at the most inopportune moments. And that shit with the lights and other electronics. Enough was enough.

Today that all ended.

He was a segment producer on *Live with Bri O'Brien.* A popular syndicated morning talk show that shot before a live studio audience and was shown across the US and in some foreign markets.

They were having author K.L. Henson on their show. The famed mystery writer was also a clairvoyant and could talk to the dead, not unlike Eva Clare, the detective in her popular Satan's Brook mystery series.

Jasper was taking Paul with him to the studio for the first time and today his ass was moving on. Whatever it was that Paul thought he needed in order to move on to the other side, it was done as far Jasper was concerned.

Maybe he'd give dating a try again. Things hadn't gone that bad with Kirsty last night. He hadn't had a girlfriend since Paul died and his ghost had become a major part of his life.

Two

There was a part of her that wondered if he'd figured out who she really was before she left his apartment. The strange incident of the TV going off and on by itself was straight from book three in the Eva Clare mystery series. Add in the lights flashing in the kitchen and last night was hazy but she was pretty sure the blender had been going at one point.

God, had she accidentally hooked up with some superfan? *Shots were always a bad idea.*

The Uber dropped her at her hotel and thirty minutes later she was showered, had downed two ibuprofen and was now drinking her creamy, sugary coffee delivered by Gia the publicist who was working with her on the tour on behalf of Periwinkle Press, her publisher.

"So a bunch of semi odd things all happened? Were they all ripped from your books?" Gia asked.

"Well, the *Judge Judy* thing was new. I mean the guy clearly has a thing for America's favorite judge."

Gia Spring was tall with the kind of curly hair that Kirsty wished she had. It always looked perfect, the curls tight and full, cut into a shaped bob that made her friend even taller. She was slim with playful brown eyes and gorgeous medium-brown skin. She didn't wear makeup except for a tiny bit of eyeliner and sometimes lip gloss. But she didn't need it.

Really the thing she envied about Gia was how comfortable she was in her own skin. Instead of putting on makeup and straightening her hair like Kirsty. Gia never wore a mask. She was one hundred percent the woman she wanted to be.

They'd met after graduation and had been thrust into each other's lives at a time when they were both unsure of the future. Gia always had her back and Kirsty did the same. Gia was one of the few people other than her mom who really knew her.

They'd bonded during her first book tour which, without much of a budget for a new writer, was pretty much the two of them driving around in Kirsty's car, going to a few bookstores in her region and eating lots of fast food. The tour hadn't been super successful, but it had gotten her books into hands of readers and word of mouth had slowly spread.

Now Kirsty was on book five of her series and readers were living for it. The goth heroine, born out of Kirsty's own love of The Killers and dark academia, had been embraced.

It also didn't hurt that her publisher had let readers and booksellers believe that Kirsty had a touch of clairvoyance just like her main character. At first, she thought it was funny, a gimmick, and that no one would believe it.

But once in a while, something unexplainable would happen at a book signing or event and Kirsty would playfully warn that they weren't alone. The first time she'd been on a local morning news show, the guy interviewing her had asked if she was into creepy guys. Kirsty had let her eyes roll back in her head and "felt" a spirit on the set. That interview had gone viral.

People started to show at events expecting her to be in touch with the supernatural. Which she always delivered.

"Did you feel anything supernatural?"

"No. You know that's just PR garbage. I can't really talk to the dead," Kirsty said as she started to straighten her hair.

"Yeah, I know, but I've always thought you must have a touch of ability. Why else would your books be so realistic." Gia walked around the hotel suite, adjusting the outfit that Kirsty had laid out.

"You know I don't. I've mentioned it a bunch of times."

"Last time we were here for the Chicago Mystery Lovers reader event, I'm sure there was something otherworldly in the room."

"There wasn't," Kirsty assured her but a chill went down her spine just remembering that room and how cold it had gotten. "Regardless, I'm not into dudes who are into ghosts and shit. That's K.L.'s stuff not mine."

"So I guess you're not seeing him again," Gia said sarcastically.

"That'd be a definite no."

"Aren't you curious about what he would have been like in the sack?"

Curious?

"Maybe." But she'd never know. K.L. was in charge today and then Kirsty had a flight home and the return to her real life.

She just shrugged as she finished her hair, then put on her trademark thick black eyeliner and bloodred lipstick. She stood to check out the temporary tattoos she'd applied earlier. The largest was the all-seeing eye held by two hands just below her neck. It stretched between her collarbones. The hands were detailed with runes for courage, energy and grace. The basic lines giving her strength as much as they enhanced her image.

Glancing at the butterfly on her wrist, she shook her head. It was bigger than she'd expected since she hadn't known what size a 50 cent piece was. But she loved the dark purple wings and the delicate black-and-white dotted details. Running her finger over it she smiled.

This was something that was always the same. K.L. or Kirsty. Her one permanent tattoo came after a night of doing shots. Clearly she had a pattern with tequila and questionable decisions.

She looked nothing like she usually did.

There was a big part of her that felt like this was her true self. The hair, makeup and tattoos changed the way people reacted to her. And she felt seen. No longer the invisible "Kristy" but someone people wanted to know.

Gia came over to check out the new tattoo design for the sleeve she wanted to get permanent at some point. She was slowly filling in a sleeve design in the shape of a ribbon that had the titles of all of her books. In between the titles were elements from each of them. Such as the haunted dagger from the third book, and the mirror that had held the spirit of an English gentleman in the second one.

"I like the rose, it turned out really well," Gia said.

"Pablo is a genius. I'm actually almost ready to commit to getting them for real," she said.

"What? I thought blood creeped you out." Gia's laughter made Kirsty smile.

"It does. Maybe I'll do some shots to get through it."

"Ugh, was that what you did last night?"

"It was good. He just…was so bizarre this morning. But nothing looks as good in the light."

"I see K.L. has arrived." Gia wiggled her eyebrows. "Ready to head to the studio?"

Wearing the Doc Martens that her mom had scrimped and saved to buy for her senior year she tromped down the hall after Gia. Last interview and then she'd be home.

"How's the book coming?"

"Great. Just like I hinted at to my editor."

"Like you hint at talking to the dead?"

"You know me too well."

Gia wrapped her arm around Kirsty.

"I love you. You've got this. Writing on the road never works for you."

"What if I can't finish this one? My readers have been waiting for Crispin's story."

"You did a great job of teasing us with him. You can definitely finish your book because you need the money."

Kirsty laughed. "Right. Forgot I wasn't born with generational wealth."

"That's what makes you so cool."

"Yeah, that's it."

She was going to be confident and witty, despite the hangover that was stubbornly refusing to go away. Weird night or not, Kirsty was a professional, and she'd worked too hard to let something so minor get to her. Putting on her dark sunglasses she followed Gia to the Uber. For a hint of a second, the image of Jasper singing with her last night flashed into her mind.

There was no denying there had been something between them.

Live with Bri O'Brien was broadcast weekday mornings in most markets and streamed on their TV network's app. The uplifting daytime chat show was billed as the destination for humor, heart and connection.

Bri O'Brien had started acting at age seven and transitioned into a popular talk show host thanks to her down-to-earth tone. The books featured on the show usually hit all the lists and most got optioned for film or TV.

They featured a book segment weekly, and the third week of every month featured mysteries. Bri's viewership was huge, and this was the first time that Kirsty's publisher had been able to get her on.

She was nervous. Though no one had explicitly said it, she knew better than to screw this up. Every author that had been on Bri O'Brien's show and had a successful interview skyrocketed.

The few who stumbled or screwed it up were destined, at best, to being bad internet memes. That meant she needed to be funny, smart and give the audience something that would make them want to see her again.

"Damn. No matter how many times I do this I start to freak out."

"You got this. If you start to lose it maybe you can pretend there's a spirit in the studio. Really ham it up?"

"Thanks. But I really don't want to do that on national TV."

"You might go viral again."

Ugh.

"I want my books to be viral, not me."

Gia squeezed her hand before heading out the door. "You *are* your books."

A PA refilled her water bottle and Kirsty downed two more headache tablets. For a minute she couldn't even remember the title of her book. So she put her head in her hands and took a few deep breaths.

Smart.

Check. She'd always been an A student and liked to learn, so that was an easy one. Talking about the research for her books always seemed to get some interest.

Funny.

If she died of embarrassment that would bring notoriety…

Sell my book.

Girl could write. Making up stories was the one area where her confidence was strong.

She could do this.

The door opened and she looked up, hoping for Gia and her infectious optimism.

But instead it was the dude from last night. Jasper. Standing in the open doorway. He didn't have eyeliner on today and his hair, which had been spiky and styled last night, was combed back neatly. He wore a button-down shirt and a pair of khakis. There was hardly a trace of the person she connected with.

Looks like I'm not the only one wearing a mask.

"Five minutes until you're needed on set, Ms. Henson. If you have a moment I'd like to talk to you…"

If Jasper had dressed like this at Zombies, she probably wouldn't have flirted with him. She would have pegged him as boring.

Judgy, much?

"What are you doing here?" she asked. "Did you recognize me last night?"

"Uh, Kirsty? Wait…are you K.L. Henson?"

She wasn't about to answer that since it was freaking obvious who she was. The TV this morning was the giveaway. There was no way he'd just randomly create that scenario, unless he was familiar with her work and wanted to mess with her.

"You need to leave. I'm not even sure how you got in here." She pointed at the door to underscore her order.

"I work here. I'm a segment producer. I told you that last night."

"Of course you do," she said. "Well the PA already took care of everything, so you can leave."

It didn't seem like he was in charge of her segment or anything that could harm her reputation. Although now she was freaked out all over again.

"Uh…"

"Uh?"

"I sort of need your help," he said.

"With what?"

"This."

He thrust a book at her. Instinctively she reached out to take it and then wished she hadn't. It was heavy and the pages were yellow with age. A battered copy of a textbook, *University Physics with Modern Physics with Mastering Physics*. Convoluted title, but then all science felt that way to her. "I don't do physics."

"Great. I need you to get the ghost of my roommate out of the book. He died junior year and has been haunting me ever since."

Of course he did. Maybe this was a setup from the show. He'd been playing her this morning with the TV and now had a book with his dead roommate in it.

Was this concocted? Had Bri sent Jasper to "meet" her last night to make her appearance more interesting?

Or…

Was Bri trying to prove that Kirsty was a fake? The bottom dropped out of her stomach. Was Bri O'Brien the one who'd dispel the rumor she could talk to the dead?

Her hands were sweating and shaking. She put the book

down. Crossing her arms under her breasts to hide it she gave Jasper her most severe glare.

Whether this was a joke or an attempt at throwing her some good publicity, she had to refuse. She wasn't pretending to exorcise this guy's roommate on TV. "No."

"You saw how chaotic my life is with him. Last night and this morning. The TV and the lights…"

There were notes of frustration and sincerity deepening his voice. Jasper definitely believed his roommate was trapped in that book.

"I saw a fan who's a little too into my books. You know that everything that happened in your apartment was pulled from them. I'm here to talk to your boss about my latest release. If you leave now and don't speak to me again while I'm here, that's all it will be," she said.

His shoulders fell as he shoved his hand through his thick hair, giving a hint of resemblance to the guy she'd met last night. A part of her almost wished she could help him. But she was an author, not a ghost whisperer.

"I can't take this anymore."

"Me either. Get out," she said.

"I'm serious, Kirsty. I didn't know who you were last night or I would have talked to you about Paul then."

"Paul?"

He gave her a hard look. "My roommate who's trapped in the book. Supposedly that's what you do, right? Talk to ghosts that can't pass on?"

"I'm a mystery author, not a clairvoyant," she pointed out. "I'm here to talk about *Roses for the Dead*. Not an actual dead person."

"Yeah, but even your bio says occult experiences are a part of everyone's life."

That damned bio. Her white lie may have helped her career. But the consequences…

"The answer is still no," she said.

"Fine." He glanced at her, desperation plain on his face. "And if we hadn't met last night…"

"The answer would still be no," she admitted.

He touched the earpiece he wore, switched a button on the receiver on his belt and told someone that "the talent" was ready and he would bring her to set.

"Ready?"

"The talent is ready."

He just rolled his eyes and shook his head as he turned on his heel and walked to the door.

It was like Paul was determined to haunt him forever. That would be on-brand for his cousin. From the moment they'd become roommates freshman year. Making sure he remembered his assignments, taking him to the dining hall when he hadn't eaten all day. Paul was the stability to Jasper's chaos. Had he ever been anything else?

Seemed like from his earliest memories he was behind everyone else. Meandering on some path that no one else saw. It was only now, when he was halfway through his twenties, that he'd begun to understand that this trail might lead to nowhere.

His mom always blamed herself for his tendency to wander through life. Like it was her fault that she was dealing with the death of her husband, and a newborn baby, at the same time. He could barely handle himself without all of her emotional baggage in the mix.

He'd been Googling exorcists during the meeting when the pitch for K.L. Henson had come up. He'd only been half listening since book segments weren't his thing, but the moment he'd heard her bio read out loud, he'd started to pay closer attention. Then of course forgotten about it until last night when Fern had reminded him that she was coming on today.

He was the one who pushed hard to book K.L. Henson. He needed her to get rid of Paul.

It also didn't help that she looked nothing like mediums he had seen in TV or movies. He'd never expected someone so quirky, young and interesting. Maybe he should have actually researched her online and taken a look at her photo. Now he was stuck leading her to the set, haunted textbook in one hand, metaphorical disappointment in the other.

Stan the tech dude came over and checked her mic before she was given a moment with her PR person. Stan finished with Kirsty and headed over to Jasper.

"Hey. What's up?"

"Bri asked me to mic you up, too," Stan said.

"Why?" This was unusual. Bri never had him miked. There was no way she could know that he'd met K.L. last night, right?

"You want to ask her?" Stan moved around Jasper's body, threading the lavalier mic under his shirt, hooking the battery pack to his belt, and finally testing it. "You know how to work it?"

"Of course I do." Fern, their boss and showrunner, walked over to him.

"Did you talk to K.L. about your problem?"

"Yeah, it's a no-go."

"Oh no. That stinks—at least you tried."

"Bri's on the move," Jasper heard in his ear minutes before she strode in.

"Alright, people, let's make some joy," Bri said as she breezed into the backstage area to wait to be introduced. She was a tall woman, almost six foot, with long reddish-blond hair that was stick-straight for today's show. His mom said Bri reminded her of a young Cher. But to him, she just looked like his boss. One who could be very generous but also didn't like screwups.

Like the one he just made when he'd asked their guest to exorcise his physics book.

It was fully within Kirsty's rights to bring it up to Bri, but he hoped she didn't. Bri would be disappointed. She wouldn't chew him out but he'd know he let her down. Something he hated doing.

Maybe this was the universe reminding him to solve his own problems. He shrugged to himself as they got ready to start the show. Whatever would happen, it was a problem for after filming.

Bri liked to film her show in order, but that wasn't always possible, then go back to do their non-audience cutaways and B-roll at the end.

The set was meant to be casual, so there was a long sofa in Bri's signature emerald green, with bookcases behind the couch that held props from Bri's film career and other mementos from famous guests. The seating was thick and luxurious. Up to three guests could fit on it. Then there was a large armchair with a low back so that Bri stood out. There was a table between the host chair and the sofa where props and water were kept.

Bri got into place and, once action was called, they started filming her opening monologue and Jasper got to work doing his job. Today it was harder to pay attention than usual.

Not that he ever was super engaged. This was fine and paid well. But he had no passion for broadcast. It was just the one degree he'd been able to get with his haphazard course selection. Plus they'd needed interns at this show years ago, and after graduation they offered him a job. His mom called stuff like this serendipity, Jasper leaned more toward dumb luck and opportunity.

Kirsty was called out to start her segment. Onstage, she was so different from the woman who'd laughed with him and done tequila shots the night before. The short black skirt, dark kohl eyeliner and chunky Doc Martens set the vibe but her attitude did the rest. This woman gave zero fucks but had an easy charm about her. The deep red lipstick made it hard to comprehend anything Kirsty was saying. She was mesmerizing.

Last night, she'd been blowing off steam. Just enjoying a night where she could be anonymous. Something he would do well to remember, instead of how she felt on his lap. How she kissed him like she was starving and he was the only thing that would satiate her. If Paul hadn't gone all poltergeist...

Story of his life.

If.

There was something about Kirsty that had made him feel like none of that mattered. Or maybe that was the shots. Whatever it was, last night he'd felt something he hadn't before. Like maybe he was in the right place at the right time.

Three

The interview was going pretty good. Bri was an engaging personality and immediately Kirsty felt like they could be friends. It had just been Bri and her mom growing up. Bri had been forced to be independent at an early age similar to Kirsty. But it had been Bri hustling to support the family, not her mom.

"After the commercial break we are going to get a chance to learn more about the special aspects of K.L.'s writing and how her personal experiences form the backbone of her books."

Kirsty sat until they were given the all clear. As soon as the "Recording" sign hanging above the cameras dimmed, Bri shot her a look, her eyes twinkling.

"I hope you don't mind, but I overheard Jasper talking to you about his book when we were backstage."

Someone took a deep breath. Glancing to her side she saw Jasper walking toward them.

"I'm just fascinated to see you in action. My cousin was at an event last year at the I|O Godfrey Hotel where you called a halt to the talk because you felt something. And then you

Ghost of a Chance

went to try to help the spirit to move on! She had chills and said after you left, the room immediately felt more at peace."

Well, fuck her. Of course Bri O'Brien's cousin was in the audience the day she had menstrual cramps and faked feeling a spirit so she could go lie down before she started moaning and crying from the pain.

"My gift isn't always accurate." Better to try to manage expectations. "I've never dealt with a spirit that was trapped in an item. It's usually been in rooms or houses, you know?"

That was the only time she'd used it as an excuse to leave an event. She never should have faked feeling another presence in front of people. Now she was trapped. Lies were like that. One lie led to another one, and you had to commit to continuing to lie. And this one was getting away from her.

"First time for everything," Bri said. "I'd love for you to give it a try. We've never had anyone like you on the show before."

"Uh…" Like the power of speech had deserted her. This would be the perfect time to fake "feeling" a poltergeist except that wouldn't help her out. Not now.

All of her K.L. confidence was gone. Invisible Kirsty was here and freaking the hell out.

"Will you try to talk to Jasper's ghost?" Bri asked.

I should come clean. As the thought hit her, she glanced over at Gia who was shaking her head so hard that her Murano glass earrings were bobbling.

"Can I have a moment?"

Bri nodded as her makeup artists stepped close to do a touch-up.

Kirsty bolted to Gia. "Was that a no don't do it or a no to my panic and me blurting out—"

Gia put her hand over Kirsty's mouth. "That one. Go back and try. Just…use your storytelling gift and sell it."

"Sell it?"

"I believe in you." Gia gave her a little push toward the sofa.

Stomping heavily back to the couch she gave Jasper a glare that made him sink back as she flopped down next to him.

"I'll do it."

"Great."

Jasper looked a bit pale and sheepish. Catching her eye, he sat straighter next to her on the couch holding his textbook. Bri was having her makeup touched up. The host raised her eyebrow but stayed silent. Based on their earlier conversation, Bri probably saw this as an opportunity to catch Kirsty's powers at work.

"I'm so sorry. I had no idea she'd do this," he said under his breath.

"Sure, you didn't."

Like she was going to believe this guy. Even if he was telling the truth, she was over him and this pushy city.

He looked like he wanted to say more, but Bri's makeup was finished and everyone started returning to their filming spots. Instead he took her hand and squeezed it.

Surprisingly a feeling of warmth traveled up her arm. She pulled her hand away. She didn't want to feel anything toward him but that potent cocktail of anger and regret, and she wasn't in the mood to change that attitude.

The producer had explained earlier that this segment would be Kirsty's last and would be about five to seven minutes. She could get through five minutes of talking to Jasper's supposed ghost.

Clairvoyance involved awakening the third eye and seeing into the spirit world around her. After reading a few books

38 — Ghost of a Chance

and watching some TV shows, Kirsty had come up with a theatrical routine to make it seem legit. The rest was a mix of improv and telling people what they wanted to hear. So at least she already had that in her back pocket.

"Welcome back. Before the break I hinted that we might get to see K.L.'s real talent for extrasensory perception. That's talking to the dead. One of my staffers Jasper has been haunted for years, but I'll let him tell the tale," Bri said. "Jasper, tell us what happened."

Jasper looked at the correct camera and smiled that toothy grin of his bolstered by sheer nerve. "Well, my college room-mate—um, Paul, died of a brain hemorrhage during our junior year while studying for his physics exam. After the funeral I started noticing certain things...the TV would come on and *Judge Judy* would be playing—"

"Love me some *Judge Judy*, she tells it like it is," Bri interrupted.

The audience applauded.

"Yes, she does." Jasper took a deep breath. "When I turned the TV off, it would come back on," Jasper said.

"Is that all?" Bri asked. "Your ghost is a malfunctioning TV?"

Bri's skepticism made Kirsty almost give her a high five. But she kept her hands in her lap.

"No, there are also lights going on and off in all of the apartments I've lived in. Usually whenever I do something that annoys Paul. And...when I try to get rid of the book, it shows up back in my apartment a few days later."

"That sounds like a lot to deal with. Have you heard anything like this before?" Bri turned to Kirsty.

"Not per se, but it does sound like you have some unresolved feelings about Paul's death. It's common for spirits to haunt people that can't let them go," Kirsty said. "Do you feel guilty about anything surrounding his death?"

"No. I mean we had a fight before, but it wasn't that big a deal. I know he would have forgiven me."

Kirsty turned toward him. The spicy scent of his aftershave reminded her of being in his arms. Of that strange night that matched his totally fake story. For a moment she lost track of the question she was going to ask. Bri jumped into the silence.

"Do you have the book with you? Could you bring it out and see if you can get Paul to do something?"

Jasper flushed, the red tone washing over his cheeks and the side of his neck, and he took the book from the couch next to him. He lifted it up, presenting it to Kirsty…and nothing happened. They all stared at the book, waiting for something.

Kirsty actually felt embarrassed for him. Why did he start this if it was going to be so anticlimactic? Maybe he just wanted attention and never thought it would be televised. But he'd taken it way too far.

"I wonder if bringing Paul into the studio has forced him to move on," Kirsty said. "Maybe he doesn't like being in the spotlight."

"Not everyone does," Bri said, disappointment clear in her voice. "Well…that was—"

She broke off as the lights in the studio burst one after another down the line. There were gasps and screams from the audience. Kirsty felt a cold chill along the back of her neck and she rubbed her arms, looking at the book that had slipped from Jasper's hands and was now lying open on the floor of the studio with the pages fluttering despite there being no breeze.

The cameras stopped rolling and the house lights went up. Bri turned toward the two of them, all smiles. "Well. That was something. I mean I had no idea what we'd get from your ghost, but that was good TV, Jasper."

Jasper was freaking out. That had been too much. Paul always had a flair for the dramatic. Such a diva. Of course he'd gone big. Even if it meant causing chaos at his job. But now at least Kirsty couldn't say that Paul wasn't real.

"This is what I've been dealing with," he said.

"Shut up," Kirsty said. "That was insane. Did you two set this up?"

Bri wasn't near them, and before she could overhear and butt in, Jasper took Kirsty's arm and led her away from the crew cleaning up the shattered lights. The debris had hit the stage and hadn't harmed anyone in the audience.

"Definitely not. Bri will be hurt if you suggest anything like that," Jasper warned her. "I know she has a reputation for being ratings driven, but Bri has a strong ethical code and genuinely cares about everyone."

Kirsty's skin looked even paler than it had before. Her hand shook as she shoved it through her hair. "I need to talk to Gia."

She pivoted, walking away from him without another word.

Resigned, Jasper helped out by clearing the set and picking up his book. Making sure everyone was occupied he brought the closed book up to his face. "That's enough. No more outbursts here. Got it?"

Of course there wasn't a response. And when had Paul ever listened to Jasper. He tossed the book on the sofa and went to find Bri who was buzzing with excitement.

"That was way better than I expected. Not gonna lie, at first I thought we were going to have to cut the entire haunted book segment before it aired, but you came through. Why didn't you mention Paul before this?"

He rubbed the back of his neck. Usually people thought he was nuts when he mentioned that he had a haunted physics book. Not that he ever talked it up. He'd only told his mom and his housemates senior year after they kicked him out for blaring music at 2:00 a.m. and playing *Judge Judy* every day.

His mom humored him when he'd said he thought he had a ghost. Had even sent a Halloween card for his ghost each year. He hadn't mentioned it was Paul…not to her. There would be too many questions. He wasn't sure she bought into the ghost but she loved him.

"It's not something I like to talk about. I didn't expect you to bring me on the show."

"I wasn't planning on involving her psychic skills…when I heard you asking her in the greenroom I knew I had to step in. My gut told me this would be a good segment and let's face it, that was phenomenal."

"It was…expensive. He's never been destructive before," Jasper agreed.

"Worth it! I'm going to talk to her PR person about filming her while she helps you get rid of Paul," Bri suggested. "We can air it on the show after he's gone."

"Uh…" Kirsty wasn't going to like that.

"No need to thank me. It's good television. Let me talk to her people," Bri said, disappearing before Jasper could stop her.

"Wow. Had no idea your book was that powerful," Fern teased, coming up to him. "Want to watch the playback?"

No. He didn't. But he followed Fern to the monitors where everyone on the crew was gathered around watching it happen again and again.

Paul seemed to be getting stronger and manifesting differently and more frequently. The first few times Jasper watched

42 Ghost of a Chance

the replay his eyes were on the book, but this time he watched Kirsty.

Her eyes were wide and she rubbed her hands on her arms as if she felt a chill...

Had Paul spoken to her?

Jasper noticed Kirsty appearing back on set and picking up the textbook. He went to join her.

"Can you talk to him?"

She shrugged. "It's not that easy. I... I'm not really in the right state of mind to do it."

"Yeah, don't blame you. Those lights were loud and freaky."

"They were. Can't say I've ever experienced that before. How often does that happen?"

"The lights?"

She gave him a hard duh look.

"Like never. They're maintained and kept clean and changed. Paul usually limits himself to *Judge Judy*, the odd song and lights...though he has recently started fucking with the blender," he said. "You look really different...where did the tattoo come from?"

He pointed to her chest. Last night her skin had been smooth and unmarred by the designs that were there now. The design showed off her delicate bone structure while indulging the unapologetic person she was. He liked them. They suited her.

"I put them on when I'm doing press," she said. "If anyone asks, they're real."

"Why aren't they permanent? You have the butterfly on your wrist."

"None of your business," she said. "I don't want to be buddy-buddy with you."

"Why not?"

"Because I'm ticked and feeling bitchy and cornered," she admitted. "I don't like being forced to use my…abilities. Sort of makes me feel cheap. Like I'm doing a trick."

"That's okay."

"No, it's really not," she said, turning away from him and stalking backstage to the greenroom.

He let her go. He had five years to get used to Paul. Even if she was used to dealing with spirits, she must not have expected this today. Maybe he should apologize or tell her to forget about it…if she'd even talk to him.

Before he could figure out what to do, he was summoned to the greenroom where Kirsty, Bri, the show's producer Landon and Gia were assembled.

"Okay, we've all had a chance to talk, and Kirsty's publisher Periwinkle Press has agreed to pay her expenses for a few weeks while she helps Paul's spirit move on," Bri said. "We sent them the raw footage and they agreed that it could be a huge moment for all of us. I'm going to supply the crew and Jasper, we'll have someone cover for you while you're filming with Kirsty. We've decided on a four-to-six week time frame. As soon as we have enough footage, we'll have you back on and share it with the nation."

Kirsty's mouth fell open. She turned to Gia, whispering fiercely to the other woman. He had the feeling she wasn't into this idea, but Jasper was secretly pumped. He might actually be able to help Paul move on after all.

"Thanks, Bri. This means a lot to me." Trying to keep emotion out of his voice but failing.

"You're welcome, kid. I can't wait to see why Paul's hanging on and what it takes to help him finally leave this book. He must really love physics."

Jasper felt a hint of guilt but brushed it aside. This wasn't the time to open old wounds.

Kirsty had her arms crossed over her chest and looked like she was seconds away from letting loose on Bri. Gia strongly gripped her shoulder, holding her back.

Gia nodded. "That's all settled. I just need some details about where you went to school, Jasper, so Bri's team and I can get their permission to film. Then I'll set up an Airbnb nearby." She turned toward Bri. "I also need the names of the crew you're sending."

"Landon will handle that." Bri glanced around the room. "Our temporary lighting setup is finished so I need to get the audience back in and finish the show. Kirsty, I'll plug your book and the follow-up segment we have planned. The audience is getting a copy. Gia mentioned you'd sign them before you leave."

"I'm happy to," Kirsty said, following Bri out of the greenroom.

And just like that, everything changed.

Jasper went back to work but he was distracted. Excited to see what happened next. He'd always wanted to know why Paul had lingered…

At her book signing later that day, Kirsty had all but shrugged off the incident on Bri's morning show. For now she wanted to focus on staying in the moment.

Meeting her fans was the best part of being an author. She'd always felt like the odd one most of her life. But her readers were her people. They were funky dressers who talked to her not just about her book but about true crime which Kirsty often used as the backbone of her plots. When she was here she felt like she belonged.

She enjoyed hearing about how they loved the series and what they were excited to see next from sleuth Eva Clare. It did stir a bit of guilt since she was struggling to write the next book. Everyone was telling her how excited they were to read it. Somehow that made it worse.

Especially since the more she thought about writing it, the harder it was to actually get the words on the page.

But right now that didn't matter. Today was about connecting with her fans and appreciating what she had. Along with signing her books, she posed for photos and handed out smaller versions of the temporary tattoos that matched the one on her chest.

Gia showed up toward the end, chatting with a few readers they'd met before. Kirsty put away her pens and swag and headed over to her friend. "So. Where are we going for this ghost disaster?"

"Burlington. You'll love it. University town in fall. It's just like your fictional town of Satan's Brook. I even found an atmospheric house that's near where Jasper was living when his roommate died."

She grabbed Gia's arm and pulled her outside so they wouldn't be overheard. "Are you sure we should be doing this? You know I have no real ability."

"I know you don't think you do. But you have felt things before," Gia reminded her.

"When I wanted to get out of something. I *really* don't feel anything spiritual or otherworldly. I'm as normal as it gets."

Gia shook her head. "When we were in the Godfrey, I felt *something*. The air was cold and heavy. It felt like all the energy was being sucked from the room until you left and the spirit seemed to follow you out. I wasn't the only one who thought it was real."

"That's coincidence."

"Too bad, it felt real. You're stuck anyway. The publisher loves the idea of getting this kind of publicity with Bri's show. Plus the internet loves this kind of stuff, even if it ends up being a hoax. It will go viral. They were happy to pay for the Airbnb and expenses but it's a small per diem for food."

"I have a deadline," she grumbled. "I really need to be at home writing."

"I'll clear that with your editor. We can add however many weeks this ends up being onto your deadline."

She gave a weak smile. Great. Like an extra four to six weeks was going to help when she practically had nothing written. But she knew there was no getting out of this. "I need to go home and get my stuff."

"Of course." Gia glanced down at her phone. "Looks like Bri is sending one cameraman and Jasper will manage him. I'll be there too. I figured we'd all meet on Monday. That gives you the rest of this week and the weekend to yourself."

"Thanks," she said sarcastically. But it wasn't Gia's fault. None of this. Right now it was a toss-up between herself and Jasper who she was really angry at.

She'd been trying to manifest getting on this show since her first book came out, so really Kirsty knew that it was her own fault. She wanted people to talk about her work. She wanted to be famous. But she hadn't ever really considered what it would be like.

Definitely not like this.

"How am I going to do this? I can't talk to Paul."

Gia dropped her arm around Kirsty's shoulder. "Treat it like one of your books. You may not be able to talk to ghosts but you know how to put evidence together and tell a story.

If Jasper resolves his feelings, maybe that'll be enough. You're very good at getting closure in your books."

"Thanks," she said, meaning it this time. She turned and hugged Gia. "Sorry I was being bitchy before."

"It's okay. I get it. It's a lot more than a book tour now. But this…this is going to be really good for your career," Gia said.

"Yeah?"

"After this your books are going to fly off the shelf."

"They are," Kirsty said without any real confidence. "That would be nice." Then maybe she'd stop feeling like a fraud.

"It will be." Gia gave her a reassuring smile. "Ready to go? You have two hours before you have to be at Dark and Stormy."

"Yes. I'm starving. Good news is that my headache is gone. Maybe that ghost scared it out of me," Kirsty said.

"Or the ibuprofen started working," Gia replied with a wink.

"I thought you believed in my powers."

"*Yours.* Not some unknown textbook ghost's."

Her flight home was smooth. Her mom met her at the airport with a small sign that said Favorite Girl in one hand, carrying a to-go cup in the other. A big smile lit up her face. Kirsty hugged her mom and took the mug of pumpkin chai latte, her favorite drink from their local cafe.

"How'd it go?"

"Mom, it was nuts. Some guy has a ghost trapped in a book," she said, then told her mom the entire story.

"I guess you're going to need all of Dot's books," her mom said. Kirsty's great-aunt had been a clairvoyant and had sent Kirsty a box of books when she was thirteen with a card…

To my favorite little weirdo. Reading those books had laid the groundwork for the Eva Clare mysteries.

She pulled into the driveway of the duplex that she and her mom owned. Kirsty's apartment was on one side and her mother's was on the other. Being a writer didn't pay that well, and living close meant she had a house sitter whenever she went on tour.

"I can't bring too many esoteric books," she said. "That'll completely give away that I'm a fraud."

"Okay. You can text me then, and I'll look things up for you. Do you think there's a real ghost?"

"Maybe. At first I thought Jasper had set everything up, but Bri—"

"Oh my God, my baby's on a first-name basis with Bri O'Brien."

Her mom got so excited by her success.

"Mom…but sure. She's really nice. You'd like her."

"I would. Maybe I should come with you when you go back," her mom said, taking Kirsty's suitcase to her front door. "I just restocked the fridge. Dinner tonight?"

"Thanks, Mom," she said.

"You okay?"

"No I'm not. I'm feeling cranky and scared. Like everyone's going to find out I'm a fraud."

"One—you're not a fraud. You're a fiction author. Your job is to make stuff up and get people to buy into your world. I know you're going to be awesome and get this Jasper some closure."

A warmth engulfed her and she spontaneously hugged her mom which took her mom aback. Kirsty wasn't touchy-feely. But her mom had soothed her fears.

"One thing, kiddo, to keep in mind is playing at being a

medium and talking to ghosts needs to be light. Summoning might awaken something inside of you."

"Moooom… I'm not a real clairvoyant."

"Maybe, but you have an affinity for the occult. Just be careful."

It took all her willpower not to roll her eyes. Mom cared which was why she was giving her advice. But the last thing that Kirsty was worried about was awakening anything.

"Thanks."

"Better?"

"I am. Thanks."

Kirsty went into her own home as her mom disappeared next door. She wasn't feeling as panicked as she'd been when Gia had first agreed to the entire ghost hunt. Talking to her mom put everything in perspective. And she'd be back on a college campus at the start of the fall term—something that always inspired her.

She could get her dark academia on. All those dark plaid miniskirts, romantic blouses and chunky cardis she kept in her closet but never wore because she rarely left her house.

Maybe solving Jasper's mystery would help her with her own story. Even if he had known who she was the night they met, the connection felt real. The way her pulse raced when his warm hands had touched her in the rain. The sparks when their eyes met as their favorite band began to play…her mind was full of possibilities and the question of what it would be like to kiss him when she was sober.

He couldn't be as good of a kisser as she remembered, right?

Four

The Airbnb looked creepy AF as Kirsty pulled into the driveway on Monday. She'd had the weekend to reread all of Aunt Dot's books and get ready for the haunted textbook. In reality, a lifetime wouldn't have been enough time.

She rolled her eyes as she sat there imagining the joy lighting up on Gia's face as she found the perfect background for some ghostly-themed social media posts. Being all into the creepy aesthetic was one thing but she couldn't do real haunted houses. Like if there were creaking stairs and breezes she couldn't explain…she'd want to bolt but honestly those things would probably be perfect for her fake abilities.

Resting her head on the steering wheel, she moaned.

This right here.

This was why she stayed home in her tiny office with her fall rain scented candles wearing her favorite once black, now gray-from-so-many-washings sweatpants and a variety of different long-sleeved tees with sarcastic sayings on them. Home was safe. And home didn't look like it had seen a few murders.

Normally, a bit of darkness and rain was her sweet spot

when it came to setting the scene in her books, and honestly also for her internal life.

But this…wet, muddy, cold. And a house that looked more haunted than that freaking textbook. She was in for a long four weeks.

Ugh, there was never an excuse to whine. Not even now.

She was here. And maybe on the verge of fixing her writer's block. That was the end of her bitching internally about it. Maybe. Time to be K.L. and leave invisible Kirsty.

The door opened and the largest, shaggiest dog she'd ever seen bounded outside, tugging someone behind him.

Jasper.

As soon as Jasper hit the first step, he stumbled and took a huge leap down the other three as the dog bolted for a maple tree that still had a fair amount of leaves on its branches. Jasper landed solidly. She admired his athleticism.

As much as she didn't want to watch him, her eyes were drawn to his long legs and those faded jeans that clung to his surprisingly taut butt as he chatted to the dog. He was too far away for her to hear what he was saying, but his tone was firm and patient.

He wore a hoodie and his black hair was more like it had been the night of the Dead Boys concert. Falling around his face and neck. It was wet from the rain, but Jasper didn't seem to be bothered by it.

He pushed his hair back from his forehead, mussing it, which just made her fingers itch to touch him. There was a rugged, outdoorsy element to him. No more Mr. Khakis from the TV studio.

Sitting in her car, she was so tempted to put it in Reverse, but she'd already promised—and broken said promise—that she'd stop thinking about being back home.

Ghost of a Chance

She wished she could say that watching him didn't make her hot, reminding her of what he felt like under her that night on his couch, when his mouth and body had driven her slowly out of her mind…

She reached for the serviceable black backpack that her mom had bought her senior year of high school, that yes, she still used. That Jansport had been built to last. It still had patches she'd sewn on senior year. Two *Scott Pilgrim vs. The World* ones and then a few she'd added over the years. Most recently, she picked up a Dead Boys one off Etsy and would add that when she got home.

Tearing herself from admiring Jasper, she got out of the car. Plonking her Doc Martens straight into a puddle. The muddy water splashed up her leg, hitting her calf. She shouldn't have been surprised when she felt the nudge of wet fur against the leg that was still on the edge of the puddle.

"Want a hand with your stuff?" His voice was low and gravelly, muffled by the rainfall and the barrier of her open car door. The tone was hesitant like he didn't want to incur her wrath again.

She'd been a bit…let's call it out of sorts when she was first cornered into doing this. He was partially to blame, but Kirsty could have said no. But being an author meant being a publicity whore even though she hated the spotlight, talking about herself, and engaging with strangers.

"That'd be great. I have a suitcase in the trunk and two writing bags."

"What's in a writing bag?" he asked, with slightly less hesitation this time.

She tried to get out of the car but the dog was looking up at her, tongue lolling out the side of his mouth. With a heavy sigh, because she couldn't resist those big eyes, she held her hand out. He sniffed, then licked it and pushed his nuzzle under her hand. She scratched his nose.

"Who's this?"

"Chewie."

"*Star Wars*, right?" Her mom was a massive fan of the original trilogy and had raised her on the prequels.

She'd even dipped her hand to writing some Reylo fanfic under a pseudonym, envisioning them as a modern Scully and Mulder both trying to prove/disprove the actual existence of the Force throughout the galaxy at her mom's suggestion. Mostly she'd just wanted to explore that crazy sexual tension they'd had in *The Last Jedi*. Even though she was still mad—well, sort of—with Jasper and didn't want to have anything in common with him, it felt good to know they'd at least have something to talk about besides music and his troublesome ghost.

"Yeah, I know. Nerd, right?"

He looked like a jock despite his unruly hair. She knew he had a lean muscled body under the hoodie. There was no way anyone would ever call him a nerd to his face. "Don't diss my fandom."

"Cool. So you're into Reylo, right?"

"Who isn't? But I'm a big fan of the OGs."

"Han and Leia?"

"Definitely. What about you?" she asked, aware that this wasn't what she'd intended to do. *Get in, fake-solve the ghost problem and get out.*

"Big fan of Obi Wan in the prequels and I like *The Mandalorian*."

As if he was listening to their conversation and satisfied with her level of knowledge, Chewie finally settled down, taking his head off her boot. She eased her way around the dog. Jasper was already waiting for her, his biceps bulging under his hoodie while he hoisted her heavy bags with ease.

54 Ghost of a Chance

Maybe this wouldn't be so bad after all. Determined to give herself a fresh start. She was armed with knowledge…and as her mom always said knowledge was half the battle.

Gia stepped out onto the porch. "Great, you're here."

Kirsty waved at her and Gia's head tipped slightly toward Jasper as if asking what that was about. Kirsty would give her a debrief when they were alone. Talking to Gia always made it easier for her to process her little problems.

Though there was nothing little about Jasper. Jasper pulled Chewie back and turned to the other woman. "The house has a study that I think will be perfect for a séance."

Ugh.

Just ugh.

That was all she had when faced with Gia's gold-blond hair. Sometime in the last two days her friend had dyed the tips orange and black. No doubt for Halloween, which was at the end of the month.

"Super." Not bothering to hide her sarcasm.

Good thing she'd packed the séance book that her mom had from her own teenage years. In her mystery series, she always put a séance in for her sleuth to contact the dead. Readers really loved it, and it was a great way to move the plot forward by bringing suspects onto the page.

Kirsty slung her backpack over one shoulder, her tote bag full of Dot's books hanging off the other. Jasper forged ahead with Chewie at his side with her duffle and rolling case.

He grunted as he put it on top of the luggage. "I guess that's your arm workout."

She couldn't help her smile as she followed him toward the house. Maybe she'd linger a few days before she "freed" the ghost. *Maybe.* Just to see if she and Jasper could pick up where they left off.

Katherine Garbera

★ ★ ★

How was it possible for her to look even cuter today?

It was hard for Jasper to keep his mind on the job, but that was the only reason they were here. He wanted to show her that he wasn't the flake she probably believed him to be after everything that had gone between them.

They were officially coworkers now. Not to mention she was his last hope for finally having a normal life. Reigniting their fling could put that in jeopardy.

Don't fuck this up.

His dog Chewie was an old English sheepdog, big and hairy and friendly as hell but not conducive to filming, so Jasper got him settled in the kitchen and then closed the door. He'd had Chewie at a dog sitter the night of the Dead Boys concert. He and Dan got the first shot set up while she and Gia went upstairs to unpack.

With his shaggy hair, Iron Man–trimmed beard and mustache and baggy clothes Dan gave off an I-might-care vibe. He was about ten years older than Jasper and a tech whiz when it came to capturing shots.

Base of operations would be in the dining room because of the large floor-to-ceiling windows that overlooked the rain-drenched wooded area behind the house. The dining room had a large chandelier over a table that would easily seat twelve. There were heavy wood chairs with faded and worn velvet padded seats.

On the sideboard there were two candelabras with a layer of dust covering the melted candles. Frankly, everything about this place was creepy AF. Which almost made him chuckle. Paul didn't like haunted houses. Served the bastard right for haunting him for so long.

Gia came in later with Kirsty behind her. "It would be

56 Ghost of a Chance

more atmospheric if this house had a library wall or something. Let me check with the library on campus. Maybe we can get permission to film in there if this doesn't capture the feeling enough."

"Great," Kirsty responded without much enthusiasm. Dan gave her a lapel mic.

"Are we filming now?"

"Might as well. I want to get as much footage as I can," Dan said.

"I'm not really made up."

"That's fine. It's better if you're just yourself," Dan said.

"You look great." Jasper couldn't help telling her.

"Thanks. You too."

He smiled because she made him feel good.

"Super. You're both great. Let's get your mic on." Dan was all business.

Which Jasper totally should be as well. But this was Kirsty…

She clipped it on herself. Jasper already had his on. "For now will this do?"

Gia nodded and went back to typing on her phone.

"Where do you need me?" Kirsty asked.

Dan cleared his throat. "We're not sure what's going to happen when you open the book, so let's start there. Jasper wants me to capture you examining the book. Then maybe you can get the ghost to talk, come out and shake his hand."

The glare she gave Dan would have melted any man who was more aware of social cues. But Dan, who was notoriously oblivious, calmly waited for her to answer.

"I get feelings from them. The ghosts don't take corporeal form." She sat down heavily in one of the ladder-back chairs around the table.

Jasper slid into the chair next to her, reaching for the physics book. "What should I do?"

"I think for the sake of the camera you might want to explain what's going on and why you feel like the ghost is in the book," she said.

She'd been almost friendly earlier but now…well, she was probably ticked about the state of the dilapidated Victorian. It didn't help that Dan had no clue what it was she did.

"Mostly Paul just puts on *Judge Judy* and flicks lights," Jasper said to Dan.

"Yeah, that's it. But tell it to her." Dan indicated Kirsty with his head. "We will start with that shot. Like explaining it all to Kirsty."

"Okay. I'll do that later in the living room. For now let's get a shot of me reading the book for some B-roll, and then Dan can capture me looking up into the camera," he said.

"Like you're the lord of the manor? Dog at your feet and everything?"

He flushed. "No. Honestly, I thought it would look mysterious like we're in a gothic film."

"Maybe it *would* be best to leave Chewbacca in the kitchen."

Chewie wasn't always the best at a long down anyway. He wanted Kirsty to know that he valued her input.

"For now I'd like you to examine the book or whatever you do. This is really about you and Paul."

She picked the book up and began to leaf through it while Dan recorded. He noticed that the polish on her index finger was chipped and her nails weren't that long. So she wasn't the type to get herself perfect before going on camera. Her skin was fairly pale in the dim light of the old house, but it was fall and had been chilly lately.

He wanted to ask her where she lived, what made her happy,

how she got these crazy powers at all since he hadn't gotten the chance...but that had nothing to do with the shot they were trying to get. Kirsty cleared her throat. "What do I do now?"

Jasper pulled himself together. He had to stay on task.

"For the camera?" Dan asked.

The hard look she shot Dan made Jasper hide a smile. Kirsty definitely wasn't one to suffer fools. Dan missed it totally fiddling with the settings on his camera.

"It'd be best if you forgot I was here. Talk to Jasper about what you're doing and I'll film it. Don't worry about showing me the book or anything. I'll do a bunch of additional B-roll shots later. Ready?"

She tucked a strand of her hair behind her ear, then pulled it back nervously.

"You're going to be great."

"Thanks."

Again with the sarcasm.

Dan started filming again. It was time for Jasper to focus. "Have you dealt with a ghost trapped in an object before?"

"No, this will be my first time dealing with this in real life. I did write about one in my first book *Dead Flowers For The Living*."

He hadn't read any of her books, so he wasn't familiar with it. She relaxed when she mentioned the book. Calmer now in a way which made sense given she was a published author rather than amateur clairvoyant.

"My heroine, Eva, noticed that every time she put fresh flowers into a particular vase she picked up at a garage sale, they immediately wilted. That was her first clue that something was amiss. What kind of strange events occur around your book?" Turning toward him, a strand of hair brushed her cheek as he met her gaze. For a minute, words just left his head. All he could think about was how her hair had brushed his face when they kissed.

"Jasper?"

"Uh…so the TV turns on once or twice a day, always to *Judge Judy*. Without anyone touching the remote, of course. There's some random stuff like music suddenly playing from my smartphone or lights flickering on and off as well. And, well, you saw what happened in Bri's studio."

"Is there a pattern to the random stuff?"

"Like what?"

"Does music play when you are experiencing a specific emotion…like, are you a jock?"

"Huh?"

"You sort of have that vibe."

"I played basketball in high school and have a pickup game when I'm home."

"Knew it."

That shouldn't have made him feel special. But it did. No matter that he'd decided they were coworkers, he still saw her as a woman he wanted to get to know better and kiss again.

"So after your team scores, does 'We Are The Champions' play?"

Laughing, he shook his head. "More like when I have a long day at work 'Batshit' blares."

"Whatever is that?"

"Oh, you'd love it. The band is called Sofi Tukker, they are electronic/dance. I'll play it for you later."

"Sounds good. So there is purpose to the music."

"Odd I never realized. Probably because I like the songs so they don't annoy me like *Judge Judy*."

"Maybe. What would be best is if we observe things around this house for a few days and establish a pattern. Next, we need

60 Ghost of a Chance

to retrace Paul's steps and understand more of who he was and what might be motivating his spirit to stay on this earth. What was he doing the night he died, that kind of thing," she said.

"How's that?" she asked Dan.

"You're doing great. I set up cameras in the living room. The lighting needs to be turned on. Let's go in there next," Dan suggested.

Jasper had forgotten Dan was in the room with them.

Kirsty flipped open the cover of the book. "All of this stuff sounds weird, but most of it could be explained away by malfunctioning technology or accident. Does anything else unexplainable happen that might be easier to observe?"

"No," he said. "I mean, other than the times when I've left the book on a bench or thrown it away. Each time it shows back up at my place."

"How often has that happened?"

"Three times."

"How do you know it's the same book?" she asked, skimming through the text itself.

"That right there." He pointed to an inky sketch of a tree that was clearly out of place.

"Good that you have that as a marker. Did Paul draw it?"

Tracing the sketch to avoid letting the sadness he felt overwhelmed him. He'd never had the chance to fully process his grief. The fight had filled him with guilt when Paul had died.

He'd freaked and lost it without Paul's anchoring friendship. Then after he'd moved to a new apartment he'd noticed the book and of course *Judge Judy* which he only associated with Paul.

"I have no idea. I never looked through the book before he died," he said.

"Well it's not a lot, but I can start there."

"By asking him about it?" He wasn't sure that talking to Paul's poltergeist was going to actually work. But she was the expert.

"Possibly. We'll see how he feels about talking to me."

It didn't work.

They spent fifteen minutes filming in the living room. Kirsty did her best to "talk" to Paul while holding the book—nothing from her research was particularly clear on how talking to spirits even worked. Was she supposed to sound casual? Or use some kind of exaggerated fortune-teller voice? She ended up doing a mix of both, but nothing happened.

Gia left to go talk to someone about filming at the college library, and Jasper hovered in the doorway to the living room observing her failure.

This might be quicker than even she'd expected. One day in and she was close to being exposed as the fraud she was. "I need a break. I'm going to head into town and stop by the bookstore."

"For research?"

"Uh…no," she said sheepishly. "I have a new book out. Figured I'd go sign stock, clear my head a bit."

"I'll go with you," he said. "It'll give us a chance to talk."

"About?"

He gave her a look, his eyes sharp and penetrating. "That night."

She arched one eyebrow. "What about it? It was an almost one-night stand with a guy I met at a concert. As far as I'm concerned, that's it."

"Cool. Me too. But we're going to be working together. Might be nice to clear the air or whatever you need to do. And not in front of Gia and Dan."

"Fine," she said, getting her black wool peacoat and putting it on. It was cold today thanks to the rain from earlier. She gave herself a once-over in the mirror near the front door, noticed her lipstick was wearing off and touched it up. Double-checking she had some bookmarks and pens in her bag, she heard Jasper call out to Dan that they'd be back later.

"If anything paranormal happens use your phone to film it. Use the highest quality settings and landscape, not portrait."

"Will do," Jasper said. At this rate, she'd almost welcome something paranormal happening if it meant saving her skin from complete humiliation.

"Ready to go?" Kirsty turned to see Jasper approaching her in the hall leading to the front door. He'd put on a UVM hoodie, different from what he was wearing earlier.

"Mind walking?"

They weren't that far from the town center. Kirsty knew she thought better when she was moving. Lord knew she needed to think and figure out her next step with the book and Jasper. She ignored her own car and Jasper fell into step beside her. Seeing him in his college sweatshirt he looked younger than she thought. This might play a part as to why he was so attached to the book and needed it to be Paul. "How old are you?"

"Twenty-five. You?"

"Thirty." Wow, younger than she guessed. She'd matured a lot when she hit twenty-eight. Sure she'd felt all adult at twenty-one but looking back she'd still basically been a kid.

"I knew you were young. How did you sell your first book?"

She shook her head. There was something about him that reminded her of his dog. He was eager and completely unaware of how she spent most of her life preferring to be left alone. "By submitting it."

He drew to a halt.

"What?"

"Is this seriously how you're going to be?"

"It's a legit answer."

"Just say what you have to say to me," he said.

"I'm not sure—"

"Really? Even though I don't know you, I can tell that you want to unload on me for something I must have done to you."

She took a deep breath and forced herself not to clench her hands into fists. But it really had no effect at all. She'd been chill but the truth was underneath her K.L. calm Kirsty was ticked off.

"*Something?* You fucking brought some dumb book on a talk show and then started this entire thing. I was on my last stop. On my way home. Back to my life in which I don't have to be on all the time. And now I'm somehow the only person who can help you out of an absolutely bonkers situation."

"You could have said no."

"You're totally right." But she wasn't going to pass up this opportunity for publicity for her books. She'd worked too hard to let it all fall apart now.

"I'm sorry for that. I thought you did this kind of thing all the time. Bri mentioned that in Chicago—"

"*Oh my God.* That was one time. It wasn't really a big deal. And nothing like…like this."

Jasper crossed his arms over his chest. Briefly her eyes betrayed her, lingering on how the fabric of his sleeves stretched taut against his muscled biceps. "I'm not going to apologize for wanting your help. I don't have your experience with the paranormal."

64 Ghost of a Chance

She was being unreasonable. No one needed to point that out. At this moment she didn't care.

Even so, she couldn't help but deflate. He was cute and young. The five years between them felt huge at this moment. Because he seemed still…well, still figuring out who he was going to become. And apparently this ghost was part of what was holding him back.

She was twenty-five when she sold her first book. Her life had changed. Not in a huge way at first, but it had focused her. Propelled her into figuring out what she wanted for her life.

Drums started thumping and a deep voice sang "Oh, you're bad enough to me."

Jasper fumbled for his phone, hitting the mute button.

"Was that Paul?"

"Probably. Now that you asked about the music, I wonder if he's trying to help me."

"Was that how he was in life?"

"Definitely. He was a year older than me."

The song playing wasn't something she could explain. Maybe his phone had a glitch. She couldn't talk to the dead but could try to figure out what his relationship with Paul was like. Why was this incident still weighing on him. Then Jasper could move on and she could go back home and pretend like this never happened.

"I bet you miss him."

"I do. But not enough to manifest him into a book or whatever it is you think I'm making up."

He had a point. It didn't seem as if he were just making this all up. "I'll try to be more gracious."

"That's all I ask," he said, starting to walk again.

She fell into step beside him. If she was going to do her best to help, she might as well start gathering information. "What drew you to UVM?"

"They accepted me."

That cheeky grin of his was infectious. She almost smiled back.

"I got in-state tuition and a scholarship." There was a note of shyness like he didn't want to talk about himself.

"I did the same thing. Ole Miss."

"You're from the South?"

"Nah. I meant the scholarship. I graduated high school with an AA degree so was a jump ahead."

Her mom had been working long hours at her job and they both knew that college tuition was going to be a stretch. So Kirsty had done what she could to ensure she graduated with as many college credits as she could. It suited her to study all the time. She'd always been a bit of an emo girl after her dad had left, preferring her music and books to socializing with her classmates.

"That's cool. Were you always into ghosts? Or were they always into you?" he asked, a sly grin on his face.

Ghosts. Everyone had them. Her mom spent most of her life running from the specter of Kirsty's father cheating and betraying her trust. And Kirsty felt haunted right this very moment by that little white lie she told all those years ago. So...

"Sure. I guess. You?"

"Nah, this is my first. I mean I thought it was pretty much bullshit and people like you...well—"

"Were conning everyone," she finished for him.

"Uh..."

"I'm not taking money to help you find a ghost. I also don't need you to leave me anything in your will," she said, mentioning two common ways scammers who posed as mediums like to be paid. She'd researched plenty for her series. "Also, you asked for my help. I would have been happy to just go back home and back into my writing cave."

He rubbed the back of his neck, checking the street before they both crossed it. "Is that where you got the idea for your heroine? Your life?"

Her first book had come from a bouquet of dead flowers in a vase and an ex-boyfriend who she wished would die. Instead of going off the deep end, she wrote about a bloody crime scene and then solved it. It had been cathartic in a way she hadn't intended.

"Not really. I sort of stumbled into it."

"Like us."

She stopped. "What?"

"We stumbled into each other...and look at things now. After years of dealing with Paul, my life's finally about to go back to normal." Jasper paused, a faraway look in his eyes. "Maybe it'll work out for you too."

Five

She ignored his last statement and kept walking as a light rain began to fall on them, the droplets sticking to the top of her head. The temptation to brush one of them off was so strong he shoved his hands into the pockets of his khaki pants.

He *liked* her. He'd liked her the night of the Dead Boys concert. But Paul had fucked that up. Or, if he was being honest, he fucked it up for himself by not recognizing her or explaining himself properly the next day. "What are you going to do when you get to the bookstore?"

"Check and see if they have my book. Then introduce myself to the staff and ask if I can sign the stock and put some bookmarks in them," she said.

"Do they let you?"

"Indie booksellers do. Some of the chains, just depends," she said.

Once again it was easy to see writing and being an author relaxed her. Her entire demeanor changed when she discussed it.

"Interesting. Have you ever seen someone reading one of your books?" he asked.

"No."

"What would you do if you did?"

"Nothing." Her mouth quirked up in a secretive smile. "Well, that's not true. Maybe I'd try to sneak a photo of them reading it. I don't know. It's never happened so it doesn't matter," she said, turning onto a street that was lined with small shops. There was a café and bakery on the end that he'd frequented as a student.

She paused in front of it, studying the sign before glancing up at him. A shiver went through him.

"You know this place?"

"Paul and I used to hit it at least twice a day."

"Tell me more about him," she invited.

"Nah. I don't like to think about him." Everything with Paul was complicated. And he felt like an ass that he was still mad at Paul for dying. For not being around to see his influence had turned Jasper into a productive, functioning adult… and the book didn't count. He wanted to talk to his friend, not be haunted by him.

"Dude, this entire exercise…me being stuck in Burlington with only a cameraman, Gia and you is about Paul. You're going to have to talk about him," she said in that direct way of hers, cutting right to the core. Leaving him no choice really.

Paul. He didn't mention that they were cousins or that he'd been more like a brother to him. That was too personal. They'd roomed together sophomore and junior year because the frat they rushed was too expensive. Their place was shabby and a little run-down but had suited them.

"What do you want to know?"

She tipped her head to the side, studying him. What was

she hoping to find? When she laughed, he realized he must be pulling a face and shrugged, a blush creeping over his cheeks.

"We were roommates and friends. He was like a brother to me. We had one class together but liked to study either here at Joe's or in the library. Being at our place…we kept for chill time. Plus, Paul was in a lot of study groups for all his different classes. He liked to discuss topics he studied."

"Not you?"

"Me not so much. So I usually found a quiet corner and wore my noise-canceling headphones."

They were walking again toward the bookstore at the end of the block. "Sometimes I go through phases where I'm really into things then not so much."

"Even now?" she asked.

"Yup." No use lying. She'd figure out soon enough that he was a drifter, stumbling into things that took hold of him. Like the job at Bri's show. Like meeting her. He couldn't say why, but he was starting to feel like he'd been drawn to Kirsty from the first moment because of something bigger.

"Why?"

He stared into the shop window to avoid answering. That was his way. "My dad."

"Is he one of those real intense and demanding ones?" she asked.

"No, he's dead." May as well rip off the bandage. "Is yours demanding?"

"Oh, I'm sorry about your dad." He quickly glanced at her face. Her eyes were cast down on to the gray sidewalk below them. "No, mine ghosted me and my mom when I was six. Been just the two of us after that."

"My dad died the night I was born. Car accident on the way to the hospital. Never met him," he admitted.

She reached out to touch him. Her hand hesitated over his wrist before she seemingly realized what she was doing. She squeezed it and then immediately pulled her hand back, tucking it into the side pocket of her tartan pants. "That's tough. So how did he affect how you are?"

Man, she didn't want to hear this. Or rather, he didn't want to talk about it. This was what he got for trying to avoid telling her anything personal about Paul. "My mom wanted me to know my dad and had his baby book and some sort of school years book left. So everything my dad was pictured doing as a kid, I had to do to 'connect' with him. She pushed me to live not just for myself but for him as well. Except he died when he was twenty-four. After college, it was like my life went from being all planned out to just being empty. So I guess I'm…"

"Not sure what to do," she finished for him. They were in front of the bookstore now. She stepped out of the light foot traffic to settle under the store's awning, gazing up at him. "What do *you* want? Your job with *Live with Bri O'Brien* seems like a good one."

"It is. Pays decent, Bri's a good boss. But it's a job. I bet writing's more than a job for you," he said.

Her face lit up.

His heart stuttered.

"I love it. Sometimes I hate it and wish I had chosen something else as a career. But you're right, it's so much more than a job."

"I want that. But I still haven't figured out who I am," he admitted. Being way more honest than he'd anticipated.

"I don't have myself figured out either. You're not supposed to," she said. "Every day new experiences and people force you to grow and change. That's the journey of life."

The door to the bookstore opened as a customer came out.

She caught the handle and nodded for him to enter first. He did, thinking about what she said. Maybe because he felt so rudderless compared to everyone else, he'd supposed that she had her shit together. She seemed like she did.

It was one of the things he liked about her. She didn't hesitate even when things got wonky. Maybe it was because she had been talking to ghosts for most of her life. There was something otherworldly about her and it wasn't just the way she dressed. There was an aura around her that only he saw.

Jasper was growing on her. That always happened when she got to know someone new, she was quick to remind herself. Most people one-on-one were interesting.

There was a part of her that wanted to fix him. Not that he was broken.

She'd always felt like she was thirtysomething. Her mom blamed herself, saying that Kirsty had to grow up too quickly. The reasons weren't that important to her now.

The truth was she was comfortable in her skin. Even when she hadn't fit in, she'd burrowed deeper into her own psyche and found a nice comfortable way of dealing with the world.

Her black clothing, heavy eyeliner and dark lipstick were enough to make most people give her a wide berth. Which gave her the option of deciding who she wanted to engage with.

Jasper was different because she'd met him at that damn concert. The one place where she didn't carry the worries that usually plagued her and just let herself be. He'd wormed his way into her life before she had time to determine what that would mean.

Taking a deep breath she let the smell of aging paper wrap around her. She was home. The world awaited her in the volumes housed in this bookstore. All those characters and stories waiting to carry her away from life. It still gave her a thrill of excitement to think she was an author.

That she was offering escape to others just like the ones she'd found growing up. She was fully present in a way she felt nowhere else. Except sex. She'd blame *that* mental detour on Jasper as well.

Skimming the signs above the shelves, she looked for mystery first and found it toward the back on the left. There were some armchairs and tables that looked as if they'd come from a secondhand shop. Worn, probably comfortable, they beckoned her to sit and curl up and read.

Yes. This was what she needed. Time to get in her head and out of this place of semi-panic she'd been in since this morning. Faking being a medium with the ability to awaken her third eye and communicate with those on the other side was a lot of pressure.

She slowly walked down the main aisle, aware that Jasper had fallen behind, but she was anxious to see if they had her new book and if any of her previous titles were there. Her name was steadily growing in the field, but each book was like starting over again, a reintroduction to convince new readers that she could be trusted with their entertainment.

Her newest book was face out and they had one copy of each of the previous four titles, which made her grin. She took out her phone and snapped a picture of them.

"Want me to take one of you?" Jasper asked.

"If they let me sign them, then yes," she said. She went to find the manager while Jasper picked up her newest book and started skimming it.

It totally didn't matter if he liked her book… Okay, even she couldn't convince herself of that lie. She wanted him to like it and be impressed. Her editor thought this book was her best yet, but inside, Kirsty wasn't sure. All of her books felt so unfinished even when they ended up in print.

She always thought of something that could be different later. Or worse, something that could have been improved on. One of her writing buddies offered that it was the best book Kirsty could write at the time which was totally true.

Was that why Paul was still hanging around? A lack of satisfaction with his life? She jotted that down on the notes app on her phone. Dying young had to mean there was unfinished business. And from what Jasper said, Paul was the type to push himself hard to perfection.

A guy about her age with a buzz cut and thick horn-rimmed glasses wearing jeans and a sweater with "Books are essential." knitted on it walked over to her.

"Hi, I'm Tim the manager. Can I help you find anything?"

"I'm K.L. Henson, the author of *Roses for the Dead*. I noticed you had some of my books in stock and wondered if I could sign them," she said. *Deep breaths, Kirsty.* Some things about the job never got easier.

"Of course. Nice to meet you. We've sold a lot of copies of it," he said. "Let's get you set up to sign them. Are you local?"

"I'm here for a few weeks with some friends. Doing research for my next book." *Liar.*

"Great. We have a local readers' group that meets on the second Tuesday of the month. Would you like to come back and talk to them?" he asked. "That's next week."

"Sure, if you think they'd enjoy it," she said. A room full of her readers sounded like a dream come true—or a nightmare, if they hated the book.

"Definitely." Tim led the way back to the mystery section where Jasper waited. "Jasper Cotton? Dude, I didn't know you

74 Ghost of a Chance

were back in town." In an instant Tim's demeanor changed from mousy clerk to full-on bro.

"Just for a few weeks," he said.

"You two friends?" Tim asked.

Oh no. If Jasper started talking about Paul and her amateur ghost whispering, then Kirsty was going to walk straight out of this shop. Even though she was getting filmed trying to live out this fantasy gone wrong, something about saying it out loud to a stranger made her feel ridiculous.

"She's helping me with a project for work," Jasper said. "I didn't realize you lived here."

"Decided to stay after graduation. My girlfriend and I leased this space and opened the bookstore. We've been making a go of it since."

While they caught up, Kirsty signed the books and put her promotional stickers and bookmarks in them. Noticing when she opened her bag that the physics book was in there. Something she shoved to one side until she could speak to Jasper. Her joy at signing the books dimmed slightly. She truly didn't believe in ghosts but how else could she explain the book being here and the music on Jasper's phone?

Jasper snapped a few photos of her signing, as well as one with her and Tim before they left.

Once outside she pulled Jasper to a stop. "I don't want anyone to know about the Paul thing."

"I sort of figured. You went even paler than normal when he asked what we were doing. But you know Dan's filming us and Bri is going to air that segment, right?"

She was about to make a massive mistake, but if she kept implying she could just ring up a ghost and have a conversation with them, she was never going to recover from this.

"Of course I know that. Also did you put the physics book in my bag?"

"Definitely not. Why?"

Opening the bag she held it out to him. Jasper rubbed the back of his neck looking awkwardly around them before pulling her around the corner. "Can you ask him why he's here?"

"I don't talk to poltergeists," she said through gritted teeth.

"Do they show you things?" he asked.

Since that was pretty much what she'd intimated every time she'd used her "ability" to get out of something, she nodded. "It's not all the time. I guess this explains your phone."

"Maybe. So what's the problem with people knowing about your paranormal skills?"

How could she say she wanted her books to stand on their own? That the only reason she'd added the joke to her author bio was to make it a part of the fantasy she'd always imagined for herself. One where she stood out?

The joke was on her. As Jasper had rightly pointed out, she was known as someone who had a psychic ability. At least in her small corner of the world. There was no way she'd ever truly know if her books were popular because of her writing or because people were intrigued by the woman behind them.

"There isn't one."

"Good. So what now?"

"Let's go to the coffee place and you can tell me more about Paul."

Joe's had a certain timelessness to it. As he stepped through the door, the scent of roasted coffee beans and the chatter of the patrons took Jasper back to the first time he'd come here. Freshman year. Paul had just transferred in after studying at

Ghost of a Chance

another university and flunking out first semester. Too much pressure, he'd said.

Jasper hadn't anticipated coming back here ever. Especially without Paul.

Of course his friend was technically here, just trapped in a textbook.

Kirsty needed to know about him, and Jasper wasn't sure where to start, even after they ordered their drinks and sat in a corner booth near the back. There was a tradition for students to write their names on the walls and they were covered with signatures and years. His and Paul's were scrawled on the other side of the café.

"What do you want to know?"

She pulled her tablet from her bag and set it on the table next to her double espresso with one sugar cube. Her fingers moved quickly over the keyboard. He noticed that chipped paint on her index finger again. He liked the slight imperfection. It showed him that there were cracks in that formidable facade that she presented to the world. To him.

She said that no one had themselves figured out, but she did a cracking job of faking it. Shoving his hand through his hair, he waited for her. He took a sip of his cappuccino with two cubes of sugar. Deliciously sweet and just what he needed.

Closing his eyes, it was almost as if he was a sophomore again. Nothing had happened. Paul was still alive; he was still dithering about his major, but not so erratic in his class choices that he was limited to a handful of degrees.

"What did Paul want to do with his life?" she asked. "I think maybe if we can figure out what was left undone, we'll have a good starting point."

Jasper had no clue. They hadn't talked much about the future. Or rather Jasper hadn't really listened. He'd mostly partied, discussed their individual classes, complained about the daily minutia of college social life, and worried about their grades. "I'm not sure. We didn't talk about shit like that."

"What did you talk about?"

"Homework, how hard certain classes were, people we hoped to hook up with," Jasper said.

"Did you both like the same girls?"

"No. Paul was into guys."

"Sorry, I shouldn't have assumed," she said. "Did he have someone?"

"Yes. He and Victor were pretty serious about each other. They met sophomore year," Jasper said.

Jasper knew he should have talked to Victor before he came back. It hadn't seemed right that Paul would be haunting him instead of Victor. They'd been so close. Honestly the most solid couple out of their entire friend group.

"Could Paul be trying to get you to take him to Victor?"

"No." He'd sent the book to Victor once, and Victor had returned it to Jasper. Though Victor hadn't included a note or anything. Probably because of how Jasper had shut down after Paul's death.

"What did he say when you told him Paul was in the physics book?"

"Nothing. I never talked to him about it. I sent him the book in the mail and he sent it back."

She closed the lid to her tablet and put both hands flat on top of it. "Are you kidding me?"

"No. Why would I tell him? It would hurt him that Paul was with me and not him," Jasper said.

"Or maybe talking about the book with him was what Paul needs," she stated.

When she put it that way, it made a lot of sense. "Good thought."

"Ya think? So where is he now?"

He didn't know. What did it say about him that he hadn't kept in touch? There had been a bit of guilt, but also the smallest bit of anger. Jasper never wanted the responsibility of shouldering the burden of his friend. Mourning him once had been hard enough.

"I'll have to find out."

"Okay," she said. "Let's keep Victor on the down-low in front of Dan until we find him."

"Works for me. Do you think we should have that séance Gia mentioned, to try to talk to him?"

Her eyes went wide and then she opened the lid to her tablet and keyboard and started typing. She looked nervous. "I don't usually do them."

"Why not?"

She chewed her lower lip, which drew his eyes to her lush mouth. God, he wished none of this was happening. That there was no ghost or TV segment to film. Just two people on a date, so he could lean over, take her mouth and show her how beautiful she was to him.

"It opens me up to too many spirits," she said, the words coming out in a low rush, as if she didn't want anyone to hear anything. "I'll consider it if nothing else happens when we get back."

There wasn't much more to discuss on that. She sipped her espresso. "So the music...even though the book's with us. Could your phone be on the fritz?"

"Oh...maybe. Hadn't considered that."

"You're probably so accustomed to the book doing freaky

things so it makes sense. Has it happened before without the book being around?"

Trying to remember. "This is only the fifth or sixth time."

"And?"

"Before it was always at home."

"Good to know. Let's keep an eye on it."

"Don't you mean ear?"

She groaned but he saw a hint of a smile. "That's a total dad joke."

"Does your dad tell them? I mean do you ever see him?"

"Not really. Not to take anything away from your situation, but it's sort of like he's dead. He never wanted to be a part of my life," she said.

"I'm sorry." He knew his father had wanted to be a dad more than anything. His mom had told him more than once that his father had read every parenting book to ensure he'd be the best father he could be. "My dad was apparently different."

"Was he? Did your mom talk about him a lot?"

"All the time. It was hard. She lost her husband and she missed him so much. Plus, I was a colicky baby, so she was sleep-deprived on top of being depressed."

"Cried a lot...that tracks," she said without cracking a smile.

"Hey."

"Kidding. That's sweet that you're close to her."

"It was just the two of us for so long," he admitted.

"Same with me and my mom. It wasn't cool to call your mom when I was in college, but I still talked to her every day. It was nice to have that one solid thing."

"Me too." He hadn't thought about it that way before. But he'd always known that whenever things went shit his mom would be there. Even if he was the one who fucked it up.

Six

The reaction to the word *séance*—from someone who claimed to be a medium, no less—was exactly the reason why he hadn't sought out any help to get rid of Paul earlier. There was something about it that brought to mind Hollywood theatrics and con men. Of course Kirsty didn't look like either of those, but still.

Her mouth tightened. "Are you sure you want to go through with it?"

"Want to? No, but I think it's what we need to do."

With an expert at his side, he was confident that this would be key in helping Paul move on.

What if this was fake? Or she was a fake? That everything with the book was a result of him slowly going insane. Still his options were limited and dwindling. A part of him hoped that Paul would be about to speak about the past to Kirsty so he wouldn't have to relive it all by himself.

They were all sitting in the study two days later. Kirsty had insisted she needed time to prepare herself and the room for the séance.

For the last few days she'd used sage to purify the space. Sat quietly in her room for hours doing who knew what and then she'd emerged this morning wearing all black jeans and a turtleneck like a sexy cat burglar and declared today was the day.

She put on a purple kimono that had mystic symbols on it. Like the all-seeing eye and moons and stars. Her hair was braided into one long plait that fell over her shoulder ending on her left boob, something he was desperately trying not to notice.

The room itself had large windows framed by heavy blackout curtains. In preparation, Gia drew them shut, blocking out any residual light from the street, making the room feel heavy and very dark. There were floor-to-ceiling bookshelves down one wall jammed with framed pictures of strangers, board games and knickknacks collected from around the world. An overstuffed leather couch faced them with two armchairs on the other side.

Everything looked antique and well-worn. There was normally a low square table between the seats, but Kirsty insisted it needed to be moved.

"How about we skip the séance?" Jasper asked, coming back in to wait for further orders to make the room *just right for talking to the dead*. Now that the moment was here, he was nervous.

"Yeah, and do what?" She glared at him over her shoulder as she pointed to the corner of the room where Dan wanted to set up the camera. "Not there. That's the place I'm going to banish unwanted spirits to. It's close to the window so they can leave."

"Gia, open the curtains a crack and then the window behind it," Kirsty ordered.

He couldn't help but clock that, despite her insistence, she didn't seem superconfident about how this all worked. "I'm

82   Ghost of a Chance

sorry you were pressured into doing this. If this isn't your area of expertise…maybe we can try to find another expert."

"It's not my area of expertise at all. Do you know of someone else?"

"No. You seem so tense."

"I've never done this with an object before…just want to set the expectation that séances aren't a guarantee. I don't want you to be let down."

"I won't be. I'm just glad that you're trying something. I really believe in you."

Her face softened but otherwise she didn't even acknowledge it. "Do you know how to build a fire?"

"Yeah."

"Great. Start one in that fireplace." Gesturing to the large stone-faced one on the wall opposite the bookcases.

"I was a Boy Scout."

"Of course you were."

"What's that mean?"

"Just that you give off goody-goody vibes."

"We can't all be Ms. Goth Girl."

"Suits me. I'm not really a joiner."

"You're unique."

Slight pink tinged her cheeks before she angled her head toward the fireplace, turning back to her preparations. The braid she had her hair in swung out as she pivoted away from him, and he was tempted to catch it and stop her from dismissing him. But he was smart enough not to follow through.

Maybe her prickly personality would be enough for Paul to ditch this earthly plane and move on.

He lit the fire at Kirsty's request, then shifted the furniture around so they could bring in the kitchen table. They draped it with a cloth Kirsty uncovered in the dining room cabinet, after knocking away some of the dust. It had black and navy stripes with an old puddle of wax in the center. Not very occult looking, but it would do.

The lamps scattered throughout the room flickered as he went to get to the book.

"Are any of you allergic to different scents?" Kirsty asked the room.

Jasper shook his head as Chewie padded in and nudged his hand before curling up at his feet.

"I am. But I can finish setting up the camera and then wait in the hall. Jasper, you know how to start and stop the recording?" Dan verified as he edged his way to the door.

"I do. Will you keep Chewie? I'm not sure he'll stay quiet while we're filming," Jasper said.

"Sure."

Gia came back into the room dressed in a lime-green turtleneck and a miniskirt in a matching plaid. Who even made lime green and bright yellow tartan? She had black leather boots and a bandanna wrapped around her head like a headband. Apparently this adventure was turning into an episode of *Scooby-Doo*.

She gave him a once-over. "Are you wearing that?"

His UVM hoodie and jeans were comfy. "Unless you object."

"Kirsty, do you think he should change?"

Kirsty glanced up from her bag, a bundle of candles in different shapes and sizes in her hands. "He's fine. Did you wear that faded hoodie when you were a student?"

He nodded.

"Perfect. That will give Paul something familiar to hone in on," Kirsty said.

He couldn't keep his eyes off of her as she glided around the

84   Ghost of a Chance

room, rearranging objects and pulling décor out of her bag. When she bent over, he couldn't help but notice the way the kimono fluttered around her lithe frame. The room was taking on an occult feel and Kirsty shone in it. Her nerves were starting to abate as the room came together.

He tore his eyes from her. This was business, he reminded himself.

His nerves were starting to settle down as well. She was probably here for publicity for her book. He got that. He'd seen what her career meant to her.

Also knew what she meant to him. Kirsty was the key to everything, and he was determined to make sure that this worked. Whatever it took.

That meant ignoring the way she made his heart stutter and his palms sweat, pretending that one night with her was enough.

Kirsty felt a little sick to her stomach. She'd never conducted a séance before. Sure, she'd played the Ouija board game as a teenager, but that wasn't the same thing at all. Besides what little she and her mother could find in their books, all she had to go off of was what she remembered from shows like *Buffy* and *Charmed*.

Closing her eyes, she steeled herself. She needed to just do this. She had already committed to it. Now she had to get into the spirit. All of this medium nonsense was much easier when she wrote about Eva Clare doing it.

Her hands sweated. She wiped them on her thighs and then cleared her throat. Gia watched her eagerly.

She took her time setting the table up. Discreetly she checked her phone and the wikiHow séance page she'd decided to use for tonight.

"Jasper, I know you're eager to talk to Paul and find out why he hasn't moved on. We can assume that means you believe in what we're about to do." Her research indicated that believing in the séance was necessary to get a result. "Gia, do you believe in ghosts and the afterlife?"

"Uh, totally. I have a Ouija board and everything," she said. "Let's do this."

"Ouija isn't the same thing." Never mind that she'd just thought the same thing. "So, you two are the sitters while I'm acting as the medium. If I'm successful in contacting Paul then you'll be able to ask him questions while I channel him."

"Perfect. There's so much I want to ask him, I wouldn't even know where to start."

"I think the simpler the question the better. Something that has a yes or no answer," she suggested. The wiki page had also suggested that. Plus it would be easier to moan a *yes* or *no* without raising too much suspicion.

She was going to hell for this. She was sure of it. She didn't even believe in hell as a construct, but she was definitely going down there for masquerading as the ghost of a dead man. Probably to endure all the layers that Dante had sent Faust through.

"Okay, so like…do you have unfinished business?" Jasper suggested.

"Totally stuff like that. But maybe more specific, add *with me.* You both should jot down your questions before we start. Then you won't forget it in the moment."

"Uh, I don't know the dude," Gia pointed out. "What would I even ask him?"

"He might have beef with Jasper depending on what his unfinished business is. You're a neutral party in case he's temperamental."

Gia and Jasper bent their heads together and jotted down

their questions on the paper that Kirsty provided. She'd banned phones except her own, citing that modern devices would interfere with her channeling. Of course, that didn't apply to any of the cameras they needed to film...but for now, no one was directly calling Kirsty out on her contradictions.

It was decided that, since the book was the focus, they'd suspend a smartphone over the table using a rig Dan set up earlier in the day and then use the proper film camera placed on a tripod far back from the scene to get all three of them in frame.

"We're ready. What now?" Jasper asked.

Kirsty surveyed the room, eyeing the heavy mixture of lit taper candles in different colors including white to invite spirits in, blue which enhanced communication, and orange which welcomed positive spirits and kept negative ones away. She didn't have any incense but improvised with cinnamon she found in the kitchen and dusted in a small bowl.

"Do you have a photo of Paul?"

"On my phone," Jasper said, going out into the hall and coming back with it.

"I have a pocket printer. AirDrop it to me and I'll go print it out," Gia volunteered. She left and then returned a few minutes later, handing it to Jasper.

"Let's put the photo in the middle of the candles on top of the textbook. Also it's important to stay calm, we don't want to frighten him off if we get him."

Jasper seemed lost as he stared at the photo. His expression was inscrutable, which given that he was normally a bit easier to read told her volumes. For his sake she hoped this séance worked not just for her own credibility. If ever a man needed closure it was him.

Gia leaned over Jasper's shoulder and touched the photo. "He was cute."

"Yeah. Cute, smart, kind, Paul was all of that and more."

"You need a minute?" Kirsty asked. She didn't know how she'd feel if it were her trying to talk to Gia. She'd be a mess.

Jasper gave the photo one more look before placing it where she asked him to. "I'm good."

She doubted that but wasn't going to let on that she saw through him. Right now they both needed this séance to work. She had to concentrate on that. If she could...who was she kidding...her chances of actually connecting with Paul were very slim. But maybe something would happen to give Jasper some closure.

"Then we're ready to begin. Do you want to start the camera?" she suggested to Jasper since Dan was watching from another room, wanting no part of the séance.

He did it then sat back down.

"Let's start with a meditation. Try to be calm and reach out to Paul. I'm going to try to open my third eye while you both close your eyes."

Keeping her eyes open, Kirsty made sure they followed her instructions. Jasper's eyes were tight in concentration, while Gia's seemed at ease, like she was taking a mini meditation break. She rested her hand on the textbook and let her head fall back, her eyes rolling back in her head.

She'd done this a couple of times. She knew it looked authentic, like a spirit was invading her being. Truth to tell it had never gotten her any results. Truthfully she always felt like the biggest fraudster on the planet.

Except maybe you're not.

What?

Her eyes flew open as she looked around the room but there

wasn't anyone else there. Jasper and Gia were quiet and still. An icy feeling shot up her spine. Whatever voice she heard didn't sound like either of them. Could it be…?

Kirsty closed hers again and concentrated, but the voice was gone.

That was freaky. Maybe she'd imagined it. Probably because she was putting so much stress on herself to make this seem real. Doing some yoga breathing helped steady her pulse and she slipped back into the role of medium.

"Are you both ready to take part in the séance?" she asked.

"Yes," they said in unison.

"Join hands." A shiver went up her arm when Jasper's warm palm rubbed against hers. Gia's fingers were cold and shook a little, either from nerves or excitement.

"Focus your energy toward the book in the center of the circle of candles," Kirsty said. She slitted her eyes so she could keep an eye out for any more interference.

"Tonight we are here to contact the spirit of Paul…"

"Lester. Paul, it's Jasper."

"Slow down. Let me do the incantation first," Kirsty warned him. She had to keep a semblance of order or her ruse would fall apart fast. But she felt how eager Jasper was to talk to his roommate.

"Sorry," Jasper said, squeezing her fingers.

"We welcome friendly spirits who can help us contact Paul Lester. All good spirits who are near our circle are welcome to contact us. We seek information and mean no harm," Kirsty said.

A cool breeze brushed against her neck and Gia's hand tightened in response. The candles flickered. She wasn't sure if there was a draft coming from a vent or the window. The idea that this was actually working seemed preposterous.

"Someone's here," Gia said. "Paul? Is that you?"

Kirsty took a deep breath, prepared to channel Paul but she felt the weight of a hand on her shoulder.

No more lies.

The words were so loud in her head that she jerked her hands away from Jasper and Gia. Breaking the circle.

Neither of them seemed concerned. Jasper was in the middle of asking a question, but Kirsty couldn't pay attention. Her hands were shaking. That was fucking weird. This was probably her imagination, her conscience playing tricks on her because she didn't want to do this.

"Paul? Are you here?" Her voice came out ragged and frantic.

Nothing happened. That cool breeze was gone, and Kirsty was afraid to go back into playing her role.

After a moment, she calmed herself. She was clearly freaking out over nothing. She had to keep pushing forward, if just for her reputation. They tried a few more times but nothing happened.

"Sorry, guys, I think we'll have to try again another time," Kirsty said.

"I wonder if he left for good because he doesn't want to talk to me." A note of sadness in Jasper's voice.

The lights in the room flickered on and off at Jasper's words. And then the sound of the TV blasted loudly from the other room.

"My guess is no."

Seven

Jasper wasn't too sure what he expected. That Paul's haunting would end as quickly as it had begun. But it seemed like his friend wasn't ready to go. The candles were still burning and the scent of the pine logs in the fire filled the room making this gothic atmosphere almost cozy.

"Well… I guess that didn't work," he said after Dan had gone to his room to review the footage and edit it. Gia had gotten a call during the séance and rushed out to return it, leaving him and Kirsty alone.

"Ya think?"

"Sarcasm really isn't that attractive." Which was a total lie—sarcasm was a part of her charm. He knew she used it when she was on edge. The séance had to be disappointing for her.

"Did it seem like I was trying to attract you?" This time her voice had an edge, razor-sharp.

"What's wrong?"

Refusing to answer him, she gathered up the candles, cooled wax droplets peppering their edges. Then she hesitated over the book.

Had Paul talked to her after all? Had Paul indicated that Jasper was the last person he wanted to talk to? Something about haunting him? Jasper didn't believe for a moment that Paul was petty enough to hold a grudge for five years because of a fight.

Kirsty on the other hand looked wan and unsure. Two things that he didn't associate with her. His gut signaled something must have happened during the séance.

"You okay?"

Her hands balled into fists and she closed her eyes, hesitation clouding her face. "Uh-huh. That's a lie. I'm not okay. I told you this isn't my area of expertise."

"You did great. I bet it was me. Paul isn't the type to hold a grudge but this is the first time I've actually had an outsider try to help."

"That's good to know. Paul sounds like a wonderful guy. Did he ever call you on anything?"

"All the time."

"Can you give me an example?"

He wasn't sure how that would help but the color was returning to her face. Relaxing her a bit. "One time I faked that I was sick for a week because I wanted to get to the end of *Star Wars Jedi: Fallen Order*. You get to battle Darth Vadar."

"That sounds cool. What happened?"

"My boss fired me and I complained and Paul was like I hope fighting Darth Vadar was worth it. Stuff like that."

"You're a real *Star Wars* fan, aren't you?"

"I thought we established that already."

"Just didn't realize how deep your obsession was."

"Ha. I didn't write fanfic about it."

"You're not a writer."

"Ouch."

Ghost of a Chance

Staring into the flames of the fire, they sat in silence until she leaned toward him. "I think we should contact a real medium."

"Uh, no. I don't trust people who charge for this kind of thing," he said.

"But you trust me."

He thought about it for a long minute. Did he trust her? As much as he could trust anyone with this. Plus he didn't want to talk about Paul to anyone else. The four of them in this house were about all he could handle. "Sure."

"Took you a minute."

"Sorry, this entire occult thing…it's not something I normally believe in."

Throwing her head back, she laughed hard. "You're the one with the haunted book."

"Point taken." He paused, looking around the room. The house suddenly felt too quiet. "I need a drink," he said.

"Me too. But not tequila."

"Why not?"

"Just…listen, I'm not doing that again. This is my career on the line," she said as she led the way into the kitchen. She opened the fridge and took out a can of Coke. "I think I saw some rum in the pantry."

He fetched it and they made themselves rum and Cokes before he realized he needed to take Chewie out. The dog was whining impatiently by the door. But he still wanted to talk to her.

"Want to take a walk with me and Chewie?"

"Yes."

Once they were on the sidewalk, he gave Chewie a bit of the lead and then looked over at her. "What did you mean your career is on the line?"

Katherine Garbera   93

"Just that if this goes south, then everyone will look at my books differently. Look at me differently," she said, taking a large gulp of her drink.

"I thought you wrote ghostly murder mysteries."

"I do. Cozies really. So the murder takes place off the page. I don't really depict any real violence. And the ghosts are benign."

"So…how is this going to affect your career?"

She paused, eyebrows furrowed. "Wow, you really aren't a fan."

"I told you I hadn't read any of your books," he said sheepishly. He was curious now, even thumbed through her latest at the bookstore. He'd heard that authors often put a lot of themselves in their books. Was that what had her worried? "Your heroine is a medium, right?"

"Not by choice. She hates her gift and never uses it publicly. It's more like the ghosts come to her while she's working at her little bakery and then she ends up helping them to solve their own murders."

"Wouldn't the ghost know who killed them?" This was new ground for him. His only ghost knowledge came from Paul, who seemed to be anything but a normal ghost.

"In my world they can't remember their death. They only know they can't move on and that there was something violent about how they died," she said. "You have to make up the rules for your world. Readers will go on a ride with you, but if you fuck up the rules then they don't believe anything."

"Do you think Paul can't remember and that's why he's—"

"I have no idea in the real world. That's fiction. I do it that way so Eva has to dig around and find clues."

Interesting. Did that mean her medium skills were even harder to believe? "Why did you start writing?"

94   Ghost of a Chance

"I always liked to read, and my mom suggested I take a creative writing course. I was working full-time at a bakery and took a night course. The teacher was really great and very encouraging…and after I wrote my first book, I got an agent and thought that I was going to be big." She said the last part sardonically.

"And you are. Lots of readers wrote to ask for tickets when we were going to have you on the show," he told her.

"That's nice. But my first manuscript didn't sell and my agent wanted me to write a bakery mystery instead…then we had a fight and I dumped her."

"Is this the breakup you mentioned at Dead Boys?"

"Yup. I went home, put on *Umbrella Academy* because it's one of my comfort watches and there was Ben aka Number 6."

"Never seen it."

"I love it. It's about these kids with powers who were all born on the same day and a billionaire adopted them all, training them to be a team to save the planet. Except their powers aren't easy to control. Anyway Ben is killed and the only one who can talk to him is Klaus. We can watch it together sometime."

"I'd like that. So your idea was born from the show? That's so cool. I could never do anything like that," he said, stopping while Chewie did his business. The feeling of wanting to create something, to be something, seemed so much out of reach for him. He and Paul had been working together to try to finish a project left undone by his dad. Paul was doing the science bit and Jasper had been meant to finish writing some pages in a science fiction short story his dad had started.

He'd tried but the words just never really came to him and the pages he'd written felt clichéd and forced. Just another thing he hadn't followed through on. With effort he shook that failure off.

Kirsty looked beautiful under the illumination of the streetlamp. There was something softer about her out here. Talking about her writing had relaxed her.

The dark lipstick she had on earlier had worn off. His eyes were drawn to her mouth, and then all he could think about was kissing her.

"What?"

"I want to kiss you." There you go. He'd never had a filter.

"I…sure."

"Sure?"

"Kiss me, Jasper."

He didn't give himself time to overthink it. He leaned over and bent down. She went up on tiptoe, her hands on his shoulders, and their lips met. Hers parted under his, a moment of surrender. Fuck, she tasted better than he remembered. Faintly of Coke and rum, but mostly something spicy and addicting.

It took all of his willpower to lightly touch her waist and not pull her fully into his arms. She was hesitant, he respected that. They were working together, even he had his doubts if this was a good idea. But he felt like he'd combust if he didn't keep touching her. Just his hand on her waist was enough… for this moment.

Her lips were swollen. "I'm trying to be smart here."

That's right. She was worried about her career. And getting caught fraternizing with the man she's supposedly helping could make it all seem like a hoax. "Got it. I'm a dumb idea."

"You're an idea. Nothing dumb about you, Jasper."

She nestled her head on his chest. He hugged her with one arm, listening to the steady sound of her breath. Chewie came back and nudged between their legs like he wanted to be part of the hug.

Was this the friend zone?

It felt like it. But somehow he felt better about where the two of them were now than he had earlier.

The more he got to know her, the more he liked her.

This night had been a ride. The first and probably last séance she'd ever conduct had weirded her out. That voice had been so deep and dark. A warning, and not one she wanted to ever hear again.

While kissing Jasper was a little salve for her battered soul. But one-night stands were for the road and book tours, not for people she had to work with, so a kiss was all she'd allow herself. Too bad that her body didn't seem to get the message.

Her breath still felt heavy, her entire being still reaching for Jasper. But her mind was too busy. Monkey mind, they called it. The chaos of trying to figure out so many things. Who was the voice? Was Paul still in the book or was he in danger? Would she get her book written on time? Should she sleep with Jasper like every fiber of her being craved? Right now that voice she'd heard during the séance was still at the edge of everything.

It had frightened her. Jasper with his sweetness and kisses was the balm for that. Comforting her in a way that she really didn't want to unpack right now.

Her mom had been pretty clear that, if she was going to play at being a medium and talking to ghosts, she needed to keep things light. Inviting herself into their realm could awaken something unexpected. But her warning had fallen on deaf ears. In no way had Kirsty ever believed any of it was real.

Now she had this faint feeling that it might be.

She might have called a spirit forward... "What did Paul sound like?"

"Huh?"

Jasper gave her a funny look, his attention on Chewie who was inspecting something. She repeated the question.

She didn't want to divulge that she'd heard a voice in that room. No one else had mentioned hearing anything, so it was probably in her head. And if it wasn't, she didn't want to reveal it before she understood who—or what—it was.

"Let me see. Can you hold Chewie's lead? I think I have a video of us from before he died."

She took the dog's lead from him and bent down to pet Chewie, letting the dog nuzzle closer to her as she did so. Jasper was a lot like his dog: big and comforting.

"Here it is. But it's just a voice note from him."

She stood up and leaned over his arm as he hit play.

"Don't forget I'm going to the lab tonight. If you get drunk Uber home. Later."

Not the voice that she'd heard during the séance. Not even close. This one was lighter and there wasn't a tone of warning. But then, his attitude might have changed after he died.

"When was that from?"

"The night he died," Jasper said roughly. His voice was choked with emotion.

She didn't have to be Eva Clare to figure out that Jasper was trying to keep from crying. The way he'd laid out the facts.

"Do you miss him?"

"I do. Usually...well, he's so irritating that I have that as a shield to keep from admitting it to myself."

"I'm sorry," she said.

"Thanks."

"I thought you said he died at your place."

98   Ghost of a Chance

"Oops, I forgot about the lab. Sorry, guess I blocked it out. I just associated him with being at our place."

"What lab?"

"The physics lab on campus," he said.

Hearing he'd blocked out where his roommate had been the night he died made her want to dig deeper into the fight he'd mentioned they had.

Since the séance was a bust and so far Kirsty hadn't felt anything supernatural around the book, she was going back to plan A which was to investigate this issue like it was a mystery. "Let's go there and see if we can find out what he was working on when he died."

"I'll check and see when the lab is open as soon as we get back," he said. As sunny as Jasper usually was, he sounded resigned. Maybe because of the toll this was taking on him.

Or maybe because there was more to the fight he had with Paul that fateful night.

"Anxious to get this over with?" she asked as they started walking back. She'd finished the last of her rum and Coke, as had Jasper. The alcohol left a light buzz behind.

"More than you know. It's not like I didn't love Paul, but it's time for him to move on. I feel like I'm stuck in some sort of stasis."

"Like when Han was in carbonite at the end of *Empire Strikes Back*? We'll figure this out," she promised.

She wasn't one to let go of something once she started it. One way or another she was going to figure out why Paul was trapped in a textbook and help Jasper move on. The possibility that it was Jasper's guilt and unresolved emotions around his roommate's death still felt the most plausible. Even with tonight's oddities.

"Except I'm walking around and talking… I feel more

like a hologram. Here but not really." But they were back at the house and Gia was outside smoking weed, waving them over to her.

Jasper let Chewie into the house so the dog could get water and then head upstairs to his bed in Jasper's room.

Kirsty was a little jealous.

"Do you think Dan captured any paranormal activity?" Jasper's deep timbre brought her back to reality.

"He texted earlier that the curtains moved at one point, so I think that's where the cool feeling came from," Gia mentioned.

"That explains it," Jasper said, his voice deflating. "I'm a bit disappointed. I mean, I wasn't sure it would work. But still."

"You should have said something, Jasper. If anyone has doubts it makes the spirits leery of showing up."

She'd read that on the wiki. It resonated with her.

"I thought that was obvious."

"How? You have a haunted book and brought it on live TV. Sounds like you believe in it to me."

"Oh, well when you put it that way," he said dryly.

"Most of the things I do are predicated on belief. So if you're not into it, say so. It can have a big impact on the environment around me." She was in this lie so deep that she was swimming now. If anyone was at fault for a lack of belief, it was her.

He nodded; his forehead creased in thought. "Sorry. I didn't know."

"I'm just cranky. I should turn in. See you both tomorrow." She left as they both were saying good-night.

From the beginning she'd known this was going to be hard. She had no way of freeing a ghost from a book. Of talking to the dead and bringing someone peace. That was more apparent than ever. Yet...

Two things haunted her as she made her way up the stairs. That voice warning her not to lie. And Jasper's kiss.

It was going to be hard to keep her distance from him. Relationships weren't really her thing. She didn't trust anyone except her mom. Probably it was down to her dad abandoning them sprinkled with the few guys she'd dated in college.

No more kisses after dark. Tomorrow she'd be her most buttoned-up self. All business. She would solve this mystery whatever it was and get the fuck out of Vermont and away from Jasper Cotton.

Chewie lay across the bottom of Jasper's bed, snoring. He should be sleeping himself, but he couldn't get that last voice message from Paul out of his head. His phone pinged.

Night, Jaspy. Love you.

Goodnight Mom. ☺

They'd had a fight earlier that day about Jasper's grades. He'd been close to flunking two classes. Focus had been hard to find while working with Paul to finish that sci-fi short story of his dad's. He hadn't wanted to admit that he couldn't do it. It was the first time he hadn't been able to do something his dad had done. Paul also worried Jasper spent too much time at the frat house and not enough at the library.

Having flunked out of one college, Paul had been determined to make the most of his second chance at UVM. He was also a year older than Jasper. Like a big brother watching out for him.

But after a lifetime of being watched and helicopter parented by his mom, Jasper hadn't been interested in that. Had started to choke on the chains of family. He didn't need to be told by another person that he only had four years to figure out the rest of his life.

From his earliest memory his mom had been warning him to make the most of every day.

He tried.

Until Paul's death.

Then everything shut down. He pulled himself back from experiencing new things, buckled down, got his degree, and then fell into the job with Bri. A real job. A grown-up job.

As he absently scrolled online, his phone started playing "No Such Thing" by John Mayer. A song that he personally didn't like, but it was on a playlist that his mom had made for him. She was inspired by watching *Guardians of the Galaxy* and seeing videos online of a parent and son who exchanged playlists. She got her best ideas from seeing what other parents did. She'd told him that more than once.

"Not tonight."

The music shut off and he fell back sideways on the bed, staring up at the ceiling. No closer to finding answers now than he had been the day he worked up the courage to ask Kirsty for help.

Unbidden the memory of her face when "Batshit" had started to play...a little startled but then totally into it. He liked that nothing seemed to faze her. Guess that was par for the course when she could communicate with the dead—but *not talk to them*.

Laughing a little at the remembered firmness in her tone. Which he'd been reading as stress. God knew she had to feel the pressure of getting Paul to leave the book. No amount of kissing and hugging was going to make up for his part in that.

Still no regrets. If not for Paul then he wouldn't have spent a rainy afternoon walking around town with her. He still wasn't sure why he'd hadn't suggested hanging out tonight.

"Because she asked you to give her space, you douche," he said out loud. Chewie snorted at him. After a few more minutes of tossing and turning, it became clear that sleep was not on the agenda, so Jasper got to his feet, pulled on a pair of sweatpants, forgoing a tee since he was hot and went down to the kitchen.

He'd dealt with insomnia in seventh grade, and his mom had him see a sleep therapist who advised him to leave the room entirely if he wasn't sleeping. To only return when he was tired. Something about not associating the bed with restlessness.

Maybe one of the girls had brought Sleepytime tea. He started opening cabinets when he heard footsteps behind him and jumped, pivoting to see Kirsty standing at the entrance to the kitchen in a long black cardigan.

"Sorry."

Fuck. His heart was still racing, and it was all he could do not to curse out loud and try to appear chill. Like she hadn't genuinely scared him.

"It's fine. Did you bring any Sleepytime tea?" he asked.

"I think Gia has some tea with valerian in it." Her hair was down, hanging around her shoulders as she brushed past him toward the cupboard and found the tea.

"Want some?" he asked as he filled the kettle with water.

"Sure," she said. "I don't know if it'll work. This place is… different."

"It definitely is." He hadn't even considered that the house itself was part of the problem. Paul seemed real enough, but the idea of other hauntings unsettled him. "Too big for my tastes. I'm used to my apartment and its sounds."

"And flickering lights," she teased.

"Especially those. Even Paul feels a bit subdued here," he mentioned. Other than earlier when the TV and the lights went off, he'd been pretty quiet.

"Probably realizes that you're serious about getting rid of him this time," she said. "Might scare him."

"Can ghosts get scared?"

"Hey, if they're our souls that are lingering for a reason, I'm pretty sure they can get scared."

She had a point.

They both took their teas to the kitchen table, which had been moved back in after their earlier theatrics, and sat down. He noticed she kept glancing at his naked chest, and he tried his damnedest to keep his eyes on her. That sweetheart-shaped face with her thick black brows and big brown eyes that he could just sink into.

There was something young and innocent about her when she wasn't wearing her dark eyeliner and lipstick. As if she was a different person entirely.

"Possibly," he said, not wanting to talk about Paul. "What's your biggest objection to hooking up with me again?"

Right now he needed her to give him something solid so he didn't make a pass. They were becoming friends and he didn't want to screw with that. Not tonight when for the first time in a really long time he didn't feel unsure.

Her hand went to the top button of her sweater, unbuttoning it and then buttoning it again as if it would help make up her mind.

"Too in your face?"

She flushed and forced her gaze up to his face. Their eyes met. He held his breath as a flash of longing and want appeared in her eyes. The spark between them went both ways. He reached across the table and touched her hand, ran his finger along her knuckles. Her skin was smooth and cool to the touch. She opened her palm and then turned it over until the tips of her fingers brushed his.

Then she pulled back. "Like I said, I'm here as an author and my publisher wants results." She started to say more, then shook her head, moving her gaze down to her tea mug.

Jasper just stared at those pretty brown eyes of hers. She really didn't like to reveal anything about herself. That much was clear. It was a wonder that she'd come home with him after the concert.

It would be easier to have this conversation if she wasn't so damned sexy. He couldn't concentrate on anything right now. As mysterious and guarded as she was, he felt like he understood her.

"That's just an excuse." She sighed, worrying a strand of her hair between her fingers. "I don't trust people."

"Why not?" He had no trouble trusting people but honestly, that was easy for him because he expected nothing from them.

"I suck at relationships. I don't want to sleep with you because one time I can write off, but more than that…things get complicated."

"Maybe we can make up rules and build our own world, like your books," he said. He'd do anything to hold her again. Sober this time. Feel her moving with him, exploring each other.

He wanted to cling to her to remind himself he wasn't going through this alone. So yeah, he'd play by her rules. Let her set the tone or whatever she wanted.

It wasn't like either of them was going to get a reprieve from the tension that flared between them.

"Like what?"

Eight

Like nothing. She didn't want to have rules for hanging out with a guy that she'd already almost hooked up with. It felt dangerously close to a relationship. "Forget it. I need to get back upstairs and write."

She started to stand. Better to leave now than do something she'd regret later.

"I never figured you for a coward."

"Excuse me?" Now she was awkwardly towering over the table as he sprawled on the other side. Those long arms of his draped over the tabletop, defined and tempting. From this angle his long bladelike nose, combined with the expression on his face, painted him in a harsh light. There was something of a playful warning in the way he watched her.

"You heard me," he said, taking the most exaggerated sip of his tea that she'd ever witnessed.

Screw him. "I'm not scared of you, Jasper."

"But you're definitely running from what you feel for me," he said.

She wanted to roll her eyes and walk away without looking back. That would be the easiest way to show him just how wrong he was. But she couldn't.

"Maybe you're projecting."

Ugh, that was her great comeback? A grown-up version of *same goes for you but double.* For a professional writer, she needed to work on her dialogue.

"Am I?"

Maybe it was the creepiness of the Gothic house or some lingering energy from the séance, but it seemed he'd moved around the table with preternatural speed. He placed himself right in front of her, pushing her back, the edge of the table digging into her butt.

With his big naked chest, his silver-blue eyes swirling with lust, and the subtle spiciness of his aftershave, she was a goner. Surrounded by all Jasper. Right where she wanted to be.

"I'm not backing away."

"You can't," he said in a low voice, sending shivers coursing through her.

Her heartbeat sped up as she inhaled his scent and felt the heat of his body circling her.

"I could climb up on the table to get away," she pointed out. "Also let's not rule out the ever graceful option to drop to the floor and crawl under it."

He threw his head back and laughed. Something wild and sensual sprung to life inside of her at the way he could be both sexy and ridiculous.

That was it. Trying to be smart had never worked for her. It wasn't like she was going to stop craving him. She liked him even though she didn't want to.

One-night stands only worked because there was no chance to start weaving little fairy tales deeply buried in her psyche. Family, happily-ever-afters—all things that seldom showed up in real life. In the past, she wove fairy tales in her head around the men she dated. The first one had been in high school so she could excuse herself for being young and naive. The second had been in college. He seemed different—at first. It had taken a humiliating event at winter social to wake her up.

"What the hell is going on in your head?"

She remained silent, refusing to meet his eyes.

"I like you, Kirsty. I have since the Dead Boys concert. You're funny, different and difficult. I can't stop thinking about the fact that we are both sleeping in the same house."

Another flare of heat went through her, pooling at her center. "So?"

"Fine. If you're not feeling it then that's cool," he said, watching her with that laser gaze of his. "I didn't figure you for a liar."

The séance's eerie voice would disagree. But she didn't lie most of the time…except about having paranormal gifts. "I'm not."

He arched one eyebrow at her. So arrogant. He didn't have to point out she was being ridiculous.

"Fine. I like you. Being around you is fun. Is that why you're all I like you and we should hook up?"

"No, I'm like that because I do like you. And I want you." He shoved his hand through his thick straight hair, making it stand up for a moment before it fell back into place. She remembered how silky and cool it felt. How effortless it all seemed for him.

A slow hum was going through her body. Her mind and good sense were losing the battle with her libido. But she had to stay strong. Their time together had an end date. He wasn't going to move back home with her. He lived and worked in Chicago, for crying out loud.

The lights flickered above them three times. Judge Judy's voice blared from the other room. "I am not going to ask you to leave. But, the next time you come into my courtroom, dress more appropriately. You are not going to a beach party."

Jasper let out a string of curses as he left the room. This was the perfect chance for her to go back to bed and pretend like this never happened.

Run away.

Like the coward he accused her of being.

Fuck that.

She wouldn't let him be right about that. Instead she followed him. It didn't mean she'd allow herself to fall back into his arms. But she wasn't running away again.

He'd see how strong her control was. She wasn't going to fall for a sexy, high cheekboned man with lips that were made for kissing. Not again.

Except as she entered the living room and saw him standing in front of the TV, illuminated by its blue-tinted glow, an unreadable look on his face, she knew she was lying to herself.

Honestly, what did he have to lose? Kirsty was in his head. Always the embodiment of mysterious except when she kissed him tonight. A dam had broken inside of him leading to an epiphany. Life was too short not to go for it with Kirsty.

Then of course Paul had to come in and break it up once again. Thankfully Jasper managed to turn down the television to a reasonable volume before it woke the others up.

Judge Judy was on a rip, crisply pointing out in that sharp, intelligent way of hers that the litigant was dumb. He really didn't like the show because it displayed people at their worst. A woman suing her best friend over getting burnt eating cheese fries… Stuff like that made him realize how fragile trust was between people.

"You just don't give up," he said to the textbook. It remained on the living room table.

"Does he answer you?"

He jumped at the sound of Kirsty's voice. "No. I would have told you if he did."

"Tell me more about him." She came into the room and sat on one of the big leather chairs, curling her legs under her. "I want to get a complete picture of him. You told me about his study groups but I want to know more."

"Like what?"

"Something funny," she said.

"Do you think it will help you figure out how to contact him?"

"It can't hurt."

Shaking his head as he smiled at her, he sat down on the sofa, putting his feet up on the coffee table. He reached over and pulled the book to him. Absently he flipped through the pages.

Physics hadn't been his favorite subject in high school even though his dad had been studying to become a physics teacher. When he applied to school his love of watching TV and movies had steered him to a BA with Major in Film and Television Studies. Though he and Paul had been in the same physics class so that Jasper could get a better idea of what his dad's fictional theory was based on. "He liked a puzzle. On my last birthday he gave me a map and some scrambled clues."

Was that all this was? Some puzzle he had to solve? That would be just like Paul, getting a one-up on him even in death.

"Did you figure it out?"

"Sure did, but it took me about two weeks. When I finally

showed up at the location, Paul had left me a present and a cupcake in a watertight box."

Remembering that stale cupcake and the copy of the latest *Assassin's Creed* game made him smile. Twigged something in his mind about the game where you could travel back on your own timeline. Was that what Paul was doing?

"What kind of clues did he leave you? Is there anything he might have been doing for the last five years that reminds you of that puzzle?"

"There's this one TV show that's always on when Paul's ghost acts up. Tonight, I was thinking that most of the cases she sees involve people who knew each other. Who break each other's trust."

She took her phone from her cardigan pocket and started tapping her fingers on the screen. "So, a soured friendship? You said you'd had a fight with him, right?"

"Yeah. But really it wasn't friendship ending. I just thought he needed to take a break. Party a bit more instead of always hitting the books."

The look she gave him wasn't hard to figure out. He made himself sound like an entitled prick who'd come to college to just have fun. "There was a Reddit thread on how blowing off steam helps you to focus better when you come back to studying. Paul wasn't retaining half of what he wanted to because he worked too hard."

"You sound defensive."

"I know. I went to the party he refused to go to…and he died that same night. If I had been there with him, I could have called 911 or taken him to the hospital."

He'd never denied the guilt he carried about that evening. The thought of Paul dying alone…the way Jasper's dad had, broke his heart.

112   Ghost of a Chance

"You said he had a brain hemorrhage. I'm not sure there was much you could have done," she said.

"But he wouldn't have been alone," he said quietly.

He didn't hear her at first as she sank down on the couch next to him, wrapping her arm around his shoulders and hugging him. He put his hands on her arms, taking the comfort from her. It was nice to have her next to him, not because he was pushing her to be but simply because she cared.

Though he wished it wasn't the fact that he was getting a response from her by showing her his hurt.

He leaned to the right until the side of his face was on the top of her head. Her shampoo smelled like fall, all apples and cinnamon. Her breath was warm against the column of his neck. Even the glow of the TV with Judge Judy bringing down her gavel and handing down her judgment couldn't distract him from this moment.

This was…nice. Comforting. Something that he hadn't experienced in a long time. He seldom talked about Paul. There was no reason to rehash his past.

He missed his friend, *still*. But no one wanted to hear that.

Kirsty was the first person in a long time to put her arms around him and make him feel like he wasn't alone.

Jasper's head was a comforting weight on top of hers. One that made her feel fuzzy and confused. Something she was doing her best to ignore, but it was tough when he was this close. She wanted to be just another girl to him, but there was no going back from this.

Things were changing.

She was almost willing to forgive him for surprising her on Bri's show. *Almost*. But she held on to grudges. It was one of her flaws. But considering she was lying through her teeth about her abilities, holding on to a grudge here felt pretty difficult.

This close, she noticed a small circle-shaped scar on his left pec. She reached over to touch it, drawing her finger around it in a slow circle.

His nipple puckered and goose bumps covered his entire chest. Lightly she traced her finger around the scar and then moved lower to his nipple. His hips shifted, and she noted a substantial bulge in the front of his sweatpants.

He placed his hand over hers as she started moving lower. Lacing their fingers together.

"Why do you think Paul was reluctant to enter the circle tonight?" she asked as he stroked the back of her hand with his forefinger.

Delicious little sensations spread up her arm. Her nipple tightened and heat spread down the center of her body. The room was chilly but being this close to Jasper, she wasn't cold.

"I don't know. I have no idea why he's doing any of this. He should have gone to Victor in the first place."

She shifted to look directly at him. "From what you said, it seems like Paul wants to be with you. Why do you think that is?"

He wouldn't meet her gaze as he stared toward the open door. Was he contemplating leaving?

He did have trouble opening up. She was onto something with these questions. This was the key to getting Jasper closure and maybe never having to do a scary séance again.

"Hey, whatever it is, you can tell me."

"It's dumb."

"Deep feelings always make me vulnerable and sharing them out loud always sounds, I don't know, ridiculous. But it does help?"

"Who do you share with?"

"My mom. But yours isn't here so spill," she said in a joking way. He was deflecting. Something she couldn't allow.

"Fine. He sort of grounded me. Kept me from going too 'Jasper' about things. Since he's been gone I'm drifting."

So having Paul in the book…was starting to make more sense. Jasper needed to see that Paul was safe to move on.

Taking her phone out she added that note to the ones she'd been compiling.

"He's with you for you," she pointed out.

"I guess. Who knows? I'm more listless than ever," Jasper admitted. "And this—" he made a wild gesture toward the book and television "—really isn't helping."

He was getting agitated. "Did the book 'return' to you by mail the other times you left it?"

He let go of her hand and she sat up.

"No. Only when I sent it to Victor. Do you even believe any of this?"

Sure she did. She believed that he believed it. And with everything she'd witnessed since meeting Jasper, it was hard to deny that something strange was going on.

Trying to get to the bottom of what was really going here wasn't as easy as she'd hoped.

There was no one except her mom that she had let into her life that way. There was a lot going on with Jasper. A lot more than she'd been prepared to unpack tonight. This wasn't just a college story of fun and games and one-upmanship.

This was his life.

He needed answers, and she had to find them for him.

When she went to her room later, she'd contact her cousin Liberty who was a tarot card reader and witch. Maybe she'd be able to give her some insight into that voice from the séance and how spirits might interact with the human realm.

"Sorry. I can see how much this means to you," she said.

"But you think it's just guilt—right?"

"There's no denying you feel guilty."

"Of course I do. Paul had his life planned out. He was going to get his degree and a job in his field. Ask Victor to marry him. I'd be best man even though Victor was technically the best man that Paul knew. You know what I had in junior year?"

She stared at him. It was clear he wasn't expecting an answer.

"A low C grade average and not enough credits for a degree in anything but media. I had a reputation for being a serial dater who broke up with women after two dates. I had no map to my future. So yeah, when I think about the one who was left behind, I wonder if fate got it wrong."

"Jasper—"

"Don't. Survivor's guilt has been discussed at length with my therapist. I get that part. But the fact that you might think I'm just manifesting the idea of my roommate into a book because I can't get over it…that pisses me off. You've seen what he does."

"I have." There wasn't much more to add. Jasper's pain was raw and she hated that she'd driven him here. All to prove something to him. Was there really anything more cowardly than what she'd just done. Forced him into a corner emotionally so she didn't have to admit her own feelings?

The answer was a resounding no.

"I'm going to bed," he said, getting to his feet and walking out of the living room.

For a moment it had seemed as if this time she was going

to be different. But no. Turns out at the end of the night she was still the same Kirsty, whose real talent was keeping people at arm's length, never admitting just how much she wanted to let them in.

Nine

Kirsty got up at six as was her habit and sat on her bed writing on her laptop for an hour. She usually liked coffee when she was writing, but after last night's disastrous encounter with Jasper she made do with her water bottle. It was still dark outside and the fall of rain against the windowpane made her want to curl on her side and scroll on her phone.

Words didn't write themselves, so she forced herself to prop two pillows behind her back to make herself comfortable. Then she hopped out of bed, cracking the window and letting the damp, chilly morning air into the room.

Taking a deep breath, she tried to expel the tension that had dogged her all night making it impossible to sleep. As soon as she finished her pages for the morning, she googled around for mediums in the area. Maybe there was someone she could talk to and find out what she was doing wrong. Faking her way through wasn't going to work.

There were two she could find, but both weren't open until ten. She put the numbers in a new note on her phone and then set an alarm to call them later.

118   Ghost of a Chance

A quick shower and change of clothes and there was nothing else she could use to delay going downstairs. The TV had blared on at six thirty before being swiftly shut off.

Feeling surly, she slicked her hair back into a low ponytail, ringed her eyes in black kohl liner and then dressed in her armor of all black. The frown on her face was just an added bonus. When she got to the kitchen, she found Gia dressed in head-to-toe pumpkin orange and making pumpkin spice pancakes. Dan and Jasper both had loaded plates and "Autumn Leaves" by Ed Sheeran was playing on someone's portable speaker.

She liked the song but this morning she was more in the mood for "Black Parade."

"Great, you're awake," Gia said. "How many pancakes?"

"One."

"Did you hear the TV this morning? I mean honestly how could you not? Woke me from a pretty good sleep," she said, pouring pancake batter in the sizzling pan.

"I was already awake, writing."

"I jerked straight up and fell out of my bed," Dan said. "After that I came downstairs and set up the camera in the living room to try to catch the ghost. But nothing."

Dan had a wide grin, probably looking for some reinforcement. Why did all of the men in this house remind her of Chewie? "Cool."

"Shouldn't that have worked?" Dan asked around a huge bite of pancakes.

"Jasper would know better. Does the book have to be near the TV to turn it on?"

Jasper glanced over her, only to answer Dan. "Nah, I keep it in a drawer at home and it still fucks with the TV."

"Well that's not great. I mean how am I supposed to capture the action," Dan said, more to himself than them.

Gia handed her a plate with one pancake, carrying a second plate with one for herself. They sat down next to each other, eating slowly. The earthy pumpkin and the rich brown sugar were almost enough to melt Kirsty's frown.

"I guess you could follow Jasper around. He seems to be the trigger," Kirsty said. "I have to make a call at ten this morning, so why don't you two focus on that?"

"Focus on what? I have no idea when Paul is going to be active," Jasper said.

He was ticked. Looks like she wasn't the only one good at holding a grudge.

"I made a list of some information we need to gather. We could divide it up and work on it this morning."

"Like what?" Gia asked. "Dan, you could film that. Maybe if we're all distracted Paul will show up to scare us."

"Maybe," Kirsty agreed.

The list she'd made was simple.

·Paul's class schedule (G)

·People Paul saw on a daily basis (J)

·Reasons Paul doesn't want to move on (J)

·Paranormal activity in Burlington/rental house (K)

·Ways to free a spirit from an object (K)

She passed the list around the table.

"I wanted to check out the campus anyway. I'll bring back lunch. I'll text y'all later," Gia said.

"I don't have an answer," Jasper said when he saw what she'd marked for him.

"I know. But you're the only one who knows his family and friends. I think you should make a list and then we can contact them later," Kirsty said.

120 Ghost of a Chance

"I've just added everyone to a WhatsApp group. Let's put our updates in there. Dan, are you staying here?" Gia asked the other man.

"Actually I'll catch a ride with you. I want to try to get some small cameras to install in the living room. That way I can get footage of the TV and anything else that goes bump in the night around here."

"Good thinking," Kirsty said. "They use infrared cameras on those ghost hunting shows."

"I'm not sure what my budget is," Dan admitted, scratching his head. "I'll see if I can rig something up with my phone at least."

Seemed like everyone had a plan of what to do. It didn't take a mind reader to see that Jasper wasn't thrilled that it was just the two of them staying at the house. He immediately took Chewie out for a walk after Gia and Dan left.

Kirsty settled in the living room with her phone and the two books she'd brought with her. *Awaken Your Psychic Ability* and *Mentor Medium*. Both books really weren't helpful with getting rid of spirits, but more on questions she could ask the other realm. She was a bit scared she'd drawn in a negative spirit last night.

Maybe something slumbered in the house that she awakened the night before. Or the wiki she'd followed for the séance might not have been accurate. Not her most rigorous research.

It wasn't like she suddenly believed she had psychic powers, but she owed it to Jasper to take this seriously. Bringing down candles and salt from her room, she made a circle on the floor of the family room, which was empty except for a treadmill pushed into the corner and an exercise ball.

She took her time with the circle, reciting a mediation she'd read in a newsletter she got about moon magic and the divine feminine. Mixing magic probably wasn't the best idea. But at this rate she'd try anything.

Sadly, it was a bust. Her only other idea was to try the incantation from last night one more time.

"I welcome friendly spirits who can help me find answers. All good spirits who are near this circle are welcome to contact me. I only seek information and mean no harm."

Keeping her eyes closed she repeated it, chanting in a low voice, reaching out with her senses. If her third eye was really going to awaken…it needed to do it now.

Nothing happened. No cool breeze. No flickering candlelight. No creepy detached voice.

Nada.

Not even Paul seemed interested in his normal shenanigans. Her legs were starting to get numb when the front door opened. Chewie ran past the exercise room as Jasper's tall frame darkened the doorway.

She got to her feet, blowing out the candles.

"Any luck?"

"Nothing." She paused, giving him an expectant look. "We need to figure out why he's so shy," she said. It was the closest she was going to come to apologizing to him for her words.

"Yeah. So now you think I'm not lying?"

"Take the win for fuck's sake. I never said that you were lying…just that it wasn't always easy to believe. You and I both know that if we're at odds he's never going to perform on camera, and then Bri and Periwinkle Press will cut the funding and we'll go home. That means you and Paul *together* for the rest of your life," she pointed out.

"Yeah, right." He sighed. "I texted Paul's mom. Hopefully we'll hear something soon."

He glanced down at her books spread out on the floor. Standing a bit straighter, she waited for him to comment.

"Brushing up?" he asked.

Taking a deep breath and then exhaling slowly, she forced herself to let go of the attitude that she'd been carrying around this morning. "Yeah. I mean Paul is stubborn. If we're going to get anywhere I need to be at my best."

"Fair enough. He always was a dick when I pushed him to try something new."

Apparently that was his olive branch. She smiled. "Good to know. Maybe we can make him believe that talking to us is his idea."

"How?"

"No clue. I need some coffee. I always think better with one."

Chewie had found a warm place near the back door where some determined sunlight was trying to make an appearance. She concentrated on making her coffee from the pod machine.

Her panic at trying to figure out that concerning voice from the night before made it easier to understand Jasper. For a moment, it had felt like she was the one being haunted. If that was what his life was like, no wonder he was so certain about the afterlife.

Obviously it would be better if he hadn't taken Kirsty's statement from the night before personally, but Jasper wasn't built that way. He'd thought they were bonding, getting closer. But in the end she'd dismissed him, like so many other people in his life had before.

She clearly didn't know him, no matter how fated their encounter seemed to be. She was essentially a stranger to him. A very pretty, slightly irritating one. But still a stranger.

He ranted to Chewie on the walk, trying to make sense of Kirsty, but the dog only moaned and whined, rubbing his muzzle on Jasper's sweatpants in commiseration. It wasn't the first time Chewie heard about his problems.

Finding her with the séance kit, obviously trying to figure things out, had taken him aback. She had to be as frustrated as he was at not getting results. Admittedly, it could be because of her own career and reputation…but something told him that wasn't the case.

While she started making her coffee, he lingered in the hallway like he was back in eighth grade, awkward and unsure of every move. He'd always been semipopular but inside he never felt like he belonged. So here he was again, letting his self-doubt prevail, hanging back waiting for a sign.

Just then the TV clicked on. "Baloney!" Judge Judy exclaimed as he raced to the other room to turn on the camera that Dan had left set up. But it was too late. They'd be lucky if the footage showed anything.

Kirsty joined him a moment later, two mugs in her hands. She gave him one. "Did you get it on film?"

"Too late. I got in here after it came on. But at least you heard it too," he said. The remote remained on the top of the television, in view of the camera, so any footage would show it wasn't tampered with off-screen.

She nodded toward the camera. "Should we film something so you have some footage? Maybe us talking about what just happened?"

"We can do that as a voice-over. The sound quality will be crap from where we are."

Both hands wrapped around the mug, she stared at him over the rim. "You've never mentioned this but… Why *Judge Judy*?"

"I wish I'd asked him when he was alive," Jasper said. There was a lot he wished he'd talked about with Paul, but honestly, at twenty it had seemed like they had a helluva lot more time.

"I bet. I wonder how he always finds the *Judge Judy* show?" Kirsty asked. "I mean I know she's on a lot, but the channels are different."

"It's always on YouTube TV. She has her own channel."

"Did you think about canceling your subscription?"

Rolling his eyes, he walked over to the remote and turned the TV off. "I don't have one and I'm sure the Airbnb owners don't either. Thanks for the suggestion."

"Hey, you don't have to be sarcastic."

"And you don't have to act like I'm barely able to get myself out of bed in the morning," he pointed out.

"I didn't meant to imply anything like that. You know Sherlock Holmes always says once you eliminate the improbable—"

"Canceling the subscription isn't improbable."

"You're being contrary."

"I feel justified."

"Why? I sort of apologized."

"Sort of."

"Fine, I'm sorry I doubted that Paul's ghost was real. But you have to admit it's a tough ask and a bit of odd circumstances," she said, going over to the armchair where she'd sat the night before.

She twisted her legs underneath her as she took another sip of her coffee. "I don't know how you like yours so you've got lots of cream and sugar."

"It's fine. My grandma used to make it that way." He leaned against the arm of the sofa.

"Mine too. You and Paul were like… Lando and Han or Luke and Han?"

"More Luke and Han. I was definitely Luke like in *A New Hope* when Han has his back all the time."

"You never got the chance to have his back," she pointed out. "Obvious right?"

"Yeah. But still true. I see what you're doing?"

"What am I doing?"

"Distracting me so I'll tell you all my secrets."

"So you have a lot of them."

He made a motion like he was zipping his lip.

"No more about you?"

He arched both eyebrows at her.

"What was the last thing you remember Paul doing?"

"He had been working on quantum transference in class when he died. Paul felt like he'd let his parents down during his first attempt at college, which was part of why he was always pushing me. *Got to make the elders proud.*"

"How would we find out what he was working on?"

Taking his phone out with his free hand, he used his thumb to do an internet search. While Jasper didn't remember much of Paul's schedule, he could remember his adviser and favorite professor. After some digging, he found that Paul's professor was still teaching at UVM and there were two classes listed for the next day.

"We could go ask his former professor tomorrow. First class is at ten. We could get there early and talk to him," Jasper said. Finally it seemed he was contributing something to this project.

"We should bring the textbook with us and see if Paul's ghost responds to the lab he spent so much time in," she said.

"Great idea," he responded, unable to stop watching the delicate way she sipped her coffee. There was something tough and don't-mess-with-me about her entire persona today.

126 Ghost of a Chance

Catching him off guard, she lifted her eyebrows at him. "You're staring."

"So."

Taking another sip of her coffee, she set her drink on the table next to her. "Tell me more about you."

Uh what?

They'd talked a lot about him. He wanted to know more about her but didn't want her to think everything he'd revealed was some sort of exchange. She needed to know about his past so that she could try to understand the poltergeist in the book. "There's not much you don't know."

"I don't even know where you're from," she pointed out. "All I know is you live in Chicago in a fairly nondescript apartment, are a fellow *Star Wars* geek, and went to school in Burlington, but where are you from?"

If she was going to crack him open, he wouldn't make it easy. He sat down on the edge of the coffee table, face-to-face with her. "I'm from Ravenpool, Vermont. It's not too far from here."

"Ravenpool? Is it a small town?"

"The tiniest. Numbers aren't my thing so I can't say how many people…but we have a Olive Garden near the interstate and some nice shops on Main Street. Just not much else. Mom grew up there and we lived with my grandparents until I was ten."

"That's interesting. Why did you move when you were ten?"

"Mom got a good job and I was getting too big for the spare room. She wanted me to have a space that was my own," he shrugged.

He'd liked the little room at Grandma and Grandpa's house. That was decorated with stuff from his mom's childhood and that his granddad had painted a galaxy mural on because he liked *Star Wars*. But his mom and his grandma hadn't always seen eye to eye on things. That tension had driven them into their own place.

"What about you? Where's home?"

"Thoms Hollow, Georgia. Mom and I lived all over the place but we've been there since I graduated college. When I started making some decent money writing we bought houses next to each other. It's a duplex," she said.

"Really? You struck me as someone who would want her independence and live…"

"As far as I could from my mom?" she asked.

"I guess." There was a softness to her face that told him she cherished the relationship with her mom.

"She's cool. She had me when she was twenty-one, so we're really close, and we have fun together. She also is totally like me. We both like our privacy but we're close in case we need each other. Also when I'm on deadline she makes sure I have dinner every night. It's just nice to be taken care of," she said.

He rested his hands on his forearms. "My mom has no boundaries. I guess it's because my dad died, but she hovers constantly. She's already texted me three times this morning just to check in. I couldn't live next to her."

"Or in the same state?" she asked, a half smile teasing her lips.

"Definitely. I haven't let her know I'm back in Vermont. Had to turn off the tracker on my phone. She keeps saying there's something wrong with hers and I'll have to help her turn it back on the next time we see each other." Which he felt bad about. Sort of. She knew he could handle himself. He wished she would act like it.

"That's evil. My mom is tech savvy so the minute I turn

Ghost of a Chance

off tracking she calls me. What are you up to—shit like that," Kirsty said.

"Do you tell her it bothers you?" His mom pulled that with him all the time, which he thought was something just she did. Maybe all moms did that?

"Yeah, because then she backs off. Like the other night I texted her 'I'm at a concert and hoping to get laid.'"

"You didn't say that to your mom."

"Yup, and she just warned me to use a condom and said if I didn't answer her text at six a.m. she was calling the cops."

"Good thing Paul woke you up," he said, remembering the blaring TV. Kirsty with her hair bedraggled wearing only his T-shirt from the night before.

A rosy blush spread over her cheeks. "There are worse ways to wake up."

Ten

"How'd the ghost hunt go while we were gone?" Gia asked as they all settled into the living room eating their lunch.

"We had another incident with the TV, but we didn't capture anything," Jasper said.

Dan was eating a sandwich in between rigging up his newly purchased infrared camera. "Bri's not going to love the quality of this camera," he said, his words muffled by the food in his mouth, "But if we can catch a glimpse of something on it I think she'll let it slide."

Kirsty hoped so. Not that she thought that Paul was taking a corporeal form but footage proving that it wasn't human intervention would still help. She'd done more research on ghosts like Paul. Supposedly poltergeists resisted being caught on film. Made sense to her.

"We are going to try to talk to Paul's professor tomorrow and find out more about the day he died. Maybe he had a paper or project he didn't finish, something important enough to keep him tethered here."

"Are you going to finish it for him?" Gia asked Kirsty with a cheeky grin.

"Uh, no. Science and me don't mix. What about you, Jasper?"

"I get the fundamentals. I think I could eke out a C if that's the only way to get Paul to move on," Jasper said around a bite. Something told her it was more than just a science paper or project, but at this point Kirsty was open to anything. "How'd you make out on the schedule?"

"Well…they didn't want to give it to me, but I sweet-talked someone in the records office," Gia said, winking at Jasper.

"Not surprising. I set up a shared Google drive for us all to use," Kirsty said. "Figured we can drop stuff in there. Updates and whatnot."

"I'll put it in there. Also, we totally can film in the library, which is pretty nice. I'd like to get a few photos of you working in there, Kirst, so we can use them for promo."

Glancing up at Gia, she nodded. Might be nice to work in a college library. She hadn't done that in years. The atmosphere would probably help give her new ideas.

"What's up for this afternoon?" Dan asked.

"I'd like to see the house where you lived and maybe Dan can film it," Kirsty said to Jasper.

"Sure. Since it's rainy it would probably be a good idea to take the car," Jasper said. He glanced at Gia. "We can leave after lunch. You coming?"

Gia shook her head. "I have to do some work this afternoon. If anything happens at the house what should I do?"

Dan gave her a wide grin. "I'm going to just run the infrared camera 24/7. I have a SLR that I'm going to set up and let run in here as well. The battery will last a few hours. Could you set an alarm and switch it out?"

Kirsty let her mind drift while they were talking. As much as she hadn't enjoyed being a medium at first, this was fun. She liked making a list of possibilities and then ruling them out. *Playing detective.*

They cleaned up after lunch and she realized she'd never called the local mediums despite the alarms she'd set. Jasper had distracted her and she'd just muted her phone. "Give me a few minutes. I need to make a couple of calls."

"Want to leave in thirty minutes?" Jasper suggested. "Chewie needs a walk and some playtime."

"That works for me."

Heading upstairs to her room she put in her AirPods and dialed her cousin Liberty.

"Hiya, famous author."

"Hi, Lib. Um…do you know anything about talking to the dead?"

"Not really. I can ask Mom but that's not our area of expertise. Why?"

"You know how I sort of let people think I'm clairvoyant; well, I'm stuck trying to exorcise a poltergeist from a physics book."

Liberty laughed so hard that Kirsty could hear her redheaded cousin's entire body shaking as her bracelets jingled.

"Nice. Let me know how that works out. You should try to reach out to some mediums."

"Yeah, they are my next call. Wanted to check with you first."

"Wish I could help. Since I have you… I'm doing Yule this year. You and your mom should totally come."

"We'll see."

It would be nice to be with family in December. Normally it was just her and her mom. They had their traditions but sometimes it felt a little small and lonely. She texted her mom about Yule before calling the first medium. The call went to a voicemail that didn't have a message. She hung up without leaving one.

The second got picked up on the first ring.

"Aza Preeti, psychic medium."

"Hello. Uh, I'm Kirsty."

"Hi there. What can I do for you?" Her voice was surprisingly mundane, sounding a lot like the librarian at her elementary school. But Mrs. Parson hadn't been a clairvoyant.

"I'm doing research for a book I'm writing. Would you mind answering some questions?"

"I don't mind, but I have an appointment in ten minutes."

"That should be plenty of time." Kirsty took a deep breath. Telling all of this to a stranger was unexpectedly awkward. "So let's say someone was pretending to be psychic and set up a séance for their friends."

"I wouldn't recommend that. My profession gets a lot of crap," Aza said immediately, irritation in her voice.

"I know… I'm an author. I'm writing a book where my heroine can actually talk to the dead and uses them to solve crimes. But there's this secondary character that's going to get into trouble for this and come to her," Kirsty said, realizing just how convoluted this sounded. "The thing is, in my story the character hears a loud voice during a séance that no one else does. Is that possible for someone who isn't a medium? Or do you believe it could just be in her head?"

"Your character is going to go to the real medium about this?" Aza queried.

"She is." The same way that Kirsty was in real life.

"Well I'd say that the character probably has some raw talent that they might not realize," Aza said. "Does that play a part in your story?"

Holy shit. Talent? Her? "Yes. So how would the character contact the voice again?"

"I'd suggest going back to where she heard it the first time. Have her do some meditation and reach out asking for more answers. The spirits require patience just like us," Aza said. "I've got to go. Hope that helped."

"Thanks, it did. Can I make an appointment to come and talk to you? I'll pay for your time," Kirsty asked. Aza had the knowledge she needed. She might have insight about Paul... and about the latent talents she mentioned.

"I have some time on Thursday at two. Would that work?"

Kirsty confirmed it would. After hanging up she flopped back on her bed.

Real psychic powers...was that possible? Or was this all just in her imagination? Did that mean going forward she'd get more ghosts trying to contact her? God, she really hoped not. This thing with Paul was pushing her outside her comfort zone. And that voice...it was going to be a long time until she didn't hear it echoing in her head.

Her mom texted a midday smiley face along with a message that she'd contacted Aunt Lourdes and was making plans for Yule. Kirsty hearted it. Her mom might have some extra insight but that was not a conversation she was ready to have. So instead, she pocketed her phone, grabbed her peacoat, and headed downstairs to meet the guys.

Jasper sat on the bottom of the stairs putting on his tennis shoes. Glancing back over his shoulder he smiled at her with so much happiness. Her heart skipped a beat. You'd think she'd be used to seeing him, but it seemed each time they were together she noticed something else she liked about him.

Which didn't help her not-letting-him-mean-anything-to-her plan.

★ ★ ★

It was one of those quintessential dark, rainy autumn afternoons, and Jasper was about to revisit the last place he saw Paul alive.

Dan left in his own car because he had to go home for a few days after they visited Jasper's old apartment. He had all of the cameras in the Airbnb rigged to go off on timers once they were set up, and Jasper was going to manage keeping the batteries charged and downloading anything captured from the SIM cards.

He'd called ahead and the current tenants had agreed to let them take a look at the place and to film inside. Dan was going to get them to sign the necessary forms when they got there.

Kirsty sat quietly next to him, her fingers moving on the keyboard of her phone making more notes. He debated for a minute after he started the car, then finally put on the Dead Boys mix he had on his phone.

A look of pure joy on her face. "Figured you like their music."

"You know I do."

The driving beat and electronic riffs of the melody from "Hunting in a Killer Moon" filled the car, and some of the tension he felt about going back to that apartment eased. Not all of it. After all, he hadn't been back in years. He moved out right after Paul died. Had in fact crashed at the frat house, sleeping on the sofa for the rest of the semester.

Their eyes met as they both started singing.

In the shadows, we move through the night. Soft whispers, cut like a knife. Your kiss like poison, your eyes on fire, dancing on graves we never tire.

"Crank it up for the chorus."

Our eyes meet, promising that soon, we'll go hunting in this killer moon. Facing our fears, chasing away doom. We go hunting in a killer moon.

"I needed this," he said to her as the song ended.

He'd been so uncomfortable in the apartment by himself. Waiting for Paul to come out of his room. His mom had offered to come and stay, but that would have been worse.

Kirsty sang along to "Find Joy," slightly off tune but he smiled and joined in, equally out of tune. For a minute they were back to that first night, two strangers who simply enjoyed the same band and were starting to like each other.

It was too easy to blame Paul for everything that happened next in his life. He never thought things through. Like with how he tried and failed to keep his distance from Kirsty since that night.

"How did you and Paul meet?"

Hadn't he said they were cousins? He couldn't remember. He definitely said they were like brothers. He'd always felt that way about Paul. "When I was a baby. He was my cousin. My dad's sister's kid."

The look she gave him would have melted a weaker man. Frankly he felt singed by it.

"You're just mentioning it now?"

"I'm pretty sure I said he was like a brother."

She shook her head and her bangs shifted, revealing her frustrated look as she stared out the window. "Gia's like a sister to me and we share no blood."

"Sorry. I should have been clearer. Everyone who knew Paul knew we were cousins. I wasn't hiding it."

They arrived at the apartment building soon after and he pulled into a parking space nearby.

"What else?"

"Uh, Paul was working on figuring out some physics notes left by my dad."

"Okay, all of this should have been brought up earlier. Why were you sitting on it?"

"I don't know. Maybe if you knew we were related you'd think that I should have figured out how to help him on my own...lame, I know, but I can't do this on my own. I wanted you to have to stay."

"Once you brought the freaking book on the TV show that was a done deal," she pointed out. Leveling that serious stare of hers on him, she just waited.

"I don't like talking about any of it. I can't deal with the grief. I know, grow up, right? But I can't. I miss Paul and this freaky ghost version of him isn't the same. I guess...it's easier to not talk about him."

Her lips narrowed before she opened the door and got out of the car. He did the same, pocketing his keys as they approached Dan. Kirsty was pissed and rightly so. She'd stopped her entire life to help him. To help his best friend. And here he was keeping vital information from her because he was scared. She had every right to hate him.

"Hey. Before we go inside I want to say...talking to you about Paul is helping me open up. I wasn't keeping the fact that he was my cousin a secret for any nefarious reason."

"I get that. I was starting to trust you."

Dan approached them before he could respond.

Dan chatted all the way to the apartment and didn't seem to notice that Kirsty wasn't speaking to either of them. When he knocked on the apartment, it was answered by Lon, the new renter, who let them in.

Lon had on sweatpants and a UVM basketball T-shirt. His hair was short and he had a weight bench in the corner. He told them to feel free to look around and went back to the couch and his controller where he was playing *Fallout*. Kirsty stood at the edge, still simmering from earlier.

The apartment hadn't changed much since he'd lived there. The same old leather couch with a blue fabric-covered love seat dominated the space. There was a TV mounted to the wall and a small credenza under it for the cable box and game consoles. The kitchen was off to the side. Jasper couldn't see it from here but wondered if the sink was full of dishes as it had been when he and Paul lived here.

"This was my room," he said, pointing to the one on the left.

Dan poked his head into the room. "Did it look like this when you lived here?"

"Yeah, this place has always come fully furnished. My bedding was different and I had a few *Star Wars* posters on the wall."

"I'll get some B-roll of the house. Did you bring the book?"

Jasper opened his backpack, taking it out and opening its well-worn pages.

All three of them waited to see if anything happened. Maybe they'd finally get lucky and it would be easy.

…Nothing. As Jasper placed the book on the bed, Kirsty wandered over to the other room. Dan asked Jasper to sit on the bed and hold the book. "As if you're studying it. Look pensive."

"I'm not an actor."

"I'm aware. I want to capture some of what you're feeling."

When they walked into the other room, slightly more deflated, Jasper caught the scent of Kirsty's perfume. She was perched near the window gazing down at the street. There was something solemn about her. To him, keeping his secrets about Paul felt harmless. But in reality he'd hurt her, broken her trust.

He owed her a real apology.

"I'm sorry. I'm an ass. I just do what's right for me. I should have realized I was hobbling your ability to reach Paul by keeping my secrets," he said, coming closer. The urge to embrace her was so strong that he wrapped his arms around his torso to hold himself back.

"Yeah, you are. I get it. There are things I don't tell you or want to talk about either. But we both want results, so from now on, no more hiding things from me," she said.

"Deal." He went in for a handshake, but she swatted it away with a playfully mocking look.

God why did her prickliness make him feel so good?

This apartment stirred memories Kirsty thought she'd suppressed forever.

Her ex Buck had lived in a furnished place similar to this. Off campus. With a roommate that he did his best to make sure she never met. This room suddenly made her feel twenty and so insecure. How did one generic room channel one of the worst experiences of her life?

Jasper was beside her, looking all earnest and apologetic, but she was in her head and not in a good place. She couldn't shake the fucking loud voice in her head, screaming that Jasper wasn't the only one hiding things.

Standing in this jock's bedroom just served to remind her of the reasons she'd started hiding who she was. It was easy to say she gave zero fucks if people liked her or not, but that was total bullshit.

Right now she couldn't even say her mind was on her career or helping Jasper get rid of Paul. The room felt heavy, filled with something more than her own emotions. Doubt, anger, uncertainty all engulfed her. Was she channeling her rejection from Buck? Having some sort of fucked-up emotional flashback?

Humbling to realize that love and rejection had shaped her. Especially when she was liking Jasper so much and he wasn't leveling with her.

She was scared. Not about rejection. That was a solid part of the core of the woman she was.

"Hey, you okay? You look pale and—"

"I'm fine. I'm going to go outside and get some air while you finish up in here," she said.

"But it's rainy." He sounded concerned.

"I like the rain."

She walked out of the apartment, hearing the thumps of Jasper following her down the stairs.

As soon as she was outside she walked to the edge of the sidewalk near the wooded area that consisted of a few trees that had seen better days. Spreading her arms out wide, she tipped her head back so that the rain was cascading down her face.

It was her most fervent hope that it would wash away everything being in that apartment had stirred in her. The panic and fear of not being accepted, of not being good enough, were overwhelming.

Jasper's firm hand touched hers, but she refused to look at him. Until the warmth of his fingers started to register and slowly the storm of emotion started to ebb.

Glancing over at him, she could barely suppress a laugh. He was mimicking her, but his hair was matted to his head and he looked a bit like Chewie after he'd been caught in the rain. It was impossible to look at him now and not remember their first night and how they were almost together.

A slow hum started in the center of her body, spreading outward, driving away the last of the cloudiness inside of her and replacing it with a need so deep it ached. Deeper than anything she'd felt for any other man she'd slept with.

It wasn't love. Love was a childish fantasy. But this was a… craving. Yes, that was it. She craved him.

It wasn't logical in the least, but from the moment he splashed his beer over her, her world shifted. That moment had ignited something inside of her that she wasn't sure would ever fade.

His eyes opened and met hers with an intensity that sent a hot, sharp and fierce current through her. Jolting her like a lightning strike. She went up on tiptoe, pulled his head down to hers with their entwined hands. His mouth was warm and familiar. Just what she needed.

His lips parted, their tongues tangled, warming her from the inside out. The rain barely registered anymore.

This was what she'd been craving. Her heartbeat was steady in her ears, his chest solid against her breasts, sending chills even through her heavy sweater.

He cupped her butt with one hand, drawing her up to him. She pushed her right leg between his and felt his erection solid and strong against the top of her thigh. Desire was driving her now. She needed him.

His hand slipped under her sweater, the rasp of his calloused fingers against the base of her spine ecstasy as he rubbed a small circle there. Their kiss deepened, and it made her melt.

Like nearly into a pile on the wet rainy ground. She was tempted to draw him down to the concrete and get him inside of her any way she could. She was tired of holding back, tired of worrying that she'd get exposed as a fraud, tired of feeling like she was going to let not just everyone but Jasper down. It was so strong that she ripped her mouth from his, stumbling backward. Looking around for a place where they could find some privacy.

Jasper seemed to be on the same page. He thrust a hand through his hair and then took her wrist, leading her back to his car. Even those few seconds apart were more than she could stand.

As he tried to open the door, she pushed him back against the car. Her hand skated over his erection, her mouth on his. Their bodies both slick with rain. He groaned and tried to say something, his mouth moving against hers, but she just took his hand, with the keys, and guided it under her sweater to her breast.

As he squeezed her, she felt his tongue against hers again. When his finger brushed her nipple, she shuddered in his arms. God that felt good. So good she was ready to do whatever she could to keep him close to her.

Someone cleared their throat behind them, but she ignored it. Then they did it again. Louder. *Fuck.*

Jasper lifted his head. "Yeah?"

"I got the B-roll. I'm heading back to the house instead of home. Bri wants me to stay and get as much as I can. So see you back there?" Dan's voice sounded strained. The rain had slowed to a misty drizzle. She tried not to think of what this looked like to him.

"Yeah," Jasper said.

Kirsty stepped away from him. She still wanted him but the run-in with Dan put a damper on the impulse that had swept through her. She shoved her hands into her pockets and walked around to the passenger side of the car.

Jasper didn't say anything as he unlocked the car. She was dripping wet. Before she sat in the passenger seat, she looked over the roof of the vehicle to take him in. Jasper's lips twitched, and then she couldn't help it. She started laughing. He went to the trunk and dug around, finding a towel and tossing it to her.

That slow hum of sexual awareness was a returning throb inside of her as he settled in the driver's seat.

His voice was rough and so, so sexy. "Not that I'm complaining, but what brought that on?"

She had the same question. She'd never felt that kind of desire or compulsion before.

Eleven

Jasper didn't drive straight back to the Airbnb. The last thing he wanted was to be around Gia and Dan. Kirsty didn't object as he pointed the car east toward Lake Champlain. It wasn't a typical lake-going day, but then again nothing had been typical since the day he met her.

There was a secluded area that he thought she'd enjoy seeing in the misty rain. But they needed proper gear. He pulled into a gas station and she eyed him warily.

"Where are we going?" she asked.

"Surprise."

Crossing her arms over her chest, she quizzically tipped her head to the side. He suspected she was trying to decide if she was going to argue with him or not. In the end, she relented. "Are you getting fishing gear?"

"Rain gear, and maybe a condom."

A smile teased the corners of her lips. "Coffee, too. I'll come in with you."

The convenience store wasn't exactly spoiled for choice but they did find two ponchos in bright yellow. Kirsty made cof-

144 Ghost of a Chance

fees from the machine for both of them while he grabbed a pack of Hostess cupcakes and a box of condoms. No use denying either of their cravings.

He'd never thought of himself as a highly sexual person. He liked sex, but around her…it was all he thought about.

Her hair had started to curl once it dried from the drenching earlier. Some of her eyeliner had faded away, making her look more like the fun woman who'd dropped *Star Wars* references.

He wanted her so badly that he'd take whatever she offered him. Usually he could figure out what motivated women, see some kernel of who they were. With her…nope. He had nothing.

Except that she kissed him with her entire being. Like she wanted to fuse with him and take him completely. That was addicting.

"Junky snacks?" she asked, nudging him out of his thoughts.

"Gas station coffee demands it."

"I like those pink snowball things," she said.

"Uh gross," he teased as he reached around her to grab a package before leading the way to the counter to pay.

"Whatever. It's an acquired taste. Like aspartame…not really for everyone," she muttered as she took out her wallet.

He waved her off, paying with his phone and declining a bag.

"Acquired taste…that's what my mom said when I tried wine for the first time. In her defense, wine is actually good."

"Snowballs are too," she said. "There's something so satisfying about the dessicated coconut on top of that sugary cake."

"You're really selling it," he said as they got to the car. It took a few minutes, but soon they were back on the road.

"Hostess cupcakes aren't exactly gourmet," she said.

She really didn't let things go, he thought. "Definitely not.

But that's the point. We want something that's full of calories and tastes like heaven as you chew it, but then later makes you wish you hadn't had it."

Her laughter filled the car, and this time he didn't bother hiding his smile. There had been a heavy sadness around her in the apartment, and hearing her joy now made him feel like he'd done something nice for her. That he'd started to understand her enough to repay her for her help.

He wanted to ask her about what made her leave his old place, but decided to wait. When they arrived at the park, he parked the car and led the way. The shore was lined with rocks and small shrubs and bushes but he knew a spot a little farther up that they could sit down. The water was choppy today and there weren't many people at the beach. Wearing their bright ponchos, carrying their own coffee and snack of choice, he felt like they were in a Wes Anderson film.

"Oh."

Her breath caught watching the waves stirred by the storm blow across the lake and stir the surface into choppy waves. The air was heavy and damp with the remaining drizzle and the mist from the lake.

She took a sip of her coffee and closed her eyes. Staring at her, taking her in, he promised himself that he'd always try to keep her happy. Even though everyone controlled their own happiness, she deserved the support. He liked seeing her this way.

"Thanks for this."

"No problem. So…what about the apartment got to you?" he asked.

"It just reminded me of me at twentysomething. I wasn't prepared for everything it brought up," she said.

"I bet you were cute. Were you so goth and emo then?"

146 Ghost of a Chance

"Always. Die hard."

"Always?"

"Yeah, even in kindergarten," she said with a wink. "I rebelled against my teacher and refused to nap."

She was funny...and distracting. Fine, she didn't want to talk about whatever she'd felt in the apartment. As much as he wanted her to feel comfortable, she needed to take her own advice and stop keeping things from him. No one could help her if she kept them in the dark. "So the apartment..."

"You're not going to let it go, are you?"

"Nah, I'm tenacious."

"Really?" She didn't believe him. That was a mistake.

"Yup. You're being evasive and that's not like you. I get not wanting to open up but if I've learned anything from all your probing it's that it's actually made me feel a little lighter. So what's up?"

A tentative pause filled the air before she started. "I don't know. I was sucked into something heavy and emotional. My college years weren't the greatest, so it might have been that."

"Probably. College is a time for figuring out how to function in the adult world."

"So true. Guess I started buying your hype that I've got it together."

"Well compared to some... Do you feel like it was all your emotions?"

"Not sure. How do you mean?"

"You were close to the book when you went in there," he said. "Was Paul speaking to you?"

"How? The lights didn't flicker, the TV didn't blare *Judge Judy*..."

"That's how he communicates with me, but I don't have your gift. Was he trying to share something with you?" he asked. Even two days ago he wouldn't have uttered those words but now he was confident in her ability and knew she had a gift that he didn't understand.

"Uh… I don't…it was like I could sense feelings more than words," she said.

"What were they?"

"Fear of rejection, like I didn't belong. Does this sound like Paul?"

Giving her a soft smile, he said, "That sounds like all of us in college."

"Are you trying to make me feel better?"

"Is it working?"

"Maybe. Does what I describe sound like Paul?"

She didn't want to share her feelings…they had to be strong. Of course they were. He'd stood next to her in the rain and felt waves of something dark coming off of her.

Revealing any of what she felt was anathema. There was no way she was admitting to any part of that girl she'd been. If he wanted to know the emotions…but then she realized that he wouldn't necessarily know they were hers. He was positive she had a real ability, was channeling Paul.

She was the only one who knew the truth.

"I don't know. We didn't talk about shit like that. I mean I know he was stressed about his classes."

"Why?"

Jasper wouldn't meet her eye and looked away finding a rock to toss into the lake. "He didn't want to fail again. You know now that I think about it he had a lot of anxiety around school. He was always telling me to make sure I didn't fall behind and shit like that."

"That's sort of what I felt. I guess it resonated with me because I felt the same pressures at school. My mom and I could only afford four semesters of college. I couldn't drop a class or fail it. The pressure was crazy," she admitted.

But that stress hadn't been what she'd felt in the room. Instead, it was closer to the lingering ickiness from Buck and how he'd treated her. But as much as she was beginning to trust Jasper, revealing that part of her life felt far out of reach.

"That sucks. I…because my dad died after being hit by another driver, we had a settlement, so my tuition was covered," he said. "Mom wanted me to have the full college experience. Dad and her met at a junior college and then she got pregnant with me, so she thought they'd both missed out."

"That's nice of her." It was sweet, the way his mom had worked so hard to make sure he was okay. But the pressure Jasper must have felt.

"Thanks. So was that it, really? You seemed way more intense than if it was just about financial stress. There was something in your eyes that seemed, I don't know, scared," he said.

He wasn't going to drop this.

Did he think she was holding something back that would help their project? Hell, she wanted to know what was going on too and get Paul the fuck wherever he was meant to go so she could go back to her comfortable place. Where she wasn't hearing loud, creepy voices or being overwhelmed by dark emotions. That place where she could keep telling herself she was pretending to be a medium.

"There were other things…but I don't want to discuss them." It was time to pivot. "One thing I've been wondering is, how was Paul's relationship? You said he and Victor planned to get married, right?"

"Yeah. They were super happy. They weren't into tons of PDA but I'd catch them exchanging looks when we'd be out. They had this connection that you really don't see all that often."

So no anxiety there. Maybe that had been how her body had reacted to Paul's stress. She really wasn't sure. "I guess that's it then. Should we head back?"

"Not yet. Snack time. There's a place over here where we can sit."

She couldn't keep her eyes off of him. There was something about him that drew her in. It had been easy to give in to that impulse when her guard was down earlier. But she didn't have that excuse now.

She didn't need it.

She was a grown-ass woman; it was okay to like a guy. She had to shake lingering doubt from remembering what had happened with Buck. It stuck to her, like she'd walked through a spiderweb and couldn't get it off. No matter how many times she brushed it away, it was still there.

Buck didn't deserve to have any influence on her life. She'd been so meaningless to him that letting him have this kind of power pissed her off. What was wrong with her that she couldn't shove that jackass out of her mind?

"Up here. Want a hand? It's a bit muddy from all the rain," Jasper said.

Jasper wasn't anything like Buck. There were his big silver-blue eyes that watched her with a mixture of desire, and sometimes fear. He wore his emotions like *The Red Badge of Courage* and she wanted to meet him halfway. But hers were buried deep inside, more like *Treasure Island* if she was comparing childhood classics.

Good luck finding a map that would allow her to finally trust again.

She took his hand; he squeezed her fingers real quick and

her heart melted. This man was too soft for her. She was hard in ways that Jasper with his sweet mom, his tender memories of his dad, and his well-paying job wouldn't understand.

He hadn't been rejected time and again the way she had. He hadn't grown up worrying about having enough food to eat or about what would happen if her mom didn't come home from her overnight job.

He'd always had security. Something Kirsty definitely envied. She was good, she reminded herself. She was no longer that dumb girl who thought a man like Buck would change her life. Now here she was with this man, a slow burn flaring between them, and she was hesitating.

"This is it," he said. They were on a higher point of the trail near an outcropping overlooking the lake.

She shifted around making sure the poncho was under her butt so she didn't get cold from the wet ground. "Hope this isn't too bad," Jasper noted.

It was the opposite of bad. She sat next to Jasper, ignoring the past and some of the present. It was about enjoying this moment with her tepid coffee, delicious empty calorie treat, and Jasper next to her. Talking quietly about the beach and how he'd always loved the water.

The slow burn kept her warm and safe. Odd that she should feel safer sitting in the rain overlooking Lake Champlain with Jasper by her side than she ever had with any other man.

Or maybe it wasn't odd at all.

When they got back to the house, Kirsty claimed she had an idea for a scene, racing up to her room to write it. Chewie playfully growled at him. "Sorry, buddy."

Normally he had a dog walker who took care of Chewie when he was working. Having Chewie on-site was fun, but unlike Jasper, he was not shy about demanding attention. "Walk?"

Chewie forgave him quickly, trotting to the bench by the front door where Jasper had left the leash. Still wearing his bright poncho, he took the dog out. Gia popped out of the kitchen and offered to join him so they could talk.

"What's up?" he asked as they started down the street, the neighborhood alight with autumnal color.

"Uh, Bri and the publisher want to see a preview of the film we have so far. Dan doesn't have anything he thinks is usable other than B-roll. Which we both know isn't great. I don't want to put extra pressure on Kirsty."

But it was okay to pressure him?

"We still have other places to film and experiment with, so why not stall them for now."

"Good idea. Kirsty's great at telling a story, even on camera. I'll ask her to share what she observed at the apartment and play up anything that could be read as psychic. I think it would be best if you interview her," Gia said, looking the most stressed he'd ever seen her. "I was afraid we were going to have to pull the plug. This is great."

"It definitely is."

"I just spent a very tense hour convincing my boss that the money was worth it. Will Bri air this, you think?"

Jasper shrugged. Gia's face fell. "Probably. I mean there are no guarantees as you know. But I think as long as we keep having things like the candles blowing with no wind...probably."

What he didn't mention was that, if Kirsty came across as a fraud, that would still be a story. Just not a good one.

"I think we've got maybe another four or five days to produce something for them to convince them it will work," she said.

"I'll talk to Dan and we'll get something together to send to Bri. Though we haven't captured a poltergeist we have some compelling footage. Also no one expected that Kirsty was going to get rid of Paul in a few days."

"Phew. That's what I was hoping for. Do you have any ideas for some dramatic shots we could get that don't involve the ghost?"

Jasper shoved his hand through his hair and tugged Chewie back onto the path. "I bet Kirsty will have a few. Let's talk to her."

"She's under a lot of pressure. She's writing one book, promoting another, and this gift of hers isn't comfortable or reliable. She's always felt spooky things in places, even if she says otherwise. I'm worried about her."

"Of course," he said. Between him and Dan they could probably fake something with their combined knowledge of film techniques. But he didn't want to do that. Bri would be pissed if they did. And none of it would solve the problem of his good old ghost Paul.

"I don't think we can fake anything."

Gia nodded. "Of course. I hope you don't think I was suggesting that."

But she totally had been. Granted, her job was on the line too.

At this moment he really didn't like Paul. Even in the afterlife, Paul could be a dick. He was putting everyone's jobs at risk now in this impossible position.

They were back at the house; his eyes drew up the battered old Victorian, and he thought he saw a curtain move in Kirsty's room. Was she done writing? He hoped so.

Their afternoon together had been so nice, and right now he wanted to be with her. When they were together he wasn't worried about Paul, or the fact that he might spend the rest of his life with *Judge Judy* blaring on at a moment's notice.

Dan was waiting for them when they walked into the hall. "Glad you are both back. I think I have something on one of the cameras."

"Let me get Kirsty. It's not Chewie again?"

"I don't think so as he's sitting in front of the fireplace when the fire comes on by itself."

"What? How is that possible? That's a traditional one with logs?" Jasper asked.

"Ghosts, right? We'll have to get Kirsty."

He followed Dan to the part of the kitchen table where his laptop and external monitor were set up to edit the film so far. A freeze frame on the monitor showed Chewie laying on the floor near the quiet fireplace.

Kirsty and Gia joined them, and Dan hit play. They all watched as a spark appeared and then small flames blazed in the fireplace.

All of them leaned in closer trying to see what had started the fire. This wasn't anything at all like what Jasper had experienced up to this point. "When is this from?"

"When we were at the apartment with the book," Dan said.

"Is this house haunted?" Jasper asked, looking over at Kirsty. "Paul's never done anything like this before."

"Is it?" she asked Gia.

"I mean maybe. Who knows for sure if they're telling the truth when people put that in their Airbnb description."

"Gia!"

"What? I thought it would be helpful. Give Paul someone else to talk to," Gia said.

"It's not helpful," Kirsty said through clenched teeth. "Now we potentially have two ghosts on our hands, and we don't know a damn thing about either of them."

Twelve

Grabbing Gia's wrist, Kirsty dragged her down to the workout room, closing the door firmly behind them.

"What the fuck?"

"What? You're the one who said you didn't really have any ability to talk to ghosts. I thought a haunted house would help."

"Help how?"

"Either by giving us some creepy stuff to film or by showing you that you *can* talk to the dead," Gia said. "You should be thanking me. You just needed a chattier ghost."

Gia had a point. Unfortunately, she wasn't really digging that creepy voice she heard. If ever she needed to project her unflappable goth girl image it was now. But she was spinning like a deranged toy in a horror movie.

Gia didn't say anything, just put one hand on her hip, watching and waiting.

"Thanks." She bit out the words. "Your plan might be working too well."

"Yeah well, not well enough. Dan's a skeptic. I'm guessing

the fireplace helped change his mind. He was totally trying to leave today."

"I could tell," Kirsty said. "So can you find out if this place is really haunted?"

"I can do some research around it. Right now I just have the spooky vibes description from the Airbnb website."

Gia watched her carefully. Kirsty had to come clean about the voice. She wanted to talk to her best friend about it and have Gia be her rational self and help her figure out if she hallucinated it or actually heard something.

"When we did the séance, I heard a voice that neither of you did—"

"I knew it! You are totally the real deal," Gia shouted. "Great. So even if it's not Paul, maybe you can get whoever you heard to talk again."

If only it were that easy. "I haven't been able to get in touch with it again. So there's that. Maybe it's whoever lit the fire."

"Sure. This is great. Let's film you—"

"Describing it? I'm pretty sure that's the boring stuff that isn't going to make it to air."

"True. I can spin what you've told me and get something going for PR." Gia paced around Kirsty. Something she'd seen Gia do before when she was unraveling a problem and figuring out the best way forward. "Tell the story. But Bri's show is all visual."

Everything was about visuals. They needed to produce something that could be aired on the show.

"What if... I just sit up all night with the book. See if that gets a reaction from Paul."

"That's an idea. Sort of a slumber party with the book? You should get Jasper in on it too."

"Yeah, he just told me today that Paul was his cousin. How could he hide they were related?"

Gia rolled her eyes. "Dudes."

"Yeah but still."

"Even if we don't hear a voice…something is escalating Paul."

"That's good."

"Yeah, but for filming. None of the things I've experienced have ever been seen by anyone. I'm feeling more like a fraud than ever. This could backfire."

Gia put her hands on Kirsty's shoulders, shaking her slightly. "Snap out of it. You aren't a fraud, you're doing great. I will send a note to both Periwinkle and Bri reminding them that you sense things. We'll still get a good story."

"Yeah?"

"Who was named as Thoms Hollow's favorite mystery author?"

"Me," she said smiling as she remembered Gia's work to get that distinction. Even though Kirsty was pretty sure she was Thoms Hollow's only mystery author.

"That's right. So get your game face on and start weaving us a tale about Paul the ghost and figure out his ending."

There was a knock on the door and it slowly opened, Chewie nudging his way in with Jasper close behind. Jasper leaned against the jamb. Their eyes met and she was instantly taken back to that moment in the rain, and a hot throbbing started deep inside of her.

"Uh, Dan admitted he used a slow burn igniter to start the fire. Gia's off the hook. I mean, that wasn't a ghost," Jasper said.

"We can't have Dan doing stuff like that," Kirsty said. It was bad enough that she was fabricating her own skills. "That will lead to all of us losing our careers."

158 Ghost of a Chance

"Indeed. He's erasing the footage. I told him he can leave if he wants to end things and I'll film us, but he felt bad and wants to stay. You two have a moment to think it over. It's up to you if he stays or not," Jasper said, snapping his fingers. Chewie ran back to his side as they went back inside.

"Goodness this is a mess," Kirsty said.

"But it's not. You heard something. That was real, and so was everything at Bri's studio. Who's to say Paul sounds the same in the afterlife." Gia paused, eyes sparking with curiosity.

"The voice was deep, but I'm not sure if it was even a guy or not," Kirsty said. She didn't want to admit that the voice had warned her to stop faking her powers. Though to be fair, if that voice was a ghost, then she might not have been lying after all.

"That's interesting. What if there's no gender after death," Gia said. "We should totally play that up. Get people thinking!"

"Sure. But I wasn't saying it *wasn't* a guy, just that it was like a…deep whisper. Hard to identify. And it didn't sound like the recording of Paul's voice."

"Why didn't you say something the other night?" Gia asked. "Jasper might have some insight he can add."

"It freaked me out. The voice warned me to stop lying. Despite what everyone thought in Chicago…" She was already being honest, so she might as well lay it all out for her friend. "I left the ballroom because my period started and I was bleeding…nothing supernatural. I have never thought of myself as having any ability. For me it was easier to think it was a voice in my head."

Gia gave her a hug, and Kirsty resisted for a second before she rested her head on Gia's shoulder. "Why are you telling me now? What changed your mind?"

"I had a freaky emotional reaction at the apartment. Like, part of it was definitely my repressed emotional garbage… but it felt like something more was egging it on. I'm not even sure if it was real, or if maybe this entire thing is making me batshit crazy."

"Ha. You're totally not crazy. You tell the truth—usually." Gia chuckled, giving her a squeeze. "So you think if you start talking to Paul you'll get another voice or emotion? Jasper never gets any feelings, right? That's odd that you are," Gia said.

"Is it? I think his frustration with the irritating things that Paul does has kept him from feeling anything else." It was a theory she'd sort of been letting grow in the back of her mind.

"Dan can stay but he needs to be on our team and not working against us with his skepticism and fakery. Agreed?"

"Yeah, you deal with him."

"As long as we make progress, I think we'll uncover one of these mysteries before long."

Kirsty was sure they would uncover something. But that didn't make her feel as good as she'd thought it would. It was uncomfortable to experience someone else's feelings, to hear a disembodied voice in her head. As many times as she'd written those exact scenes for her heroine Eva Clare, she realized now she hadn't really done them justice.

She followed Gia into the house, settling in the living room where Jasper and Dan were idling. Jasper caught her eye as Dan got up to apologize, and Kirsty half listened but really all she saw was Jasper.

That creepy voice had thrown her for a loop. None of this was going the way she'd expected it to. This new ghost could be malicious. What were they going to encounter if they kept digging?

In spite of what she'd said to Jasper, she had sort of thought she had it all figured out. But if she really did have a gift to talk to ghosts...that was a lot to take in.

It took every bit of Jasper's self-control to stay where he was seated with Chewie when Kirsty came back into the room. Gia and Dan were speaking intently, and he should have been participating, but when Kirsty was in the room there wasn't a chance.

He wanted to invite her to come and sit next to him on the couch. Feel the warmth of her body against his.

He yearned for her. Being this close was a kind of torture. And so delicious. But they couldn't make their relationship public to Dan and Gia, not when so much else was already on the line.

Kirsty drifted over near the couch and dropped down on the floor next to Chewie, absently petting the dog.

Jealousy. Yup, he was jealous of his damn dog as he watched her hand move through Chewie's thick fur. She dropped her head back on the cushion, rolling it toward him and smiling.

"You ready for tonight?"

She'd laid out her plan and it was a solid one. He liked the idea of spending the night with her. Paul...actually after all the talking he'd done lately about the ghost he wanted to try to connect.

"Not really. What am I going to say? I don't want to be all pouring out my heart to a physics textbook. I don't want to become some internet meme." He was committed to doing it because she thought it would work and he wanted results.

"Me either. I'm not really used to doing this with an audience," she said.

There was so much he wanted to ask her.

"Yeah that's part of it," he said. She waited expectantly for a response. "But more, it's that I haven't really wanted to talk to him because I'm mad that he's still here."

"I can see that for you," she agreed. The lights in the living room flickered.

They both laughed. Dan and Gia stopped talking.

"Try acknowledging him."

"How?"

"Talk to him."

"Good to see you, Paul," Jasper said. After his disappointment during the séance it was nice to see Paul up to his familiar behaviors.

"Were the cameras on?"

"Yeah. We both heard you say he ticked you off," Gia said with a grin. "So what's next?"

"Jasper, try having a conversation," Kirsty said. There was a hesitant note in her voice.

"What should I say?"

"What do you want him to know?"

The questions he'd had at the séance had been generic. But he and Paul had always been closer than that. Dan and Gia had moved so that they were sitting in the two side chairs also facing him.

No pressure.

Basically he figured it for a one-sided talk. How often had he wished his roommate would shut up and let him talk? But not like this.

"I miss you," he said, emotion clogging his throat.

Nothing happened.

"Honestly if I'd known that would be your last night in the apartment I would have stayed."

Every light in the house came on, brighter than before. "Fix

162 Ghost of a Chance

You" started playing on Jasper's phone, and the fire flickered in the fireplace, the flames leaping up toward the flue.

"Wow. That's a strong reaction," Kirsty said, pulling out a notebook from her bag and frantically taking notes.

"Yeah, I still need fixing but I'm getting there," he said to Paul.

Jasper was also concerned about Paul. "I think about that all the time. Like you wanting to work on our side project for my mom. I know you were doing it that night. I feel bad that if I'd skipped… It's not about me. I want you to know that." Jasper gave a mirthless laugh. "I finally get that."

He broke off as *Judge Judy* blared on as she said, "If you live to be a hundred, you will never be as smart as me."

Kirsty started laughing. Gia and Dan were both sort of staring at him as if they hadn't seen him before. Of course confessing to what he considered his worst moment as a human being wasn't easy.

"Fair enough," he said.

Dan clicked the TV off. Jasper knew it was because television sound would interfere with his voice on the recording.

"Keep going," Kirsty said.

"Is there any way you can tell me what you want?" Jasper asked.

Nothing. All that opening up and he was getting the cold shoulder from a damn ghost.

"It's not healthy for you to be lingering with me," Jasper said again.

Still no response.

Slowly an hour passed and nothing he said caused another reaction. Dan finally went up to bed at ten, and Gia followed him a few minutes later. Kirsty however stayed, grabbing the bottle of rum and a two-liter of Coke from the kitchen and made the two of them mixed drinks.

"Did you two have something you did together?"

"We played *Star Wars Battlefront* and watched *Game of Thrones*."

"Did the series finish before he died? Maybe we should put it on for him," Kirsty suggested. They were really running out of ideas.

"No, he saw it all. But he hasn't seen *House of Dragons*. Want to sit up here and watch it with us?" That was really reaching. "I tried watching the first episode but it made me miss Paul, so I shut it off and went out instead."

"I'm here now," she said, taking his hand. "I've never really watched *Game of Thrones*. I was waiting until the entire series was finished. My mom and I like to binge a bunch of seasons over the weekends. But that last season had so much controversy—"

"Yeah. It was nuts. I still like the early seasons. It's got lots of stuff I think you'd like," he said.

"Like what?"

"Snow zombies."

"Ghosts aren't zombies, you know."

"Yeah, I guess you're right. But they're still paranormal. This new series is a stand alone. So?"

"Let's do this." Plopping down next to him on the couch, she patted the space next to her and Chewie jumped up, curling next to her. He draped his arm over her shoulder and pulled her close. They might not be any closer to their goal, but at least he wasn't spending tonight alone.

Kirsty's mom would be giving her so much shit if she knew she was watching this show. The same show she'd dissed when it first came out.

164 Ghost of a Chance

She was going to eat her words, because the show was good and addicting. Enjoying the steady warmth of Jasper's body didn't hurt, either.

Paul's poltergeist self didn't do anything as they watched the entire first two episodes. As the next cued up, her phone pinged thanks to her bedtime reminder. Nearly 2:00 a.m.

"What'd you think?" Jasper asked, standing up and stretching.

His shirt rode up and a patch of toned, tanned skin poked through, making it impossible for her to do anything.

"Kirst?"

"Yeah?"

"Want to watch another one after I take Chewie out to pee?"

As reluctant as she was to go in too deep, the genuine look in Jasper's eyes made her melt. "Maybe."

He arched both eyebrows at her. "Want to do something else?"

They were down here alone… "Make out on the couch?"

"That works," he said, snapping his fingers. Chewie jumped off the couch and followed him out the door. "I'll be right back."

He practically ran from the room. With how hot and heavy things got earlier in the day, his reaction didn't surprise her.

She turned off the TV and lit a fire in the fireplace. Not wanting to take any chances, she took the textbook into the kitchen. With her luck, Paul would finally show up again just to interrupt.

Jasper came back in and ordered Chewie to go to bed. The dog obediently left the living room and padded up to Jasper's room. "Where is he going?"

"His dog bed. I put it in my room when we got here."

Now that he was back inside, it wasn't awkward exactly, but it wasn't totally comfortable either. He didn't know that he was the first man she was risking more than a one-night stand with since she had her heart broken.

What a dumb saying, heartbroken. Buck didn't deserve to be the man who broke her heart. He broke the girl she used to be, made it so she'd never be the same. She'd never realized how vulnerable being fearless and impulsive left her.

"Kirst. Woman, that look on your face… I'm tempted to drag you outside. There's a full moon and some mist in the air. We might as well howl and let loose like werewolves," he said.

"Let's do it."

He smiled and held out his hand. She took it and he tugged her off balance, enveloping her in his arms and kissing the top of her head.

"If you don't want to…"

"I want to," she said, looking up at him. "I'm just a bit of a mess when it comes to sex."

"You were pretty good at our foreplay," he said.

"Not the act. The other stuff," she said. What guy wanted to hear a woman talk about her feelings while he was trying to get off? Jasper scared her as much as he excited her. She wanted to open up to him completely, but she was worried that once she started, it would be impossible to stop.

"Yeah, the other stuff is scary," he said. "Not going to lie, I'm sort of in my feelings for you."

"You are?"

"Yeah. You intrigue me and I can't stop thinking about you. I want you, bad."

Being vulnerable was suddenly easier knowing she wasn't the only one.

She guided his face closer to hers. He hesitated a moment

and then she felt the brush of his lips, his hands gripping her butt, pulling her flush against his body.

They fit together perfectly. She shoved her hands into the hair at the back of his neck. Loved the cool, silky strands, lightly damp from the mist on his last walk with Chewie.

He groaned as he lifted her up and she felt the kitchen table under her ass. Jasper stepped between her legs. Slipping her hands under the hem of his T-shirt, she grazed the skin she'd been staring at earlier. He was muscular and hard, but his skin was soft.

Her memories of his bare, chiseled chest that hungover morning after were mouthwatering. She ached to see him again and tried to push his shirt up. He promptly tore it off, tossing it on the table. Perfectly covering Paul's textbook.

"Let's go in the living room. Leave Paul in here," she said.

Thirteen

Make out with me.

The heat from the fire seemed to have doubled, but his entire focus was on her. On that sweet body. On how she somehow made him both comfortable and terrified.

It was like his brain had shut down and his base masculine instincts took over. He was glad to hear that she was in her feelings, too. It made him more hopeful that this might be more than a reaction to the odd ghost hunt they found themselves trapped in.

There was no one else he wanted to be trapped with.

The first time he'd held her in his arms everything had happened so fast. A blur of drunken lust. This time he was determined to enjoy every second of it.

He pulled her into his arms, tipping her head back so he could stare at her brilliant eyes. He liked that he was taller than she was. That her curves fit seamlessly against the strength of his body. Humming a bit of a song that wouldn't get out of his head.

"What's this?" she asked.

"I want to make sure I don't miss a moment this time. Those shots of tequila we did at Dead Boys might have tinged the way I remember you."

"What song are you thinking of?"

"Not a Dead Boys' one."

She absently licked her lips, causing a groan to escape him.

"'Just Another Girl,'" he said. It was there in the back of his mind. They swayed to the beat as he continued humming. She tilted her head and her hair brushed against his arm soft and silky, leaving a trail of flames in its wake. Her breath was warm against his bare chest, sending shivers through him, making him even harder.

"Am I just another girl to you?" she asked. There was a note of uncertainty in her voice.

"No. That's what the song is about. The singer doesn't want any other woman." He wasn't one to hold back, but after twenty-five years of being this way he wasn't going to change. "Just the one he can't have."

Some risks were worth it. Kirsty definitely was.

"Ah…seems like you can have me," she said.

"Just for now?"

"For tonight, and then we'll see. I like you too." She walked her fingers down his chest, following the line of hair tapering down toward his jeans.

She caressed him right above the waistband. His cock hardened and he groaned. The feel of her fingers teasing his bare skin was addicting.

"You're a bit overdressed," he said.

"Yeah? You should do something about that," she said. Her hands refused to leave his body. He worked out and tried to stay in shape. All those early-morning runs and gym sessions were worth it.

He inched his hands under her sweater, causing her to shudder as he began to rub his hand on her back, gently scraping his nails down her spine. He wanted to share pleasure with her, to make her unravel.

As he inched her sweater up, he remembered her tattoos. The temporary ones were starting to fade. As he swept the sweater up over her head, he traced the pattern of the one on her chest. The edges came down to the inside of her breasts.

"I like this."

The pattern was intricate and delicate. Strange that it was temporary when it fit her so perfectly.

As he traced the fading lines of the tattoo, she reached behind herself, thrusting her breasts forward against his chest. She shrugged out of her bra, exposing her creamy skin. Cupping both of her breasts, he leaned down to kiss her neck and used his tongue to trace the pattern of her tattoo.

She smelled like fall. Cinnamon and rain and something else that was unique to her. He breathed deeply as he let his tongue travel over her, watching goose bumps appear. Her nipples tightened at his exploration, pressing into the palms of his hands.

He teased them in slow circular motions until she arched her back even more. Taking his time, he slowly took his hands away from her breasts, replacing them with his tongue, sucking one of her rosy buds into his mouth.

She moaned, low and feral, and her hands tightened their grip in his hair. Her hips rubbed against his erection. He needed her more than he'd realized.

Oddly this was what he'd been waiting for. She just wiped everything else away. At this moment, if he had to choose between having Kirsty and getting rid of Paul...there was no choice.

He'd pick her. Every damn time.

Ghost of a Chance

* * *

The way that Jasper looked at her body made her feel like she was the sexiest woman alive. That was a heady feeling and for a moment she indulged herself in it. It was a bit alien though. In her past relationships she'd never felt like she was enough. Buck hadn't been half the man that Jasper was. Jasper was imperfect and real.

All things she stopped thinking as his mouth closed around her nipple. Immediately she was wet and empty and needing. She wanted so much more from him than she could admit, but for tonight in front of the fire with Jasper holding her, this felt like enough.

God, actually it was more than enough.

All she could do was dig her fingers into his shoulders and enjoy his touch. She slipped her hand down his chest, the light dusting of hair brushing her fingertips, abrasive in the best possible way. Then she went lower to his flat stomach, his belly button.

He groaned and pulled away from her breast, the puff of his breath against her nipple a revelation.

She circled his belly button.

His erection jumped each time she did it. She lowered herself, kissing a path down the center of his body before he lifted her off her feet and settled her down on a blanket in front of the fire.

Thankfully she'd put it there earlier, because in romance short storys and movies couples always made love in front of a fire.

The firelight danced over his skin, shadowed patterns playing over the planes of his body. For a few moments she stilled, entranced in a sort of fire meditation. But it wasn't just the flames that captured her mind.

He pushed her gently back and lay down on his side. His hand swept down from her shoulder to her arm. Lingered at the curve of her hip where her palm rested against her black jeans. She held her breath as he slowly caressed the curve of her waist, settling on her belly button half covered by her midrise jeans.

He undid her jeans and then his finger was there. Brushing over her skin, sending delicious shimmers up and down her, heat pooling in her center.

"Like that?"

"As much as you do," she said. Her voice sounded raspy to her own ears.

"Not possible," he said.

Gooseflesh spread out across her stomach. Her panties and jeans felt too tight. Why hadn't she taken them off before?

Rolling away from him, she pushed her jeans and underwear down her legs, kicking them off her feet. Thank God she wasn't wearing her boots. Sitting up, she fumbled in her pocket for the condom she'd put in there earlier.

She hadn't even attempted to pretend that tonight would be innocent.

He took the condom from her, having stripped off the rest of his clothes. His hand stroked his erection, his eyes sharp and hungry.

"Everything I can think of sounds trite and corny but dammit, woman, I've never seen anyone more beautiful than you," he said.

Reverence laced his voice with deep guttural need that shook her to her core. Her heart was pumping hard and making her feel things…things she was going to ignore because he was so sexy and hot, and there was nothing as important right now as getting him inside of her and taking every ounce of pleasure she could from it.

A log shifted in the fireplace, flames hissing, a stray spark landing on the hearth, as if the waves of heat from inside of her had manifested. He pulled her close, his mouth coming down on hers as he rolled her under his body.

"I want to be on top this time, okay?"

"Yes." She wanted his strength on her, his cock inside of her. She wanted it all.

Pulling on the condom, the heat of the fire on his back, Kirsty spread out in front of him with her legs open and that dark brown gaze of hers... He wanted this to be perfect.

She'd been brutally honest that one-night stands were her hookup of choice so he didn't kid himself that this would turn into anything more. So he'd make it last. But of course, how could he do that when she devoured him with hungry eyes and kept touching his dick with one hand, her clit in the other.

God, there was nothing hotter than how she wanted him.

Except how he desperately needed her.

Bracing himself on one hand, he used the tip of his cock to fondle her clit. Arching her back, she moaned and shifted until his cock slid down her body.

There were still so many parts of her that he hadn't explored but he needed to be in her. Right now.

Cupping her ass with one hand, guiding her hips upward, he drove himself deep into her. She lifted her legs, wrapping them around his hips so he could go deeper. She pulled his head down to hers, kissing him deeply as he drove himself into her.

He wanted to wait for her to come, but the moment he entered her tingles ignited throughout his body. His cock was so full and hard, a moment from exploding. He drove into her harder and harder, chasing her pleasure.

She tore her mouth from his, arching her back. "Now."

He groaned as he pumped harder and faster, responding to her keening moans with his own, until everything exploded inside of her and he came long and hard. He kept thrusting as waves of ecstasy hit him, feeling her pussy walls tightening around him as she wailed in her own release.

He rested his forehead against hers, eyes closed, breath sawing out of him. Her fingers lightly grazed his back as her own breathing slowed. He opened his eyes.

Her gaze was soft, making him feel like he was the only man in the world. He rolled off of her and drew her against his side. Wanting to hold her even though the condom was sticky against his lower belly. She shifted around and pulled a box of tissues from the floor behind the couch, handing him one.

"Thanks."

"Figured it might be nice to cuddle after," she said, slightly breathless.

"No blanket?"

"You're pretty hot-blooded and the fire should keep us warm," she explained.

How had he missed this? He'd been swept up in the goth paranormal energy that veiled her like an aura. But she was a planner. She liked fixing things so that they worked out the way she wanted.

"When did you start working on making this happen tonight?"

"At your car, when Dan interrupted us. Didn't you?" she asked.

"I mean I hoped we'd connect, but until you asked me to have sex with you… I didn't really think it would happen."

"Yeah?"

"Yeah."

"You totally underestimate your effect on me."

"My effect?"

She shook her head. "I'm not going to explain it."

Well, now he had to know. "You have to. I mean is it that I'm a stud or so irresistible—"

He broke off as she started tickling him. He had to roll away to escape it. "Let it be."

It had been a long time since he'd felt this kind of joy. The freedom of being entirely himself with another person. "I'll clean up and grab us a blanket. Then we can cuddle by the fire."

"It's a bit chilly," she said.

He went and got his T-shirt. Tossed it to her and stared as she pulled it on. The fabric hung loose on her frame but still hinted at her supple curves. He wanted her to see him as he was. All the screwups and the uncertainty and the fact that when he was with her that sort of melted away.

Fourteen

There was something about being in Jasper's arms that she could get used to. The spicy smell of his cologne mingling with a hint of sweat. The way his body enveloped hers. *Dangerous thinking.* Curled behind her in his boxer briefs, holding her against his chest, he felt solid. Comforting.

Her mind was quiet for once.

"I like your tattoo," he said, quietly, his chin resting on her shoulder. "I get that you haven't decided on making it permanent yet, but it's really nice."

"Yeah? I like it too."

"Then why don't you just get it… I mean it's none of my business but I'm curious."

"It's the blood. I mean I thought I could handle it. I watch *Ink Master* all the time. Honestly, I thought the red that showed up was just some sort of dark dye they had to use to get the colors to pop."

"Uh…"

"Yeah, I get it. It just didn't occur to me. So I rolled up to get my first tattoo—like I said, slightly drunk—watching the

176   Ghost of a Chance

needle as he worked on the design. Then I got lightheaded, saw spots, and barely managed not to pass out until he was done…but it wasn't the best experience."

"Wow, that's a lot. No wonder you don't have more," he said.

Not *you're a massive wuss* which was what Buck said. Remembering that she'd let that asshole have any control over her pissed her off. He was a jerk. Why hadn't she been able to see it when she'd been dating him and trying so hard to make him happy? Why would she want that guy to like her?

"What about you? Any tats?"

"Yes. I thought you'd noticed it," he said, sitting up and twisting his leg so she could see the back of his left calf where there was a… What was *that*?!

"Yosemite Sam?"

"Yeah."

"Big fan?" she asked sitting up, crossing her legs as she looked at the design. It was pretty nice, but huge. It took up most of the back of his calf. She was surprised she hadn't noticed it before, but to be fair when he was naked her eyes were usually on his chest, or his ass, or his dick.

"Um…well I have one video that my dad made for me and it's him talking about the stuff he wants to show me when I'm older. And one of them was Looney Tunes, especially Yosemite Sam. So when I was twenty-one I got drunk and decided to go and get the tattoo."

Leaning forward she traced her hand over the hat and the two .45s that were pointed up in the character's hands. "It's really big."

He flushed and shook his head. "Yeah, turns out I'm not great with knowing what size a quarter is."

"What did you think?"

"Five inches."

She started laughing. "I'm bad with numbers but not that bad."

He grimaced. "Most of the time no one can see it but in summer, I get all kinds of comments."

"I can see why," she said. "But I think it's sweet. Like you have something special with your dad."

He grew quiet for a minute, then leaned against the back of the couch. "Do you have anything with yours?"

"No. Nothing. He left us when I was six."

"What a dick move. You know that has nothing to do with you," Jasper said.

"I don't know, he's never reached out and I never saw him again. At this point I'm good," she said. And she was. Or at least she tried to be. Closure wasn't always possible.

He pulled her into his arms, stroking her hair. "Sorry."

"Not your fault," she said. Because what else was she going to say?

That she was sorry too? It hurt that she didn't have two parents that cared for and loved her the way other kids had when she'd been in school. But now that she was an adult, she had to grow up. "It really wasn't a big deal, except for in fifth grade during the daddy-daughter dance. I really didn't miss having him around."

"Did you have to skip the dance?"

"No. My mom took me. Told the school they were being discriminatory. There were other parents, not just us that objected. Some same-sex parents also didn't like daddy-daughter or mommy-son. So they changed it to parents and kids. Actually, it turned out really nice."

Her mom could be too much and push too hard, but Kirsty

wanted to be fearless the way she was. When her mom saw something that wasn't right she spoke up.

"Sounds like it. We didn't have anything like that at my school," Jasper said.

"I'm not sure that they do it everywhere. We were living in the Midwest at the time in a suburb of Chicago," she said, remembering that rented town house that had been so different from the big house they had in Florida when she was really little. It had snowed in October right before Halloween and she'd been entranced. Never having seen snow before, it was magical and she'd wished that they would stay there forever.

But they hadn't. Her mom had to take different jobs to move up the corporate ladder and they moved once again back to the South, and then again to Texas. Her childhood had been a bunch of restarts.

Which was probably why she'd bought that duplex and given the other half to her mom. They both had a permanent home now. Her mom still traveled a lot for work but Kirsty had someplace of her own. And her mom was never far away.

Jasper was quiet, watching the fire and lost to his own thoughts. She appreciated it because once she started thinking about her past, thoughts of the future crept in. A future that was unsettled until she figured out her own possible abilities as a medium and why Paul lingered on. Otherwise this television spot, and potentially her career, were dead on arrival.

Also, now there was Jasper.

She'd told herself it was safe to sleep with him. They were only in each other's lives for a short while. It felt like that longing to stay in the Midwest had when she first sat in the window and watched the snowfall.

Like a new start. Something different.

Katherine Garbera

179

★ ★ ★

It was just too easy to talk to her about his dad. The stuff that he normally didn't bring up. It hadn't taken him long to figure out that most people didn't know how to react when he said his dad died the night he was born.

But with Kirsty it didn't feel odd. Maybe it was because she hadn't known her dad either.

"Is there anything you're not good at?" he asked after a few minutes.

"Lots of stuff. Sports especially."

He doubted that.

"I bet you're better than you think," he said.

"Doubt it. Obviously you're great at them, right?"

He shrugged, and she immediately resettled on his shoulder. "I'm alright. It's not really about being good for me. After working at the studio all day and in my office I need to move. Otherwise I get cranky. I run and work out at the gym. Sometimes I play basketball in a league with some other shows that shoot in the Chicago area."

Physical exercise really kept his mind clear, helping with his mental health on days when he battled being overwhelmed. He liked being outside and around other people but with his job and Paul sometimes he wanted to hide away.

"I walk. Somedays the words aren't flowing. And you might not know this about me, but I'm stubborn."

"What? Really? I'd never have—"

"Enough," she said, mock-punching him.

"How does that play into your writing?" he asked. He enjoyed hearing her share her writing process. There was no way he could do anything creative. She looked so excited to talk about her process.

"I just make myself sit there while the timer is on… I write

180 Ghost of a Chance

in twenty-five-minute sprints. And then finally I admit it's not working and go for a walk. There's something almost magical about moving your body."

"Especially when I move mine with yours," he said.

She gave him a disappointed look, sticking her tongue out at him. "I was being serious."

He had been too. Magic was the best way to describe it.

"So you walk and then things sort themselves out?" he asked.

"Yeah. It's like once I'm outside all of the parameters I'd been putting on my story are gone. I might see someone's dog being naughty and running away from them or kids tossing a ball and bam! Different things spark ideas."

"That's funny. I never notice people when I'm running, other than as an obstacle I'm going to have to navigate around." His head was clear when he was out which was nice since he was always overthinking everything.

"Makes sense, you're out there for a different reason. I'm just trying to refill the well and force my mind into finding some new pathways," she said around a yawn.

"Getting sleepy?"

"Yeah, but I don't want to head up yet," she said, her hand kneading his thigh.

He didn't want that either. Should he ask her to come to his bedroom? Of course, Chewie liked to sleep with him so Kirsty might not like that.

And… What if she said no? What if he made things awkward between them?

"I like this," she said.

"Me too." Whatever she meant by *this*. "I guess we should think about heading to bed. We have that physics class tomorrow and I think we're getting closer to figuring out what's going on with Paul."

"Yeah. The class should help us a bit. Maybe we can figure out why he's tied to this book at least."

Do you want to sleep with me? The words were right there.

"What do you think?" she asked.

"Uh…sorry, I wasn't paying attention," he admitted.

"It's okay. It's late. We can talk about it tomorrow. Thanks for tonight," she said as she got to her feet. "I'm going to keep your shirt for now."

"Fine by me," he said, gathering up their clothes after he banked the fire. Her insisting on keeping his shirt to wear to bed so casually was intensely hot. "Want to sleep with me?"

The words just slipped out as she waited for him, chewing her lower lip between her teeth. He knew the answer before she spoke.

"I'm not…"

"It's okay. Chewie snores and likes to climb into the bed anyway," he said, turning off the lights and joining her in the hallway. It had been a nice night. Why had he done that? He should have let things alone.

What would it take for her to let him in? To allow him into her life? She probably saw him as just an annoying guy with a ghost, the dude she slept with, a temporary friend on this weird journey.

He was working himself up as they climbed the stairs to the second floor. She was staying in the converted attic and paused at the foot of those stairs. "It's not you, okay."

Yeah. Right.

If she needed proof that one-night stands were the only way to go, here it was. He asked her to sleep with him. How much more romance movie could life get than that. Except she'd never slept with anyone. She'd always had her own bed and always went home alone after sex.

What would it be like? She was a restless sleeper and had atrocious morning breath. These were all things that she was guessing Jasper hadn't considered.

Right now he looked at her with those wounded eyes and she wanted to walk back her no. Normally she could give two craps if she upset someone else but this wasn't normal. Not one damned thing since she'd gone to the Dead Boys concert had been normal.

It wasn't like she'd subtly been asking for change in her life. She'd spent a lifetime dealing with the chaos that was change and had finally—*finally*—gotten to the point where she had a routine and safety.

People totally underestimated how much someone who'd lived a nomadic life desperately craved normality.

"I've never slept with anyone," she blurted out, trying to keep it at a heavy whisper. "I'm probably not good at it given how I am just in general. So it's really not you."

He leaned against the wall and ran his hand through that spikey, silky hair of his. What was he waiting for? There wasn't anything else to say.

"It's because everything with you is temporary."

Okay. Well, fuck him. He wasn't wrong but still, she hated being this seen. This twenty-five-year-old man-boy who told her point-blank he hadn't figured out life yet was doing a banging job of calling out hers.

Looking straight past the kohl eyeliner and heavy fall of bangs.

Not exactly a hot mess. On the cusp of change. The kind

of change that for once centered her own desires and the life she'd always wanted but never thought she'd stumble into.

"Temporary...dude, life is temporary. You know that better than anyone else," she pointed out. It was a low blow. Fully expecting him to retaliate so she could justify turning on her heels and stalking her way up the stairs.

"You're right. I do. But I don't run from life. Temporary doesn't equal meaningless or without connections. Say what you want to, but fear is something I'm very familiar with, and I know it when I see it."

With that he entered his bedroom, leaving her alone as he prepared for bed with Chewie.

Coward. Literally that's what he'd said to her more than once.

This just turned that harsh spotlight right back on her.

Dammit.

Just dammit.

"You can sleep in my bed," she bit out in the loudest whisper she'd ever used. She hoped Dan and Gia were heavy sleepers and didn't wake up.

"Oh, can I?" he asked, peering out of the doorway. He was still in his boxer briefs holding both of their other clothes in his left hand.

She was so scared and frustrated and angry.

"Yes." All of a sudden she was afraid she might cry. That wasn't like her. But this was Jasper and he pushed her into places she once thought she didn't want to go.

Slowly, deliberately, he came back into the hallway. "You are..."

"Frustrating?"

"No. Confusing."

"So, no to sleeping with me?" she asked.

"No," he said a faint smile playing at his mouth.

Fine then.

Kissing him hard, she shook her head and stalked up the stairs, very aware of him trailing behind her every step of the way.

Her room was a mess, she wasn't a neat person by nature. Her bed hadn't been made and her laptop and metaphysical books lay open on its tangled covers.

He tossed their clothes on the chair in the corner while she gathered her shit and put it on the nightstand.

"I sleep on the right," she said.

"Great. I usually just sprawl everywhere."

Of course he did. Great big puppy dog that he was.

She flipped off the overhead light and climbed into the bed. She lay there in silence for a second before he let out the biggest sigh she'd ever heard and lifted his arm over his head. "Cuddle?"

Without a word she shifted until her head was nestled on his shoulder and her arm was draped over his chest. He let out a long breath and encased her.

The beating of his heart lulled her to sleep.

Fifteen

Judge Judy blasted from the living room TV at 6:00 a.m. "I'm here because I'm smart, not because I'm young and gorgeous…although I am!" at full volume echoed up the stairs. Jasper jumped out of bed. Where was he? In the blur of the morning, it was hard to get his bearings.

Kirsty's room.

She sat up blurry-eyed and shoved her hair out of her face.

The noise got steadily louder as Chewie started barking in response. But he couldn't take his eyes off of the woman he'd slept with last night. He wanted to stay. Wanted to crawl right back into bed with her on this chilly autumn morning.

"TV!" She was not feeling the same.

"Yeah." He picked up his jeans as he headed toward the stairs. He whistled for Chewie who'd definitely need to go out and strolled into the living room to turn off the TV. Looking down at the physics book, which had clearly moved from the kitchen last night, he sighed.

"Morning, asshole."

He grabbed the hoodie he left over the kitchen chair and

pulled it on as he shoved his feet into the Crocs he kept by the door for middle-of-the-night dog walks. Chewie waited impatiently as Jasper put the leash on him and opened the door. He stepped out into a relaxed cloudy rain. The lights in the kitchen flicked behind him as he followed Chewie to do his business.

He hadn't grabbed his phone so was just staring around the neighborhood collecting his thoughts.

The lights surged again, then again a few minutes later as he and Chewie went back into the kitchen. Chewie shook himself off outside.

"Coffee?"

Dan stood there, a mug in one hand. Even though he'd been startled out of bed it seemed he'd had time to get dressed in his regular khakis and a polo.

"Yeah. TV wake you?"

"It did. I checked the infrared footage. There's a sort of blurry…well, you look at it and tell me what you think. It seems as if something is moving toward the TV before it turns on."

"For real?"

Dan looked sheepish. "Honest. I told you no more faking stuff. This isn't polished at all. That's why I think it might be real."

"I know it is," Jasper said, taking the coffee mug from Dan and following him to the monitor where he had the playback set up. "Gia and Kirsty are going to love this. Also the fact that you were wrong."

"I know. I fucked up. But after three days here I believed this was a waste of time."

Dan hit Play. The sound was up on the monitor but there wasn't much noise. A shuffling sound cut through the silence, and then there was that blurry blob that appeared on-screen just before the television came on.

"That is terrifying."

"What's terrifying?" Gia asked, joining them.

"The footage that I got," Dan said.

Gia started a cup for herself before joining them. Today her hair was all springy curls tied back with a thick headband. She had on a *Nightmare Before Christmas* sweatshirt over orange-and-brown-plaid pjs.

Dan played it again. Even seeing it a second time sent a chill through him. There was something in the living room. Some kind of energy. Paul's energy.

God, he felt like an idiot that he hadn't really taken the time to talk to Paul before this. To be fair, until Kirsty had come along Jasper hadn't been ready to do it.

At first he tried to be logical about the stuff going on, the way he knew Kirsty had when she arrived here. But logic didn't explain mysterious figures where none should be. He'd always known that Paul was haunting him but having visual evidence made it seem real in a whole new way.

"That's spooky. I love it. The film is kind of grainy though…do you think it'll be clear enough to convince Bri and the audience?" Gia asked.

"With infrared that's about what we are going to get. I don't want to enhance it in post too much or we'll end up with some of the audience thinking it's faked," Dan said.

"You're right. I didn't think we were going to get anything as good as that. I'm going to go wake up Kirsty. She needs to see this."

Gia left and Dan leaned back in his chair. "Finally I have something that Bri can use. She was breathing down my neck.

188 Ghost of a Chance

I mean no excuses for what I did yesterday, but you know how she can be."

"I do." Their boss was kind and generous but also extremely demanding when it came to her show. She wanted results and wouldn't tolerate anything less than the best.

Jasper was a bit relieved too, despite the unease the footage gave him. All these years hadn't been just in his head. There had always been a small part of him that wondered if he had been projecting, imagining it all.

Maybe that explained why he'd been so ticked off when Kirsty hadn't believed him. Part of him had always been a little unwilling to put his faith in something that was so out there. Kirsty just had the nerve to share her doubts out loud.

Kirsty stumbled into the room behind Gia, their eyes met and she gave him a conspiratorial grin before coming to stand behind Dan. The scent of her freshly showered body made it difficult not to drop his arm onto her shoulders.

But he didn't.

Keeping their relationship—whatever it was—under wraps was for the best. After all, they had a ghost to save.

Things were really starting to come together. If she didn't have to hold another séance she'd be elated. The infrared footage that Dan captured made up for the day before and then some.

Now they all were sitting in the back of a physics classroom, auditing a class before filming thanks to Jasper's persuasion skills. Jasper leaned back in the chair stretching his legs out in front of him and scrolling on his phone as students trickled in.

She'd loved school for as long as she could remember. Learning at least. Not so much the social aspects. There was a thrill in getting a new fact, in solving a problem.

"I'm pretty much crap at anything science," she said. Ever since last night, Jasper's energy was off. He'd been cordial and talkative as usual, but she could tell he was holding something back.

"I'm okay," he said. Paul's textbook was with them hiding in a large bag at their feet.

The professor came in and started explaining something about quantum entanglement. There was frantic note-taking from the students and Jasper leaned forward listening intently.

But she was confused.

Jasper leaned in close, a troublemaker's gleam in his eyes.

"Want me to give you the cheater's version?" he asked.

She nodded, so he continued, his voice a low whisper as the professor droned on. "Physics is basically studying matter and its motion through space and time, along with related concepts such as energy and force. It's the study of nature in an attempt to understand how the universe behaves.

"Quantum entanglement attempts to explain how particles can become linked in a way that's not explainable by regular physics."

So Paul was studying how energy moved through space and time when he died. "Is there any way he could have attached…"

Trailing off, she paused. This was ridiculous. She was about to ask him if his roommate had transferred his soul to a book. At this point, anything seemed possible, but from what little she did know about science and physics as a college undergrad, pulling something like that off would be especially impossible.

"I don't know. I mean if you were going to ask if he'd moved his energy into the book intentionally, that would be venturing into something far beyond college physics."

Hearing it out loud, she cringed. "More like fairy tales or

fiction. I mean in my books it would work. But I don't have to logically prove how that works outside of the page. Given my lack of science brain, that's not a good thing."

He laughed softly and continued giving her a layman's breakdown of what the professor was going over during the class.

As Jasper explained the lesson, Kirsty's mind wandered. Paul was starting to take shape for her, the way a character did when she was writing.

Paul was so much more than just a playful poltergeist to her now. He was taking shape as a person. Would he have felt like the world was limitless when he'd learned this? That anything was possible?

She wished she'd met him. From all that Jasper had shared, Paul sounded like he was a special person. He'd definitely taken care of Jasper in a way that made her like him just a little bit more.

She wasn't a detective and honestly not very good at solving mysteries but she wanted to be…for Jasper and for Paul.

"You sure know a lot about this stuff. Why weren't you taking physics?"

"Uh, that's complicated."

"Okay." He called things complicated when he didn't want to discuss them. Maybe it wasn't important to everything going on anyway.

"I just can't whisper it. I'll tell you later when we're out of class." He squeezed her hand.

A little shiver jolted through her fingers. There wasn't anyone she felt comfortable touching this intimately, but Jasper proved to be the exception.

He gave her a quizzical look, reaching up to pat his hair. "Is my hair sticking up?"

"No."

"You're staring."

"It's *complicated*."

His lips twitched as he turned to pay attention to the professor and she jotted down notes on concepts that she'd have him explain to her later.

Because there was no way she was getting anything as she sat next to Jasper, enjoying the fresh scent of his body spray, the way he tapped his fingers on the desk as he leaned in to listen more intently.

There was something about him that made it hard for her to look away.

She'd always been a loner and liked it. She hadn't wanted or missed having a bestie in school or in life. She had everything she needed with her mom and her books.

After Buck, no man was worth the pain she'd experienced. But somehow Jasper felt different.

She was so cute trying to figure out physics. To Jasper it was natural. The concepts and theories all made sense. It was probably in his genes. Another thing he could chock up to his dad.

His father had wanted to be a high school physics teacher, but Jasper never really wanted to follow in that path. Maybe because his mom always talked about his dad working on his science fiction short story.

As the lecture concluded, the professor left through the back. Next they had an appointment to speak to Paul's old professor before the lab he was holding in about forty minutes.

It felt natural to reach for Kirsty's hand as the classroom emptied, so he did it. For a second her hand was stiff, and then her fingers slid through his, sending a pulse of awareness straight through him. "What'd you think?"

"I'm trying to somehow make sense of Paul trapped in a textbook. Do you think he loved this class so much he didn't want to leave it?"

"I'm not too sure."

"Me either. I mean he'd have to be so inspired by his studying that he'd want to stay around." Grasping at straws wasn't getting her anywhere.

"I've never heard of anything like that," he said. "I don't think science-wise that's what happened."

"Dying and becoming a ghost doesn't scream science," she said. "But his emotions could have guided him."

"Yeah, I could see that. Humor me for a minute. Until the textbook I totally didn't believe in ghosts him becoming a poltergeist seems more logical."

"But what if him thinking about transference guided him to the book?" Kirsty was so serious he had to at least consider it.

Still Jasper wasn't sure that was possible. "That's not really how physics works."

"Oh believe me I know. If it was there'd be possessed items all over the place. But I'm back to Sherlock. We've ruled out all the logical things, so that leaves…"

"The illogical?" he asked.

She lightly punched his shoulder. "Don't say it like that. Makes it seem crazy."

She had a point. There had to be an explanation and she'd come upon one. It just made their project that much more difficult. "How would Paul know he was going to have a brain hemorrhage? He'd have to have an experiment set up."

"I don't think it was intentional."

She had a point. But his gut wasn't certain. "Let's talk to his teacher and see what he says."

"I agree. I mean I don't want to go in there with this theory but there has to be a reason why he's tied to the book. Even if it's not necessarily logical to us or Paul himself."

They got to the lab early and the room was empty. They let themselves in and went to one of the long workbenches placed throughout the classroom. Looking around the room, he was flooded with memories. Jasper made his way to one particular bench. "This was ours."

"Is it weird being back here without him?" she asked.

"Yeah a little. I dropped physics after he died."

"I would have dropped it way earlier," she said with a laugh. "So what did twenty-year-old you pick up instead?"

"More classes from the media and communications department," he said, leaning back against the table. "That department is on the other side of campus. I liked the courses and started spending all my time over there."

"I've found that most things in life aren't all that circumstantial. Every decision we make leads to where we are meant to be," she said.

"Like our decision to go to the Dead Boys' concert?" he asked.

Light filtered through the lab windows, highlighting the two black braids framing her face, that thick fall of bangs, and the fading tattoo visible above the collar of her black puff-sleeved top. He put his hands on her waist and pulled her slowly toward him.

Her hand came to his chest. He leaned down, their mouths met and for a moment he wondered why he hadn't kissed her sooner this morning.

He'd missed this. Missed her taste. Missed the way she grounded him in a way.

The door to the classroom squeaked open. Dammit. He quickly broke away from her as the professor entered. Mr.

Thompson hadn't changed much in the last few years. His hair was a bit grayer and maybe a little thinner but he was still lean and had a no-nonsense manner.

"The next class isn't for twenty minutes but you need to take that elsewhere," he said.

Kirsty stood straight and walked over to him, her head held high. "I'm K.L. Henson. I believe you spoke to my publicist Gia from Periwinkle Press. She mentioned we had some questions about a former student."

"Leo Thompson. I did. You don't look like...not that it matters." Leo harrumphed, setting a stack of papers on the lab table at the front of the room. "What do you want to know? Who was the student?"

"Paul Lester. I was in your class with him. Do you remember us?"

"I do. Paul had potential, you were sort of coasting through the class. I was sorry to hear Paul died his junior year."

"Yes. Well, we are trying to establish a few facts about Paul's course of study at the time. Do you know if he had any particular attachment to this book?" Kirsty asked, taking it from her bag and placing it on the lab table.

"I'm not sure where you got this book," the professor said.

"It was with his stuff when we cleaned out the apartment," Jasper said.

"Well, this isn't a textbook he would have been using. It would have been outdated long before you were in school."

Sixteen

What was Professor Thompson talking about? "Is there any other reason he would have had this book?"

"None that I can think of. That book is from the early 1990s."

"Are you sure?" Kirsty asked with an edge in her voice.

Professor Thompson gave her a look that said he was done with this conversation. Granted, she never did bother to look at the copyright date. "What book would he have been using?"

She jotted down the name of the new textbook. "Is there a chance he would have had this old one because it was cheaper? I did that for a few of my classes."

"No. If he couldn't afford the book I have some I keep on hand. I've never seen this book in my classroom. I wasn't teaching until after it was discontinued," he offered. "Is that all?"

"What was he working on at the time of his death? Jasper mentioned he'd come to the lab to study for a big exam the night he died."

"I'd have to check my class notes, but you were in the class, Cotton, do you remember?"

"Uh, no." Jasper looked dejected. She resisted the urge to reach over and comfort him.

"I'll use your PR person's email to send you the info when I find it. Anything else?"

"No. Thank you for your time," she said.

"No problem." The professor paused for a moment before sheepishly rubbing the back of his head. "I have to say, I am interested in how you're going to work physics into your next novel," he said.

"Have you read them?"

"I read the first one. My daughter recommended it to me," he said.

"I'm working on using physics to rule out how the ghost in my current manuscript is tied to an object," she said. It was easier to talk about her theory as if it were fiction.

"Ah, there is so much we don't know about matter and movement through time and space. You might want to check out chaos theory," he said. "Of course that relies heavily on mathematics but it also deals with random and unpredictable behavior. I'm not saying that something like what you described is possible in the real world but in your fictional one where there are ghosts…maybe."

"Maybe. Thanks for your time, and for reading my book."

"You're welcome. I enjoyed it," he said.

They left the classroom and Jasper, who'd been quiet the entire time, continued to brood as they walked back to the car. It had started raining again but they were both prepared with their brightly colored ponchos this time. She pulled on the hood and thought about the book in her bag and how, according to the professor, there was no connection to Paul.

Where did that leave them?

She was going to have to do another séance or take the book to Aza. She had an appointment booked with her in two days. For right now that was all she could do.

Until then, she had to contend with Jasper and what this meant for him.

"I don't think Paul is in this book," she said once they were seated at a nearby diner that Jasper drove them to.

"Why not?"

"You heard the professor, this wasn't even a book he was using." Could it be someone else trapped in the book? But then why would they haunt Jasper?

"Why would someone else want to hang around? Paul is the only logical—"

"Sherlock."

"We haven't ruled Paul out. He could have picked it up for some research into an older discounted theory. I mean that makes more sense than it not being him when this book's been haunting me."

This wasn't something that Jasper seemed ready to let go of. But she was going to start looking into anyone else who might have had this book. Idly she picked up the book, really examining it. Before, she'd assumed that Jasper had checked this, that this information was confirmed. It was time to do her due diligence.

It was obviously used. As she flipped through, she returned to the sketch of the tree in the corner. There wasn't a name in the top corner, just a stamp for a used bookstore. Pity. She wrote her name in all of her books—not that she lent them out, she just liked claiming them in a way.

Her stomach rumbled. In the chaos of their investigation,

neither of them had much to eat. They both ordered patty melts and onion rings.

"Once we get the professor's notes on what Paul was studying, we can probably figure this out," Jasper said.

"Yeah, that will help. There has to be something we're missing," she said. Jasper nodded, his face grim.

He'd shut down and retreated. She was disappointed too, and this was just supposed to be a publicity thing for her. This was his life. He'd been living with a ghost since his roommate died. It had to be a blow to realize it might not be his close friend at all.

She wanted to discuss it more, but Jasper wasn't responding to anything she said with more than a grunt.

She lost her patience with him. He kept forgetting they were in this *together*. Earlier that thought would have sparked joy inside of her. Now it felt like a warning to not let herself get in too deep. "I get it's difficult to hear that it might not be Paul, but taking it out on me isn't going to change anything. He wasn't using this book for his class. He probably was just studying for a standard test, which wouldn't have used this book at all. Is there any other reason he'd have it?"

Jasper put his sandwich down and leaned across the table toward her. "If I knew that then I wouldn't have dragged us to campus today."

"Don't be an ass. You said yourself you blocked out a lot after he died. I'm asking to jog your memory."

"Nothing's coming to mind," he said, taking a huge bite of his patty melt.

She rolled her eyes and looked away from him. "I guess we'll have to go back to the night he died. You said you left him at the apartment, but we know he made his way to the lab. We should retrace your steps that night as well. Might trigger something."

He finished chewing, then nodded. "Sorry. I was being a dick. It's just, if it's not Paul, then I have no idea what's going on. Am I being haunted by some random ghost?"

Probably. Her experience with them in real life was nonexistent, so she had no idea what kind of things would motivate them. "You're forgiven. Remember I'm on your side and want to solve this as much as you do."

"I'm grateful for that," he said. "I'll have to go through my socials to remember what I was doing that night. Do you really think it will help?"

"It can't hurt. Maybe Paul talked to someone who gave him the book. We ruled it out as a class text but there are still options," she said with fake optimism.

Jasper knew he shouldn't take it personally. But if it wasn't Paul in the book then he had bigger problems.

Kirsty had been nice enough after he apologized. He rarely lost his temper but after the professor had ruled out the connection to Paul, he'd been left with nothing. Nothing.

This was worse than when he brought the book to the studio and the lights had exploded. There was literally no reason for anyone else to haunt him.

Kirsty's suggestion that they retrace his steps was his best remaining chance at closure. Even if it confirmed the sinking feeling in his gut.

He wanted to apologize. If only he could. He finished up his food and then leaned back looking around the diner. Victor had worked here when they'd been in college.

Maybe it was time to really talk to Victor instead of hiding from his guilt and grief. Taking out his phone he DMed

Victor and then started scrolling back to five years. He hadn't really posted much after Paul's death. The three of them had a running daily Snapchat streak with each other and it had made him ache to open the app knowing that he wouldn't have a message waiting from Paul.

"I'm going to run to the bathroom," Kirsty said.

He nodded absently. It was like he'd cracked open Pandora's box. Memories were flooding him and it was hard to keep it together.

Kirsty slid back into the booth across from him.

"Just had a thought…but what if I ticked off someone else that night? What if there's something I'm missing?"

She rolled her shoulders and pulled her notebook from her bag. He took that as a good sign.

"Did something you noticed on your socials trigger that?" She pointed to his phone, the app still open.

"Nah. It was more what you said earlier about ruling out logical things. So if it's not Paul it has to be someone else… just so you know I'm not ready to rule him out yet. I mean he liked *Judge Judy* and physics was his thing," Jasper pointed out.

"Fine. But it will still be good to have other possibles. What have you got so far?"

"The night Paul died, I went to that frat party, and it seems I went to Pop's Pizza before. That was typical for us…looks like Paul was with me for pizza," he said, zooming in on the photo. His cousin wasn't as tall as he was and where Jasper had black hair, Paul's was a reddish blond. They shared the same blue eyes. In the photo they were grinning without a care in the world. Arms around each other, leaning over an extra-large pizza that filled the entire table.

He'd forgotten this. That night had started out fun. For years now he'd focused on Paul's death and not his life. He'd meant what he said about not letting go of Paul as the ghost. It seemed more logical to him that the spirit was Paul's. Little patterns that Jasper had picked up, the timing of the songs and the song choices, the way it was always tuned to *Judge Judy* first thing in the morning at the same time as when Paul used to leave for his run.

Jasper wasn't sure what any of that meant but his gut told him it had to be more than coincidence.

Kirsty leaned on her elbows to see the photo better. "You both look so young."

"Yeah," he said. Paul was locked in that moment. Now it felt like Jasper had decades on him even though it had only been five years. There was no denying that those last years had been tough. The toughest he'd ever had.

Losing Paul had been a blow. Then the haunting, slowly making him think he was losing touch with reality, until he was so angry that he couldn't remember any of the good things about Paul.

"I have an idea how I might help Paul move on."

Kirsty gave him a pointed look. "And what if it's not him?"

For now he'd ignore that. "No idea."

"What's your idea?" she asked.

"Retrace the night he died. There might be something that I didn't realize he was hanging around for. If it's not Paul, then I have no other suggestions and I really don't want to think some rando has been in my life."

Sighing. "Yeah I'd be creeped out by that too. Talking worked last night…want to do it again?"

"Fine, let's try that. Talk to the book."

"We're in public. He never acts up when we are out."

"Except that day in your studio," he pointed out.

"Yeah you're right."

"What was special about that day?" she asked him.

Not a clue.

"You were getting flustered. I was secondhand embarrassed for you and then…the lights exploded…like he was determined to make sure you were believed."

That had been it. He'd wanted to melt into the floor and then boom. He was emotionally connected to the book. Made sense as he'd been dragging it around for five years. "So Paul, right?"

"Did anyone else from your frat die?" she asked.

"No. Just Paul," he said. "When we get back to the house I'll talk to him again."

Whatever logic she was following via Sherlock Holmes didn't work. That dude was super old and the book was ancient so it made sense that new logic needed to be applied. Paul was the ghost in the book. He was sure of it.

It was dark and stormy as they left the diner.

Jasper's insistence that the book contained Paul's spirit was proving difficult.

He kept thinking that they could retread old ground, that somehow they could magically free Paul out of will alone. But she knew that it couldn't be. That voice from the séance must have been a warning.

While Jasper drove, she reflected on the open questions that still remained.

Why had the book returned to Jasper every time he got rid of it?

And why would the book fixate on Paul's favorite TV show, *Judge Judy*?

Whoever was trapped in the book would have to be someone who knew the pair of them well enough to mimic Paul's behavior.

"Did you guys have another roommate or a close friend who hung with you all the time?"

"Just Victor. I didn't date anyone seriously. No other roommates," Jasper said. "See, you think it could still be Paul too."

"It's a possibility."

"That doesn't sound believable at all, you know that, right?"

"Neither does having a dead roommate trapped in a textbook," she said succinctly.

"You're right."

She sensed a hint of resigned desperation in his voice.

This was more than she'd signed on for. She was pretty sure that her publisher would back her up if she asked to leave. They had enough for a segment, even if it wasn't as explosive as they'd hoped.

But she wasn't going to do that. She wasn't going to walk away from this, from him. Not yet.

"Are you going to tell Dan and Gia?"

"Yes."

"What if they…what do you think they'll say?"

"That this entire situation has gotten crazier. But Dan will probably back you up. He's loyal, and after that wild footage he's as much a believer as the rest of us," Kirsty said.

"Gia will do whatever you want. She'll love that it could be someone else if it means we get more hijinks."

He wasn't wrong there. If it garnered publicity for her and her books, then Gia would back it. Plus her friend was genuinely invested. "We'll figure it out. I'm not ruling out Paul yet. Even if I think you need to come to terms with the possibility it's not."

"Thanks for pretending."

He pulled into the driveway and turned off the car. "Rationally, I know you're right."

"Then why are you fighting it."

He turned to face her, his arm resting against the back of her seat. This close even in twilight she could see the flecks of silver in his blue eyes. The lines at the edges of his mouth, honed by a man prone to smiling. Despite being haunted, he was a pretty upbeat dude most of the time.

But not now. Now he watched her like he had almost no hope left.

Despite her exterior, she was naturally upbeat to an extent. She didn't run around all sunshine and daisies but she believed that if she put her mind to anything, she could work it out.

"I'm afraid you'll leave if it's not Paul," he said.

Part of her wanted to because this was hard. Being open to Jasper made her vulnerable. His happiness was on the line here, and he was placing his fate in her hands.

"I'm not going to leave until we figure this out," she admitted. "I'm sticking around."

"For the fame and the PR stunt of it all?" he asked.

It wasn't just this new information that had him worried. She couldn't blame him. She'd resisted him from the beginning, using her job as an excuse. They had no hold on each other beyond this ghost hunt.

Nothing else bound them together except for the tenuous strands of emotion knitting between them.

"Yes, and for you."

Jasper's lips thinned for a second and then he leaned forward to kiss her. Something moved inside of her. A sense of safety and comfort. That elusive emotion that she had only started to feel in his arms was back again.

Seventeen

Pizza for dinner seemed a natural place to start in retracing his steps the night Paul died. They entered the pizza place around seven, and it was busy but not too crowded. Gia and Dan joined them so they could go over their notes on the investigation.

Kirsty wore her huge black peacoat, and when she took it off he grew hot. She wore a body-skimming black-and-white striped turtleneck over a miniskirt, black tights and her chunky boots. He'd been eyeing her legs since she'd come downstairs. She looked like a dark goddess. It was all he could do to concentrate on ordering a pitcher of beer and pizza.

Her hair was stick-straight again, she'd gone for her normal heavy eyeliner, bright red lipstick and he suspected she wore mascara because this morning her lashes hadn't been that long. Her goth girl armor was strangely comforting.

"Do you like mushrooms or not?" she asked, giving him an odd look.

"Uh, yeah. I'll eat anything on a pizza except pineapple."

"Steer clear of Dan's Hawaiian then. Gia and I like olives,

mushroom and sausage…want to split a big one with us?" Kirsty asked. They were sitting side by side in a booth and he liked the proximity. He put his arm on the back of the banquette.

"Jasper."

"Yes. I'll share a pizza with you," he said, staring down into her eyes. Now that he'd confessed that he didn't want her to leave, his emotions were flowing like a river that had burst its banks.

"Great. I'll go order. Beer all around?" she asked.

Everyone agreed as they were getting Ubers for the rest of the night. Something he hadn't done in a long time. Drinks with friends. Going out after work didn't really happen that often. Though the isolation was his own doing.

"This place feels so lived-in. Reminds me of my parents' place in Detroit." Gia smirked, her eyes twinkling. "So when Kirsty gets back, we can catch up on everything. Professor Thompson sent over the class syllabus. I emailed it to you," Gia said.

"Thanks." Even if it might end up being useless.

Kirsty slid back, giving them all the amount they owed her. Everyone Venmoed her the money before she pulled out her notebook. He loved watching her write. Her fingers were elegant and confident when she held a pen. She jotted down the date and then drew a line under it.

"What have we got?" she asked everyone.

He skimmed the email Gia sent. Paul's class schedule seemed normal. It didn't ring any bells.

"While you were gone there wasn't anything to film. I edited the clip we got this morning. It might be worth it to try to be in the living room before the TV comes on at six.

Maybe see if you feel anything?" Dan suggested. "I'd love some reaction shots."

"Good suggestion. We can try it tomorrow unless we end up drinking too much tonight," Kirsty said, making a note.

"I thought the plan was to drink too much," Gia said.

"Plans don't always work out," she said. There was a shift in her voice that he struggled to place.

"Indeed." Gia gave Kirsty's shoulder a light squeeze. "I got the class info and shared it with Jasper. I've also been in touch with the local bookstore. They're excited that you're coming in next Tuesday, which has nothing to do with the investigation but I didn't really have much to do today," she admitted.

"Thanks for taking care of that. We do sort of have a new line to look into." Kirsty took a deep breath. "Professor Thompson said this book wasn't being used when Paul was in his class. It's actually from the early 1990s. Any chance you want to see if you can figure out where this specific book came from and who's owned it?"

"Uh, that's not going to be easy," Gia pointed out.

Jasper agreed. "There is a stamp on the front cover. Peterson's Used Books."

"I'll look at it. Think it's from Vermont?"

"I've never heard of it, but I don't frequent bookstores," Jasper admitted. "I'm more a comic books guy."

"I've got lots of contacts for independent bookstores. I'll see what I can find." Gia tapped a note on her phone.

"Jasper, did the course information jog any memories?" Kirsty asked.

"No. I need to dig into it a bit more. I'll start doing that tomorrow," he said.

Kirsty nodded and jotted more details on her notepad, her

face scrunching as she concentrated. He loved it when she looked serious.

"I'm going to speak to another medium tomorrow afternoon. I want her to see if she picks up anything I'm missing with the book," Kirsty told them.

"I thought you were an expert," Dan said.

"I've never done this before. I mostly write fiction books about it," she said sharply.

Dan held his hands up. "Sorry. Find out if I can film her. I think we need the entire story, whatever this is. And it'll make for a good piece of the story."

"I will ask her. She might not offer anything new. I really just want a second opinion," Kirsty said, her voice cagey.

The pitchers of beer and glasses arrived. Gia glanced around the table and lifted her glass. "To Paul, for bringing us all together."

They all clinked their glasses in a toast.

It was an odd night, and Kirsty couldn't help feeling in flux, a sensation that kept dogging her this year. She'd never sat around like this enjoying such easy company. Growing up there hadn't been money for her to eat out with friends, so she and her mom tended to eat at home. It wasn't that she'd never been in a restaurant, but as an adult she'd kept the habit, especially when writing was so solitary.

She liked it. There were lulls in the conversation, but everyone was having a good time. Somewhere along the way the four of them had transitioned from colleagues to friends.

Gia's eyes met hers and she gave one of her signature silly grins. "So, Kirsty, favorite movie of all time? Prepare to defend your choice."

"What's all this about?" Dan asked.

"Perfect. While Kirsty thinks, you can go first instead, Dan," Gia said to him. "I bet it's something creepy."

"No. Is that my vibe?" he asked her.

She shrugged. "You seemed really into the ghost hunting footage and techniques. So I'm guessing you like horror."

"I don't hate it. But my favorite film would have to be one that Roger Deakins did the photography on. He's the best cinematographer of all time."

Kirsty had never really paid attention to that. "What are some of his films?"

"Recently *The Goldfinch*, but my top film he did is *Blade Runner 2049*. The way he shot it is breathtaking and I've watched it at least a dozen times. There's something magical in the way he captures light and shadow."

"Interesting." She'd never thought much about photography before. The way Dan's eyes lit up made him seem more approachable. "What do you think, Jasper?"

"Yeah, I like that movie. I'm not as into how it's shot. I've been vibing with *Star Wars* and I'd have to say and I know it's not popular but for me *The Last Jedi* is my favorite. Though I did really like *Andor*."

"What? *The Last Jedi* killed Luke. I mean really?" Kirsty couldn't contain her shock. She liked some of the things that Rian Johnson had done in the movie especially with Leia but there were better *Star Wars* movies. And the sexual tension between Rey and Kylo Ren aka Ben Solo had been off the charts.

"Yeah but he needed to die like Obi Wan in *A New Hope*."

"Oh no. Do we have two *Star Wars* nerds here?"

Dan raised his hand. "Count me in as well. I agree with Jasper on this. Luke had to die."

"Well, my mom was super pissed about it," Kirsty said. She'd spent a whole week mourning.

"What about you? What's your favorite movie?" Jasper asked her.

Her first response was the 1997 *Cinderella* starring Whitney Houston and Brandy...but that wasn't the kind of movies they'd been talking about. Would it make her sound childish? Aside from *Star Wars* she mostly watched TV shows so she had to cast her memory back to when she'd been a kid.

"Not sure. I don't go to the movies that often."

"Come on, you have to have a go-to movie that you put on when it's a crap day," Gia said.

If they insisted. "*Howl's Moving Castle*," she said. It just slipped out. But that movie with a cursed lonely girl who doesn't fit and finds her own path was her go-to.

"I mean I prefer *Princess Mononoke*," Jasper said. "But yeah that's a good one."

"I was sure you'd say Brandy's *Cinderella*," Gia said with a cheeky grin. "You are always putting it on when we travel."

"I do like it. A lot. But when it's crunch time I do default back to Howl."

"It's Howl then?" Gia asked. "I like him too. My favorite is anything with Jennifer Lawrence. That girl can act."

The conversation moved on to actors and Dan and Gia had strong opinions while they were arguing over which was the best Chris: Pine, Hemsworth, Pratt. Jasper turned to her.

"When this is over, what do you say to a *Star Wars* marathon at my place?" he asked.

He'd asked her quietly, his voice drowned out by Gia's and Dan's playful arguing. *After this.* Right now it felt like they were going to be living here and dealing with ghosts for the rest of their lives. But it would end.

She'd go back to her life, and he'd go back to his. But he was asking her to make plans with him after this was over.

Her heart raced; her lips felt dry. It wasn't like he was asking her for anything other than to watch movies with him, right? The rational part of her brain tried to rein her in.

But the other part of her brain had latched on to Jasper and wanted more. More than she was truly ready to admit even to herself.

"So that's a no? I really thought you'd understand about *Last Jedi*—"

"It's not a no. I do understand. I just wanted to give you a hard time about it because it seemed like it would be fun, and I wanted to see if you'd back down from your opinion."

"I usually don't," he admitted. "I mean, I will if I'm wrong, but it takes a lot to sway me."

"Like with Paul and the book?" He was a stubborn ass sometimes.

"Exactly. So, are you going to come to my place and watch *Star Wars*?" he asked her. His eyes grew large and…was he pouting?

She wanted to. It was scary how much. "Will you be wearing a droid costume?"

"No. But I do have a huge T-shirt collection and I will change them with each movie," he said with a grin.

God, this guy.

"I'll think about it."

"Good enough."

Dan and Gia wanted to go to a new club that opened near campus, but Jasper and Kirsty didn't go with them. Jasper wanted to continue their investigation while he had the chance.

The Uber dropped the two of them off in front of his old frat house. It was one of those October nights that was crys-

212 Ghost of a Chance

tal clear and cold. A huge moon hung in the sky, casting light across the quintessential college street.

The large redbrick building had four Doric columns in the front and the arch over the portico had been shaped to look like a Greek temple. The white marble steps led to the front door which was open. There was a fog machine and a large ghost that flew down whenever motion triggered it.

Kirsty had the collar up on her coat. He was bundled in his own, a big heavy wool number. Winter was right around the corner, and by the time it arrived, he expected they'd be back to their real lives.

"So this is it?"

Nervous wasn't a word he'd ever apply to her but there was definitely something uncertain about her.

"Yeah. Were you in a sorority?"

"Nope. Too expensive. Mom and I were barely getting me to classes," she said.

"Did you want to?"

"Not after watching rush videos on TikTok. I mean the pressure to get into the right one, that would be too much for me. Was it like that for you?"

"Nah. I just applied and got in. Money wasn't an issue because...well, you know my dad died and we got a huge payout. My college was set." He smiled ruefully. Some luck.

"Was that weird?"

"In what way?"

"To know that he...never mind. Sometimes I don't have a filter and just ask things that I shouldn't."

"Sometimes?" he teased. He could guess what she was about to ask. He'd never really thought about the source of the money so it hadn't felt odd at all.

"Ha. You don't seem to mind it," she said.

"I don't. I like knowing where I stand with you. When I'm an ass you tell me, when I'm not you let me know as well," he said, slinging his arm around her shoulder. He'd already checked with the house and knew they were having a party tonight, which he'd gotten the okay to attend. "So is this your first frat party?"

He wasn't entirely sure why it mattered to him, but he wanted to be the first to do things with her. To have those experiences together.

"Uh...no. I've been to a few."

Dropping his arm, he glanced at her. "Was not expecting that. So did you like it?"

"There were a lot of people which made it hard to talk. The music was pretty good. I danced for a while and back then... well I was really focused on studying so wasn't into drinking."

"Probably something I should have done," he said ruefully.

"You're okay, remember?"

God, this woman. She got him. The urge to kiss was right there but he was enjoying learning about college Kirsty too much at the moment.

"I can hear the drumbeat of the music inside, maybe we can have a dance?"

"Perhaps."

But there was a smile in her eyes.

"So who'd you come to the frat with? Study group...were you in one?"

"No. I don't play well with others." She smirked when she said it.

"You play okay with me, Gia and Dan."

"Yeah, but you guys are my gang."

"So who'd you go to the frat with?"

"Just a guy that I was tutoring. Things sort of heated up

and he asked me out. Things happened and he invited me to the winter formal."

Damn. Who was that guy? "Oh so you were getting really into Greek Life."

"Not so much. He dumped me before the dance, said I was too weird. He did it at one of those Friday night parties… I guess like this one. I had finished helping him with a paper he'd been writing. I was asking him about the dance. Some other people were around." She stopped talking. "That was the past and we're here to relive yours."

"Oh, Kirst. That sucks. I'm sorry."

"Me too."

Jasper wanted to know more. "Did your friends have your back?"

"I didn't really have a friend group or anything. I felt humiliated and then mad at myself for letting him make me feel that way."

"Men can be dicks," he admitted.

"Not all of them." Having her by his side was everything. Back then he wouldn't have appreciated a woman like her.

She watched him with those serious brown eyes of hers. Pulling her into his arms, he lowered his head and kissed her. Her arms wrapped around his waist. He kept the kiss gentle, wanting to show her how much she meant to him without saying the words. Though he knew he wasn't a subtle man. He wanted her to feel in every part of her being how much she meant to him.

That the douchebag who'd dumped her had been an idiot.

He lifted his head.

"What was that for?" she asked.

"You looked like you needed a kiss."

"Did I?" she asked.

"Yup."

"That party you were at the night that Paul died…walk me through it."

"So… I forgot, but Paul rode with me in the Uber to the party because Victor asked him to come pick him up before he had to go to work. While we waited for Victor I badgered him to come in for a few minutes," he said. Knowing better than to push her intimately any further right now.

"Where?"

He glanced around. That night it had been lightly raining. "That corner over there. We waited for the Uber and I saw over his shoulder that he was going to the lab after he dropped Victor at work."

As much as he'd loved being part of the frat, and having a group of men who were his brothers, he'd wanted Paul to stay that night. To let loose with him. Their time in college was limited and he didn't want to miss out on the experience with his best friend.

"I was being mean and selfish. He pointed it out before he got in the Uber. His last words to me were 'stop playing at being an adult and start being one.'"

Eighteen

It was funny how words like that could scar someone. Kirsty had felt that way about her first agent. The one who'd said she needed to write to trends until she learned how to write, period. Her agent had been right but those words had been hard to digest.

But this cut deeper for her. No wonder Jasper was having a hard time saying goodbye to Paul. That night had been monumental before Paul's death.

"That's some tough love."

"That was Paul. In a way you remind me of him."

"The tough part?"

"Sure, but more the way you care about Gia. I think…no hedging it, I wanted that for me and Paul but we were never there."

"I'm sorry you didn't get a chance."

"Yeah. That night… I flipped him off, told him to fuck off just to prove how wrong he was. Walked away without a backward glance," Jasper said, rubbing his hand over his eyes.

His grief was like a cloud hanging over him. There was still so much that she didn't know. She hoped Aza could speak to whoever was trapped in the book. If the real medium couldn't, they were all screwed. "Want to skip the party and maybe just walk?"

"Why?"

"You look like you're about to—"

"Don't say cry, or I will," he said.

"It's okay. He was your best friend and cousin and you were close," she said, looping her arm through his. "Even you've admitted you haven't really dealt with your grief."

She started toward the corner he'd pointed to a moment ago.

Tipping his head back and, having done it herself, she suspected he was blinking to keep tears in his eyes.

There was nothing that made you feel more vulnerable than crying in front of someone. There was no disguising how deeply something hurt/moved/touched you were when you cried.

"I wanted to show you that I'm proud to be with you at a frat party," he said. "I wanted to make out with you in one of the hallways so everyone else would be jealous that I'm with the hot, cool author."

Stopping, she stood in awe at him. There was something about being with someone who emoted so clearly, like a big, fluffy dog, that really got to her. She wanted to warn him to keep some of his feelings back. That the world was going to hurt him...that she might someday, even though she liked him and liked being around him.

She was basically a loner. Eventually she was going to be back in her small safe house creating in her fictional world and he was going to be in Chicago. A few states and a world away from her.

Still, she couldn't resist basking in how he described her. "We can make out here."

"Here?"

"Definitely. On this corner," she said, hoping to replace a bad grief-filled memory with a better one.

"It's not raining though," he said a slight grin teasing his lips.

"Is that your only requirement to make out with me?"

"I thought it might be yours," he said as tugged her off balance and into his arms. His hands rested lightly on her waist, his head tilted to the side, blocking out some of the light from the streetlamp.

The moon was still behind him, big and bright. Somehow making this night seem magical in a way that normally she didn't take the time to observe. She was different with Jasper. Lighter. More…hopeful.

Looping her arms around his neck, she went up on tiptoe, canting her body into his until she felt the wool of both of their coats brushing against each other. The warmth of his breath brushed over her mouth. She parted her lips, their eyes met, and she knew that this kiss, this night was changing something fundamental inside of her.

She wasn't giving herself permission to change, it was already happening.

His lips were firm and soft. His kiss not as gentle as it had been before, when he'd been trying to soothe her past hurt.

He wasn't as kind to himself as he'd been to her. She hadn't paid attention to that fact until now. He was hard on himself. Saw his life as aimless drifting instead of seeing his own strength, his resilience. The fact that he'd had a lot of blows in his life and still figured out a way to make it something he could be proud of.

When he lifted his head, she noticed that his breathing was heavier. So was hers. Lightly she ran her finger down the edge of his cheekbone. There was something sad and angsty about him that made her heart almost break.

"We have two choices," she said.

"They are?"

"Continuing making out here and see how far we can take things without being seen," she started.

"Or?"

"Something outrageous that will make you smile again," she said.

"Both of those will make me smile," he admitted, pulling her back into his arms. His mouth came down on hers again, hard and heavy. His hands were already undoing the buttons of her coat until he lifted her off her feet.

She forgot about where they were and about cheering him up. The kiss took her out of her own mind and into this place where only pleasure existed. Needing more of him, addicted to his taste and the feel of his hands as they roved over her body.

She was trying to get her hands under his coat when the streetlamp over their head exploded.

She screamed and jumped away from him.

"Fucking hell, Paul. Really?"

Her heart was racing. Jasper reached for her bag, opening it and taking out the physics textbook. He tossed it on the ground behind them and then took her hand, walking away from it, abandoned on the sidewalk.

Jasper was done with everything. Talking about Paul today had really brought his friend back. But this was too much. He was tired of literally chasing after a ghost, of digging up his past, only for it to bite him in the ass.

"Do you think we should just leave the book there?" she asked.

"I told you, it always comes back, and I don't know about you but I could use a break from exploding lights and Judge Judy's gavel," he said. "Tonight it's just you and me, as if we met for the first time and didn't know any of this shit about each other."

The look she gave him told him she thought he was losing it. Maybe he was. There was only so much a man could take.

"Just go with it. A fun night with you and me. Maybe then your answer to seeing me after will be yes," he said.

Lacing her fingers through his. "It wasn't a no. It's just... I have a book due and—"

He put his fingers over her lips. "Life isn't allowed to intrude tonight. Just you and me. Deal?"

It took her longer than he wanted it to before she nodded. "Okay. What are we doing?"

"Well, you're going to have a college experience that you missed with me," he said. "To start."

"How much do you have planned?"

"Not a thing. I'm making this up as I go," he said. He needed this and he suspected she did too. Their lives this last week had been completely driven by their careers and these damned ghosts. "We're hitting the party tonight. You said you really didn't enjoy it last time, and I want you to."

"Uh, that's not necessary," she said but didn't resist when he drew her back toward the house.

Music was blasting from inside the house, the intense bass pulsing throughout the building, and of course since the house was off the campus drinking was legal for anyone twenty-one and up. UVM was pretty strict about drinking on campus and in student housing.

The house was a large brick one that looked like it had been here since the Revolutionary war, but it was really built in the seventies. There was a large porch that was shadowed now that the streetlamp was out. The moon didn't reach it through the trees surrounding the facade.

He pulled her toward a corner tucked away from the crowd with a wooden bench that was secluded from the rest of the party. He sat down on it and pulled her onto his lap. It had been too long since he'd held her.

It had only been last night when she'd been in his arms, but that was way too long.

She wrapped one arm around his shoulder, sitting crossways on his lap. Her head rested on his shoulder. He lowered his to kiss her. Her mouth was perfect for long leisurely kisses, when it wasn't delivering the perfect put-down or smile to take the sting off her acerbic tongue.

Tracing the shell of his ear with her finger, she sent tingles down his neck and straight to his dick. She shifted, gently rubbing herself against him as she turned to kiss him more deeply.

That slick turtleneck that hugged her body seemed to have no end, frustratingly he couldn't find the way to get to her skin.

Her soft laughter made him look up.

"You growled."

"Your shirt is a pain."

"Is it?" she asked, opening his coat and then pushing her very cold hands against his stomach.

"Yikes, woman."

"Cold hands, warm heart."

Seeing her cheeky grin was totally worth her freezing touch. He shifted her hands up to his chest and then hugged her close until his thoughs touched hers.

Her tights were smooth and soft against his fingertips, the calluses from his guitar playing rubbed against them. She shifted, her legs parting as her mouth trailed kisses and love bites over his neck.

Each breath was all Kirsty, the scent of cinnamon and fall, then the slight musk of arousal as he turned her on. Slowly he moved down the outside of her thigh to her knee.

"Stop dicking around."

"I'm teasing you," he responded. He continued grazing her inner thigh, brushing his fingers against her pussy as he slid his hand higher until he found the top of her tights and slipped his hand inside them.

Teasing her. He sure was. They were in public at a frat house. The words filtered into her head. But at this moment she didn't care. His idea had seemed silly to her and if there was one thing she wasn't it was silly. But sitting in the dark, the sounds of the party muted through the walls and the full moon overhead. There was something freeing in pretending they were just two lovers.

His kisses were addicting and he was driving her to the edge of some kind of sexual need that she'd never experienced before.

She tried to squirm around to reach his dick, figuring if he was in her hand, he might speed things up. But he kept her locked to him, his palm possessive on her stomach.

He rubbed his finger lightly on the top of her sex which was sending shivers down to her clit. She was wet, swollen. As much as she enjoyed his teasing she craved more.

Trying to move her hips was also a losing proposition, so she arched her back and turned her head until she could continue kissing the side of his neck. He groaned, bucking against her. His fingers dug into her skin as she drew his head down toward hers.

His tongue drove into her mouth with the same rhythm she wanted on her center. So she reached between her own legs, putting her hand over his and guiding his finger to her clit.

He smiled against her mouth, his finger found her and he tapped lightly against her. She arched against him and moaned into his mouth. He kept touching her until she knew she was going to come. Arching against him with more urgency, sucking his tongue deep into her mouth, her orgasm rolled through her.

She turned her face into his neck as she rode it out. Then turned on his lap straddling him and reaching for the zipper of his jeans.

He brushed her hands aside and freed himself. She shifted to go down on him and he leaned back, his hands in her hair as she circled her tongue around the tip of his erection. He moaned as she took him deeper into her mouth. Holding the back of her head as he thrust up into her mouth.

She sucked him deeper into her mouth, moving on his cock until he pulled her off of him. "I want to be inside of you when I come."

She kept stroking his dick. She had a condom somewhere. Thankfully he pulled one from his back pocket. He slipped it on and she perched top of him.

"Brace yourself on the bench," he said.

She did, spreading her legs so he could enter. She felt the tip of him at the entrance to her pussy, and then he pushed into her. Fuck. She moaned at how good he felt inside of her. Didn't even care if someone could hear. He leaned over her, his voice guttural in her ear.

"God, I love fucking you."

She shivered as he guided her into each of his thrusts.

This was addicting. She wasn't sure what she'd do when they left Burlington.

Blocking that, she focused on savoring the feel of him driving into her, praising how she made him feel, whispering into her ear that he wanted to keep doing this all night.

Then she felt the tension in her getting tighter. She was on the edge of another orgasm. She turned her head and he leaned over to nip at her lips as he drove even harder than before.

She started to shiver and then her orgasm washed over her. Calling out his name, she felt her pussy tightening on his cock as he held himself still for a moment before thrusting until he groaned her name against her shoulder. She felt his cock throb inside of her as he emptied himself.

She couldn't catch her breath. It was an awkward position to be in, riding cowgirl on a cold wooden bench, but she would stay this way for as long as he held her.

Nineteen

Kirsty finally had an idea for her story all thanks to Jasper. He was unlocking parts that she'd never focused on before. Waking in the middle of the night, she grabbed her laptop and started writing. Jasper was sleeping on his side next to her in the attic room again.

He looked so calm and sweet in sleep. Curled on his side, his hand extended to where she'd been.

Now she was distracted from writing. She was meant to talk to Aza later today and frankly she was hoping to get some clarity on who the hell was trapped in the book. It felt like cheating to go to another medium when she was supposed to be one. But her abilities were sketchy at best. If they even existed.

After their bench rendezvous, Jasper wanted to leave the textbook at the frat house, but Kirsty insisted they take it back with them. She wanted to look through it in more detail. It was large and weighty, filled with concepts that still eluded her.

Though that didn't matter. Whoever was trapped in the book wasn't trying to teach them physics.

Closing her eyes, she let her head fall back and put her hand on the cover of the book.

All of the times when she'd had any contact with the spirit in the book it had been accidental. What would happen if she tried contacting it herself? If she focused her mind? It couldn't be any worse than their other methods.

"Spirit, I invited you to join me. I mean you no harm and seek only answers," she said.

Opening one eye a crack, she glanced around but nothing was happening.

Shaking her head hard. No candles. She needed at least the white one to invite the ghost in.

Being as quiet as she could she took the candle and the book out as far away from the bed as she could.

Sitting down again she lit the white candle. Closed her eyes and reached out with her mind.

"I'm not going to harm you. I want to help you move on."

The deep voice didn't answer her. She probably needed all the candles and a better incantation. She walked to the dormer window overlooking the street. That big moon illuminated the floor around her. Maybe she should try again over here.

Putting the book on the floor, she took a moment to dig the other partially burned candles out of her bag, along with a lighter, and placed them around the book.

"What are you doing?"

She jumped at the deep rasp of Jasper's voice.

"Jesus! You scared me. Trying one last time to see if these medium powers can get us any answers," she said.

"Want me to help?" Climbing out of the bed, he came and sank down next to her on the carpeted floor.

He wore only a pair of gray boxer briefs and his hair stuck straight up on one side like a cartoon character. He rubbed his hand over his chest as he shifted one of the candles into a better position.

He crossed his legs and held his hand out to her. "I'm ready this time."

Me too. Whatever happened she was going to keep her focus. "I'm going to find out who this ghost really is."

"Fine. I want to know as well," he added. "I read in one of your books that having the window open might help. Also that you should have something they can extinguish or a pendulum to direct answers to."

"You get the window… I can't reach that one very well," she said. "I have a letter map I made for my last book."

Her book's heroine, Eva, needed to communicate to a spirit that wasn't able to talk. Her editor had suggested it would be a nice twist since the other ghosts that Eva had encountered had been verbal. The solution was a letter map.

In this case, the map was really two pieces of copy paper she'd taped together and then used some stickers and markers to decorate it. The entire alphabet was spelled out in three arching rows. There was a yes on the left side and a no on the right side for simple questions.

She even had the jade crystal necklace that she'd used as inspiration for a pendulum for the book. Breathing in the combined scents of the candles and the faint smell of rain on the breeze from the newly opened window, she closed her eyes.

"Ready to begin?" Jasper settled next to her.

She wished she was more prepared.

Tonight she didn't want to force anything.

Jasper squeezed her hand. "You sure you want to do this?"

"Yes. I have to," she said. Lacing their fingers together, they started chanting to invite friendly spirits to come and help

228 Ghost of a Chance

them. The room felt calm around them as a gentle breeze filtered through the window.

After about ten minutes, a sense of relaxation came over her and she let go of Jasper's hand, lifting the pendulum over the letter map.

"Spirit in the book: Are you named Paul?"

She opened her eyes, but the jade crystal just hung there, completely still.

God was she wasting her time?

Suddenly, the crystal began to swing.

NO.

Wait. What? "Are you Paul, Jasper's cousin?"

YOU'RE NOT ASKING THE RIGHT QUESTIONS.

That voice in her head was back again, strong and deep, but not scary this time. Probably because she was ready for it.

"Are you here for Jasper?"

YES.

"Does he know why?"

A strong gust of wind blew through the window and the candle flames pitched before going completely out. The pendulum stopped swinging, and her head was silent.

Jasper looked over at her.

"Anything?"

"I'm not sure. Uh, the ghost is definitely here for you. But when I asked if you knew why, all of that happened."

"What the hell does that mean?"

Jasper had felt Kirsty's energy change before that gust of wind. He was in awe of her talents. Somehow a woman who began as a total stranger had spoken to his ghost, however briefly.

"Did they say who they are?"

Kirsty didn't answer him, playing with the leather cord and its crystal, running it through her fingers.

"Not really. I asked if they were Paul and they said I'm not asking the right questions. Which they did the last time, too."

"So then you asked about me and the wind blew all the candles out..." Restating the obvious somehow made him feel less shaken.

There was no denying that he was disturbed. First they learned that the book wasn't Paul's textbook for class, then the light shattered in front of them at the frat house, and now this.

"What could a spirit want from me?"

Like she had a clue. She was as much in the dark as he was.

"What does it sound like?" he pressed.

She stood up, wrapping her arms around her body. "I don't know. It sounds loud and firm and sort of scary. I'm not sure what it wants."

Draping his arm around her shoulder, he tried to comfort her but she held herself stiffly, resisting his proximity.

"Do you think it's in your head?" It was the question he was afraid to ask. What if this was all just a collective delusion?

"What do you mean?"

"I figured since it was speaking and you were the only one who could hear it..."

"I honestly don't know. I have no training and until you and the textbook, most of this ghost business was just for fun to research my books." She frowned, her forehead creased in thought. "That voice could be talking to me, but it's definitely not my own thoughts. I have never heard that voice in my head before."

"Okay, well, you did hear Paul's voice on the video. So I believe you, that it's not his." He couldn't tell if he was relieved or heartbroken. "Do you feel like we got anywhere?"

230   Ghost of a Chance

Her skin was paler than usual, her body language subdued. She probably needed space, but he couldn't resist trying a little harder. "Tomorrow we'll talk to Victor, and you're going to the other medium. We have to be close."

"Yeah."

"Kirst, you will figure this out. The ghost was probably just startled. I think you were on the right track. Want to try again?"

"No," she said sounding a little put out. "I just want some fucking answers."

He did too but life didn't work that way. Sometimes you just had to settle for moving on. Ironic coming from him— he'd been stuck in the past for years, assuming that this haunting was based in his own mistakes and guilt.

"I do too. I really don't know a lot of dead people," he said, trying to lighten things.

"Great, then it should be a short list," she said. Then she wrinkled her brow. "Though maybe asking about you *is* frustrating the ghost. Both times they've run away, once when I brought you up. What if they're involuntarily stuck with you?"

"Kind of like the afterlife version of what's been going on with me?" It was a thought. One that would completely suck if it were true. But Gia was tracking down the last owner of the book, so perhaps that would answer things before long.

"Yeah, something like that."

He opened his mouth and she held her hand up. "Don't ask. I have no idea if that's possible or not. It's a theory."

"What if the book has always been haunted? Then when Paul died I got it when his stuff was boxed up?"

"That's a good idea. We need to ask Victor about it. You said you thought Paul liked *Judge Judy* but what if it was the book the entire time?" She hurried to her side of the bed and started jotting things down in her notebook.

He followed her around, sitting down next to her on the bed. That vague feeling of being stuck that had dogged him since he'd graduated was coalescing into a future the more time he spent with Kirsty.

He wanted her by his side.

And she wouldn't even commit to watching *Star Wars* with him after this, let alone something more. But these feelings that she'd brought to life in him weren't going to disappear. He wasn't about to run from them.

"Any other ideas?" she asked.

Tossing her hair, she chewed the end of her pen as he contemplated her question. All he could think was about pulling her under him and making love to her.

There was no future or past. Nothing but the two of them together in the present.

"Only one."

"What?"

He took the notebook and pen from her, placing them on the nightstand before he pushed her gently back on the bed and came down on top of her, careful to keep his weight from crushing her.

She wrapped her legs around him, the tail of her nightshirt falling to the tops of her thighs, and he felt the warmth of her center against his growing erection. The smile on her face was soft, gentle and so open that he couldn't bear it. When she looked at him like that, the love he'd been hiding from her struggled to stay hidden.

Judge Judy woke the house at 6:00 a.m. with a loud, "If it doesn't make sense, it's not true." Jasper went down to turn it off and to take Chewie out. Kirsty pulled on her headphones as she got out her laptop. Today, she was writing. Last night had been frustrating. At least Eva always found the answers when she needed them.

In fact, Kirsty had been way too easy on Eva, looking back on the books. She'd used her abilities as a tool. This time Eva wasn't going to be able to. That would push the character in a new direction. She turned on her playlist, fingers moving over the keyboard as the words just flowed out.

When she finished the chapter she was working on she felt better. Two hours had passed. Jasper had brought her a strong black coffee partway through writing and left it on the nightstand. It felt good to do the thing she was good at rather than trying to play a part.

She showered and got dressed ready for the day. She was meeting with Aza while Jasper and Dan went to get the remaining B-roll they'd been waiting to shoot. Gia had a lead on Peterson's Used Books, so she was on her way there to investigate.

They all had tasks to do. As she prepared to leave the house, she found herself lingering in her room. She was going to miss this little group they'd formed once this was all said and done.

Though she had more questions today than she had yesterday, the answers were getting close. Like any investigation she could feel it slowly coming to a conclusion. Maybe Jasper felt it too.

He'd given her a lot of space this morning and was quieter than usual. He hardly even looked at her when she came downstairs though she struggled to keep her eyes off him. Somehow, he was getting cuter each time she saw him. The way he concentrated on editing his part of the video footage this morning was impressive.

He might not have wanted to work in television but she could tell he was very knowledgeable and good at his job. He'd found something that suited him, whether he wanted to admit it or not.

As Jasper finished his edits with Dan, he glanced up and she winked at him, just to throw him off. He flushed, sheepishly coming over to her.

"Did you have a good morning?" he asked.

"Yeah. Lots of words down and I finished my chapter," she said.

"Good. You were practically in a trance," he said.

"I get that way." Nothing felt as good as hitting her stride in a new story.

"Were you thinking about your book just now?"

She rolled her eyes. "I'm heading out to see the medium."

"Want me to come? Maybe she can tell me how I'm involved," he said.

"Yeah. But Dan can't come, no cameras at all. She doesn't want to be filmed," Kirsty said.

"Figures. Be careful she's not scamming you," Dan said.

"Why would she be?"

"The lack of filming makes me think she's hiding something. You didn't have any objections?"

She had similar concerns, but at the same time she'd had no choice. "Thanks, Dan."

"No problem," he said. "I'll keep editing and get some footage around campus and town for the voice-over you suggested."

"What voice-over?"

"I figured it would make a nice story if we started with a voice-over explaining my history with Paul and the book even if it turns out not to be Paul trapped in it. The haunting definitely started here," Jasper said, explaining as they both left the house.

Kirsty grabbed her keys while Jasper got into the passenger side of her car, putting the seat back. His long legs weren't suited for this.

The trip to Aza's took all of ten minutes. The house they pulled up to looked ordinary, like every other one on the street. There was a small sign out front with a palm stamped with the all-seeing eye and other symbols.

"Guess this is the place," Jasper said. He'd been eerily quiet on the drive again.

Worrying about a man wasn't something she'd allow. Not again. It was just that now she was forming an attachment to him. And it felt almost like he was pulling back.

This was precisely why she had stuck to one-night stands.

He followed her up the walkway to the front door.

The door opened and a woman appeared, about Kirsty's height with straight blond hair wearing a purple silk slip skirt and a mohair sweater. She smiled easily at them, the scent of patchouli wafting out.

"You must be K.L. Henson."

"I am. This is Jasper Cotton. We both have some questions about this textbook," she said.

Hopefully Aza could give them a lead. Once this was wrapped up she would know for sure if Jasper's presence in her life was just a Burlington fling, or something more.

Twenty

The psychic really didn't help at all. She claimed that she sensed something in the book but couldn't talk to it, and when Kirsty tried a repeat of yesterday, only the candles blew out again.

Disappointment hung around her like a heavy cloak as they walked back to her car. He wanted to cheer her up but had no idea what to do. "She's not you. You've had a connection to the book since I brought it to the studio. I think…that the ghost is more comfortable with you."

"Well, I don't. We are no closer to figuring any of this out. I think we should just say it was a bust and move on."

"A bust? The book is still here and still haunted. I can't just move on from it," Jasper said. After years of being haunted by this poltergeist, he was so close to freedom. He wasn't going to back down now.

She put her head on the steering wheel. Her hands tightened, knuckles white against the leather, and she muttered under her breath. He reached over and patted her shoulder. "I know you can figure this out."

236 Ghost of a Chance

"Thanks," she said sitting up.

His phone pinged in his pocket. "Victor can meet us at the diner in thirty minutes."

She put the car in gear without saying a word. He noticed she got quiet when she was turning things over in her mind. Which was fine with him. He had his own shit to contend with.

He wasn't sure he was ready to see Victor again. Jasper had been a crap friend after Paul had died.

But truly, it had hurt too much to be around Victor. Around him, Jasper missed Paul more keenly. Felt his absence the most around Victor. So he'd walked away. Finishing his classes and then immediately taking the job with Bri's show, moving to Chicago without a goodbye.

They entered the diner and Kirsty headed for the booth they'd sat in the night before. He followed her, sliding in across from her so he could see the door.

"I'm sorry I just can't figure this out," she said. "I feel like I've tried everything I can."

"There might be something simple that's been overlooked," he said. "It's not just down to you to figure out. Gia is tracking down the book. Victor will probably have some insight that I've missed."

"I hope so," she said. It was clear she was used to solving puzzles and this lack of progress was frustrating her.

The door opened again and Victor walked in. He was tall and slim; his hair was curly, springing around his head in an effortlessly cool style. Victor's left hand was covered in rings. He wore a plaid coat and a scarf around his neck.

Paul's old scarf.

Jasper stood up, hugging Victor as soon as he was within

reach. Victor was stiff for a minute and then hugged him back. "What's this about?"

"Paul," he said.

"Finally got over yourself and decided to talk about him?" Victor said, glancing toward Kirsty and arching one eyebrow.

Guess he deserved that. "Kirsty, this is Victor, Victor—Kirsty," he said, gesturing between the two of them. Victor sat down next to Kirsty and told Jasper he'd have a cappuccino.

He nodded and left the two of them to go and place the order. Their heads were already bent together as they were talking. The conversation flowed smoothly between the two of them from what he could tell. Jealousy shot through him, remembering his awkward attempts at reengaging Kirsty before Victor had arrived.

But Victor was like that. He always put everyone at ease or in their place. There was something so deep and honest about him. You didn't mind when he pointed out you were being an ass because he did it in a gentle way.

Looking back on the years he'd spent ignoring Victor, Jasper regretted it. He also didn't really feel great about getting back in touch just to ask him about Paul. He should have been a better friend.

The server at the counter said she'd bring their drinks and be over to take their food order shortly. When he got back to the table Kirsty glanced up at him. "Victor mentioned that Paul was working on a special project with you."

He sat down harder than he meant to. "Yeah. We were trying to figure out some old notes my mom had found in a box in the attic. But once Paul died I stopped. He was the driving force behind it. It doesn't matter."

"What was the project?"

"My dad had some notes for that science fiction short story

238 Ghost of a Chance

he'd been working on. The story revolved around offering people the chance to buy transference for themselves after their death."

Victor looked back and forth between them. "What's this about anyway?"

"Remember when I sent you the textbook?"

"Yeah. Not exactly what I was expecting from you after all those months of silence," he said.

A small part of him was relieved that Victor had clearly mailed it back. Somehow the ghost's powers didn't extend to fooling the postal service.

Before this went any further, he had to apologize. He put his hand on Victor's, gently touching him for a moment. "I'm sorry. I was too in my own feelings to be a decent friend to you. The easiest thing for me was to just stop talking to any-one who knew Paul."

"Such a douche." Victor frowned. At least he was honest. "How'd your mom take that?"

"She hated it and came to stay at my new apartment. Just moved in until I talked to her," he said. "You know how she is."

"I do. She visits me a couple of times a year. We talk about the hot mess that you are," Victor said.

"That should keep you both busy," Jasper said, something inside of him relaxing. Victor was hurt but still willing to be friends with him. And apparently was friends with his mom—something to handle another day.

"It does. So, what's up with the book that makes it such a big deal?"

"We think it's haunted and may have been connected to Paul before he died," Kirsty said.

Victor lifted both eyebrows. "This conversation might require something stronger than a cappuccino."

Kirsty wholeheartedly agreed that something stronger might be needed. Yet as painful as it was, it seemed like it was necessary.

Jasper was different around Victor. There was clearly a bond of friendship between the two men. So much more of him made sense now. His devotion to Chewie, the way he was so laid-back most of the time. This was probably closer to who he'd been before Paul's death.

Yet it was concerning that he continued to keep things from her. He'd avoided the topic of the science fiction project he'd been working on with Paul. She was a writer, why hadn't he mentioned that before?

"Do you have the book?" Victor asked after their drinks arrived.

Kirsty opened up her bag and took the book out, setting it on the table between them. "It's this one?"

"Yes." Jasper gave Victor a hopeful look. "I mailed it because I figured that Paul wanted to get back to you."

"Thanks, sweetie. But he'd never trap himself in that book. I mean it's big and ugly, two things that you know he hated."

"You're right. But could it be tied to him?"

"Well I can't be quite one hundred but maybe," Victor said. "Let me see if I can pick up his vibes."

Victor closed his eyes, sort of like when she had meditated to talk to the ghost. But he didn't have candles or chant out loud. He just kept his hand there, his head tipping to the side as the minutes ticked by.

"I'm not sensing Paul with this book."

Jasper shook his head. "How do you explain things like *Judge Judy* always coming on. Lately it's been at six a.m."

"Why would that have anything to do with Paul? He hated *Judge Judy*."

"Uh, no, he didn't. He had it playing all the time at our apartment," Jasper pointed out. But his voice wavered. It was clear that what they'd suspected was true. "I constantly told him to turn it off."

"Yeah, he mentioned that. But he wasn't watching it. He hated that show. Said people needed to be decent, you know."

If Paul hadn't been turning on the TV when he and Jasper were roommates…then it proved the haunted book had been with them before Paul's death. Or maybe the *Judge Judy* thing was just a red herring.

"It would come on in the living room when Paul was working in there."

"I don't know about that," Victor said, taking another sip of his cappuccino. "But he definitely didn't like the show.

"What else does the book do?" Victor asked.

"It always comes back to me. I've thrown the book out more than once and it shows up back at my place."

Victor put his hand on the book again. "I'm definitely getting something from the book but it doesn't feel malevolent."

Kirsty believed that Victor had a gift that she would love to explore sometime. He was getting stuff from the book that she hadn't. She hesitated for a moment. Thinking of Jasper who needed some closure with Paul. "Have you had any contact with Paul after his death?"

"Nothing like Jaz has been experiencing with his creepy ass textbook. But sometimes I feel this warm breeze on the back of my neck, I guess. Usually it's when I'm having a bad day or feeling down. He used to kiss me there so…yeah, I think it's him."

Kirsty squeezed Victor's hand. "I bet it is."

He finished his coffee while Jasper observed him, perplexed. "Sorry I couldn't be of more help. I have to head to work now."

"I'll walk you out," Jasper said.

Kirsty jotted down a few more notes. Looking at her notebook right now reminded her of all of the failed story ideas she had on other pages. If she was trying to write this as a story, she'd throw it out and start over.

It was clear to her why Jasper had assumed it was Paul. He was roommates with Jasper, so the *Judge Judy* show and the physics connection coming from the book itself would have been present in the apartment with both of them. Jasper just had no idea of knowing it was from a haunted book, that Paul was probably dealing with the same thing he was now.

Accepting the truth was hard. But why was he still hiding stuff from her?

He needed to come clean.

He walked back in looking a bit sheepish. But she wasn't in the mood to let him off easily. He owed her some answers and no more half measures. Not this time.

Kirsty waited by her car after he finished talking to Victor. She had questions. And she deserved answers.

He wasn't sure why he hadn't just come clean about the project before except that…he hadn't. There were some things that were harder to talk about. His dad was always hard. And Paul's death had cast a long shadow over the sci-fi short story.

Even in his head it was an obvious excuse.

She didn't say a word as he entered the car, which was somehow worse than if she outright berated him.

She drove back to the house. Gia's and Dan's cars were gone. "After you let Chewie out we need to talk."

"Yeah, we do."

Fine. It was totally justified that she was upset with him. But he hated that he'd upset her again. He kept saying he wanted to make her happy and make her smile, but he had no clue how to do that.

He had a lifetime of regrets and longing, stuff that he never wanted to surface. How the hell was he going to tell her that?

Chewie was anxious for a walk and a piss, so he took the dog out around the block, hoping that maybe he'd figure out how to tell her about the tangled emotions that were tied to the secret he'd kept from her.

Would she even care?

That was a cop-out. His way of still trying to justify not telling her. He'd hurt her by not telling her.

It seemed he was pretty much an expert at putting himself first and shutting out people he loved. Kirsty might not be comfortable letting people into her life either, but she finished what she started. And she knew when to open up even if it hurt.

Was there something he could say that would change her mind? Show her that he hadn't been playing a game with her?

"What do you think, Chewie?"

The dog just barked at him. Not helpful at all.

When they returned, the smell of coffee was strong and led him to the kitchen. Kirsty had made herself a cup and left him an empty mug.

He made one for himself, adding extra sugar and milk because it comforted him and then he found her in the dining room with her laptop. Her fingers were moving quickly across the keyboard. She didn't glance up when he entered. She held up a single finger.

He took a seat across from her, sipping the coffee that was too sweet and left an aftertaste in his mouth. He wanted to go back to bed and start the day over.

Meeting with Victor had made him realize how stupid he'd been in his grief. He allowed himself those first few months when he'd needed to be alone, but these last few years he'd been running in place. Using the busyness of work as an excuse to not reach out to the people who mattered.

As he sat across the table from Kirsty he vowed he wouldn't do it again. He'd confess it all. Show her the broken boy that still existed inside of him. That one who held on to his fears and his secrets because too much of his life had been known by everyone around him.

She finished typing, closing her laptop with a resounding snap.

Leaning back in the chair, crossing her arms under her breasts she pierced him with that inscrutable look from her heavily lined eyes.

"I know you're cross with me but it's sort of sexy," he said. Immediately regretting it when she tightened her jaw.

"Sorry," he said, sighing.

"For?"

Everything.

"For trying to distract you with that comment," he admitted.

"Okay. You were writing a short story? Tell me about that."

Stretching his legs out under the table he took a deep breath. "I wasn't per se. It's not as simple as it sounds."

"Then break it down for me. You are really good at explaining things when you put your mind to it."

"Fuck. I'm sorry I never told you. It's just that it wasn't only about Paul."

"Who else could it be about? We should definitely talk to anyone involved in this. Does it have to do with quantum theory?"

"It was Dad's short story. He was working on the theory for a science fiction book idea he had. Paul and I were trying to flesh out the idea before my twenty-first birthday so we could give it to my mom as a gift. To thank her for supporting us," he said.

Twenty-One

His dad again. She understood why he hadn't gone all into it at first. But as they had grown closer, he should have mentioned it. Victor knew it was a big deal to Paul at the time of his death. Hearing now that they had been trying to finish it for Jasper's mom just reinforced that.

She had to separate her lover from the man she was working with. There was no time for hurt feelings. This could be a solid lead to unraveling whose spirit was trapped in the book.

"Tell me more about what exactly you were doing?" Pulling her notebook closer to her, she picked up her pen ready to jot it down. She thought better with pen and paper than she did on the keyboard.

She'd been ticked from the moment Victor had told her about Jasper and Paul. Mainly because he'd lied to her once more but also because she'd trusted him.

Letting him sleep in her freaking bed because he'd made her feel safe enough to invite him. Now she realized that she'd been played. Who knew what he really felt for her, if anything.

She'd tried to get over her own walls. He had his own.

He hadn't bothered to hide them. But because of that sweet, sexy way of his she'd just sort of taken to him like she did Chewie. She'd simplified him. He was complicated but he seemed to emote in big chunks so she'd thought…that he'd finally let it all out.

She had more baggage…well, that wasn't fair. They hadn't lived the same life and he was lugging stuff around too.

"It was sort of what we discussed the other day. Dad's theory was in a fictional world, could it work there, but he hadn't had time to really do much research before he died."

Jasper's voice was low, despondent almost. It took all of her hurt to keep her from reaching out and taking his hand. He needed her but she needed to get this sorted before she figured out what was going on with the two of them.

"As you know physics isn't really my thing. But it was Paul's. I asked him to help come up with a fictional way this could work so I could finish the story. He got into it and started looking over the notes my mom had sent," he said. "I don't always get it."

"That's not the only time you don't comprehend," she said, unable to keep herself on the task of just taking notes.

"You're right."

"Don't agree with me, I'm still mad at you."

"Fine, but I'm sorry I didn't mention this before. When it comes to my dad…it's hard because I want to just pretend that it's cool that I've never known him, but I'm not. Mom will talk about him all the time but it's not what I want to do. Not sure I'm explaining it right."

Of course he was. Who could resist the longing and sadness in his voice? Not her. She hadn't been kidding about still being mad. She was petty enough to want to hold on to it longer.

"You're explaining it fine. I get it. Truly I do but this is important and it gives us another link to Paul, which is helpful."

He rubbed the back of his neck like he did when he got tense. She hated that she was softening. Had been since the moment he'd mentioned his dad. If there was one thing she understood better than most it was how a missing person could take up more of your life than the people who were in it every day.

For her there were questions that she'd never asked her mom. Hadn't wanted to hurt her mom by even bringing it up. Mistakenly she'd thought that maybe it was easier for Jasper because his dad had died.

Dillon Henson had left her because he didn't want to be a father, Jasper Cotton senior hadn't had a choice. In her mind it had seemed clearer...simpler. But when emotions were involved nothing was that simple.

"I'm not..." She wanted to say she wasn't mad but she was. "I get why you didn't want to talk about him. We have had a lot of talks about ourselves and you never brought this up."

That was it. The real reason for her anger. She got that she had walls. But she had let him in. She thought he'd recognize that when she'd invited him to sleep in her bed. Why hadn't he?

"I'm sorry. You are right to be mad. What does it say about me that I didn't even feel bad about keeping it to myself until Victor told you... It should have been me."

"It says you're human." She did that too. She hadn't mentioned that her psychic talent wasn't really a thing and Aza hadn't really cleared it up. Kirsty felt like she was back to square one with that.

"Thanks. I had wondered about that."

She gave him the smile she knew he wanted but inside everything was tight. Her heart was beating steadily but there was a sense of panic in her stomach. Like she'd let him in and she shouldn't have.

One-night stands had been her gold standard for relationships until him. Something that had felt like growth until now. The hurt lashing her heart made her doubt it.

She hated that. Hated it enough to cut herself out of his life. Go back to being people who'd slept together and had a puzzle to finish solving. That was it.

Except her fingers still longed to touch him. Her eyes lingered on his mouth and her heart ached at the thought of not sharing a bed with him again.

The way she watched him now…he was pretty sure she was going to be majorly pumping the brakes. He didn't blame her. After all, he'd lied about something big but another part was almost certain she'd been waiting for him to screw up.

Waiting for a chance to push him away.

There was nothing cowardly about her, but when it came to personal relationships she was wary. If he hadn't been so tied up in himself he would have realized that she wouldn't be able to get around this one.

"I haven't touched the story since Paul died…"

"That's not what's bothering me. I invited you to sleep with me. I've always slept alone…you had to know I thought we were on the same page," she said.

"Same page. Are we business partners or in a relationship."

Her mouth got even tighter, and glancing down at her notepad he saw there was a row of skull and crossbones running down the length of it. "There's usually honesty between both partners."

"Fair enough. But I've come clean now."

"Heard that from you before."

He wanted to slam his fist down on the table but stopped himself and just clenched his hands instead. "I'm trying to be open but most of the people I've cared about...well, Paul and my dad are dead. I'm not keeping stuff from you to hurt you. I wish you could see that."

"If you were just a jerk I'd walk away no problem, but you're not. You talk to me about *Star Wars* and sit next to me when I write. Try to get into a trance to talk to the dead... That guy isn't one I thought had to keep secrets."

God, the truth hurt. He couldn't keep being defensive. He had to tell her what he felt. Show her why he'd be scared.

"There are maybe a handful of people on this planet I care for and you are one of them."

"Thank you. I care about you too," she said quietly. "I'm not just hanging on to my anger to be a bitch. Sex with you, that's easy and fun and no regrets. Sleeping with you is something else. Maybe we moved too fast. There is so much else going on.

"You are dealing with the past and the grief you never let yourself express when Paul died. I think you need to process that first."

She was right. But that didn't change the way he felt about her. Or the fact that she was shoving him away.

"Probably. But there is a part of me that believes you were waiting for me to mess up."

She opened her mouth and then closed it. Her arms wrapped more tightly around her chest as she took several deep breaths.

Yeah, that was a bit on the nose. But he wasn't the only one who was fumbling their way around here and making mistakes. She was too.

"When you care for another person the way I do about

250 Ghost of a Chance

you…you give them some grace. Take the screwups but stay together. If not, what's the point of letting anyone in?" he asked.

She was too important to him to just let her walk away. Though she'd stay to finish this thing with the textbook, it wouldn't be the same. She was already wrapping herself back into her armor and retreating. The energy in the room had changed in the last thirty minutes.

For the first time he didn't feel her curiosity and her passion. She'd shut down. Completely locked herself away.

"You're right." The words were softly spoken and quiet.

"Great, because being right is what matters," he said sarcastically.

"Hear me out. I've been sitting over here acting like the injured party when there are things I haven't told you."

What?

"Anything big?" he queried, wanting to know if her secret like his had nothing to do with who they were now.

Jasper had knocked her off from the first. Pushing her in ways she doubted he'd recognize. Tapping her into the supernatural in a way she'd honestly never expected.

He was right, she had been waiting. She'd found her nice, safe routine and settled into her life. Writing books that gave her a chance to live out her favorite goth girl fantasies. Living next to her mom who'd step in if things got too tough.

Just existing until she'd gone back to his place and they'd kissed. Magic had wrapped around her as steadily as Jasper's arms had. That ghost had tied the two of them together and as reluctant as she'd been to come on this trip…it had been the adventure she'd always secretly craved.

It was easy to point to Jasper. *You lied to me.* But she'd never been honest. He'd been counting on her to help him with the ghost and she'd never had the ability to do it.

At some point, that should have been made clear to him. Her emotional hideaway was a big comfy sweater that she could tug down to cover her knees when she drew them up to her chest. Just a place where she bundled into herself and hid.

But there was no hiding from Jasper. He pushed her with things like his smile and his big, furry dog. Nothing that had anything to do with why she was scared to really let him in.

That fear came from deep inside. From being a child that one parent didn't want. She could even understand that her father had promised them he'd be a crappy family member because he truly only cared for himself.

It took a lot to admit that…she got it. It was a him thing not a her thing, but still that feeling of not being good enough remained.

A kernel deep inside of her that had been reinforced over time by the relationships she'd allowed herself to fall into. Larry in high school and Buck in college. That had been it. Two risky moves and she'd retreated. And they'd let her.

But Jasper wasn't letting her. He sat across the table from her, looking anxious and sad and worried and mad. Showing her all his emotions without censoring himself because that was how he reacted.

His father had been taken from him and he still took chances. Sure, he sort of rolled over everything in his path and today seeing him with Victor she realized there was still so much to this man she was coming to care for that she didn't know. But it was all good things.

What if there was nothing good left for him to discover about her?

She looked just like her mom and had always feared that

meant that inside she was just like her dad. True, her relationships had ended for things other than her being selfish but she'd picked men who she knew weren't looking for long-term.

"Are you just going to stare at me?"

"No. I don't really believe I have any psychic ability. That thing in Chicago was me starting my period and needing a quick escape. Until I came to this house I had never experienced anything remotely paranormal."

Shaking his head he stood up and put his hands on the table and leaned over toward her. "Why did you pretend with me?"

"You sort of left me no choice…but now… I don't know. I'm hearing a voice from that textbook. Paranormal shit is happening all over the place. Now I'm connected to it and to you."

Turning away from her he put his head against the wall behind him. "You think that's why we got together? The ghost?"

The words were muffled but she heard them clearly.

"No. I mean not for me, but maybe for you. I'm different and probably seem exciting to you."

"For the love of— You are the most frustrating woman I've ever met," he said, and pivoted to face her. "I like that you are unique and that you don't play nice. I like you for you."

All of the fear and uncertainty she'd felt about finally telling him dissipated. "I like you too."

"But it scares me that you'll use that excuse to keep me at arm's length now. I see you, Kirsty. I see the woman you want to be with your temporary tattoos, walking into bookstores, talking to strangers and unraveling puzzles like your fictional character does. And that frightens you."

"Seeing me is the last thing I want you to do." It wasn't lost on her that the conversation had turned entirely personal and not about the ghost at all. Maybe it had never been about that.

"Why the hell not? You don't want to be invisible, Kirsty."

It had taken her a long time to feel comfortable in her skin. Telling him that there were things about herself she didn't like…wasn't what she wanted to do. But she'd demanded honesty from him and he'd delivered it in spades.

"There are things I don't like about myself. You're not wrong when you said I was looking for you to screw up. Waiting and watching so I could be right to not let myself feel safe in your arms. To not let myself admit how much you mean to me. There, happy?"

"I mean thanks for the truth, but honestly do you think so little of me that you think a few flaws would make me not like you?"

"It's not a few flaws. I am really judgy and I hold on to my anger. I'm not going to pretend I can just let things go. I'm mad you didn't tell me about the short story and how you were working with Paul even knowing I hadn't told you I have no psychic ability."

As soon as the words left her mouth the overhead lights flickered and then a bulb exploded at the other end of the table.

"The ghost disagrees," Jasper said.

He came around the table and pulled her into his arms. "You can't scare me off."

Twenty-Two

Sleep eluded her, so she spent the night writing and then reapplying the temporary tattoo that had almost worn off. Staring at her chest and arms in the bathroom mirror, covered in art that mattered to her, made it a lot easier for her to see. This *was* her true self. But at home she tried to ignore it. Tried to hide that she was K.L. Henson.

She might not care what other people thought but there was that part of her that was always trying to blend in. Pretending to be something she wasn't. Her time in Burlington had shown her that wasn't necessary. Here she was just herself.

How had she never noticed that she wasn't comfortable in her own skin in the small Southern town she and her mom had settled in. She'd stayed there because she had desperately wanted a place to call home.

But it wasn't the right place. She shouldn't be living where she couldn't always be herself.

Judge Judy shouted "Baloney!" at 6:00 a.m. The usual song and dance of Jasper shuffling downstairs with Chewie made her smile.

She'd missed him last night. The bed felt too big without him next to her. Something that had never bothered her before she'd let him sleep with her. Sourly she pounded out a really intense scene in her book where Eva confronted her longtime friend for betraying her.

Kirsty hadn't planned on Crispin doing that, but as the words poured out of her, it was definitely where the story needed to go. Eva had her own secrets, but it felt cathartic to let her rip into Crispin. The way that Kirsty had wanted to let Jasper have it last night. But in real life that kind of argument left too much emotional debris.

Holding her tongue wasn't something she usually did, but she went easy on him because she had her own secrets.

But. No use rehashing that. Today was a new day. She was happy with her pages, and when she looked at the clock it was already after nine.

Gia texted to remind her that she had a book signing and talk at two that afternoon. Then we have an appointment in town at the space that used to be Peterson's Used Books. The former owner was going to meet them afterward to check out the physics textbook and try to identify it.

Staying in her room was beginning to feel cowardly, so she got her bag with her book signing stuff before going into the kitchen. She heard voices in the living room and wanted to avoid any awkward confrontation.

Jasper stood at the back door, head down, talking to Chewie.

"Out or in, I'm not standing here all day," he said to the dog.

But Kirsty knew he didn't mean it. He'd do whatever the dog needed him to. Maybe that was what was bothering her so much about him.

Jasper was usually *that guy*. The one who cheered her up

when she had a rough moment, or made her laugh just by being silly, or turned her on by looking at her. He was always trying to help.

"Out, Chewie," she said firmly. The dog needed a command instead of options.

Jasper peered over at her, and he had glasses on. He looked somehow sexier than she'd expected. He opened the door again and Chewie went out to do his business.

"Since when do you wear glasses?"

"Since I didn't sleep last night and my eyes are too scratchy for contacts," he said, following Chewie out the door.

He wasn't ready to make nice with her. Feeling as if she were the injured party, she'd let herself forget that she'd lied to him too.

Especially since she hadn't figured out if bridging it was a smart thing to do. But this morning had been a clarion call showing her that her life needed a change. She'd sort of hoped that Jasper would have been his old normal self this morning, that this would be easy.

He came back in with Chewie who shook himself off, trotted over to her. She bent to pet the dog.

"Gia mentioned that Pete from the used bookstore is going to meet you later today. Do I need to be there?" he asked.

"Only if you want to," she said. Though she'd hoped he'd come. Seeing him would make all the difference.

"My mom is driving over and I want to make sure she's settled in her hotel."

"Why is your mom coming here?" Kirsty asked.

"It's my birthday tomorrow," he said.

"Oh, I didn't realize." That one stung a little.

"Why would you?" he asked her, washing his hands and then leaning against the counter.

This was one of those moments where her life shuddered to a halt and her head got light and it was hard to think. Whatever happened next would determine if she and Jasper were able to move past this or if they'd part ways as onetime lovers.

It had been a long time since she'd allowed herself to feel this much for a man. But Jasper with his dreamy blue eyes, high cheekbones and quirky personality had charmed his way into her life and into her heart.

There was no denying it. Or what she wanted. She'd never asked to stay, or anyone to stay with her. But now it seemed important that she did. She'd always thought she was content with the loneliness she'd cultivated in her life…but she wasn't. Not anymore.

Jasper had spent a lot of time thinking about everything that she'd said the night before. He'd replayed it, done things differently, but in the end it was up to her if she wanted to move past this.

He did, but he was tired and cranky. His mom was here to celebrate another birthday. And this morning, as Jasper performed his usual routine, he realized that he finally knew what he wanted from his life.

It wasn't a career change or a big upheaval. It was simply to have someone with him. Not just any someone—Kirsty.

But she had to be willing to meet him halfway.

She studied him with those unreadable, serious dark eyes of hers. What was next? Was this where she told him goodbye?

"I guess I figured we knew each other better than that," she said. "That this was more than temporary."

His heart almost stopped beating. Then redoubled, pounding so hard he struggled to hear anything. Had she?

"This isn't easy for me to admit but you were right. I was

waiting for you to screw up so I'd have a reason to push you away. That's not something I wanted to hear you say." She put her hand on her hip, which was hugged by a formfitting black turtleneck sweater.

"What are you getting at?"

"I want to do a *Star Wars* marathon after we leave here. I want to see you regularly. What do you think?"

Chewie was looking back and forth between the two of them as they talked. Jasper's heart was still racing. The fact that she stood before him right now was a lot. "I want that too and a lot more. Last night after you left I kept thinking I shouldn't have let you walk away. We should have hashed things out."

"I wasn't in the mood to. I needed time."

"Yeah, you like to think and analyze shit and then you have a plan," he said. "Is this your plan?"

She grimaced, shaking her head before she took a step closer to him. "Not exactly. This is me improvising and being impulsive."

"Ah…so you have no idea how this will go." He pulled her into his arms, hugging her tightly to him. "I'm an expert in dealing with impulses."

"Are you?" she asked, hugging him back and looking up at him. They were so close he could see those thick lashes framing her brown eyes and the faint dark circles underneath that betrayed her sleepless night.

"A true pro. So now you just have to keep rolling with whatever happens next. Hold on until you can get your feet back under you."

"Aren't they?"

"Not yet," he said, lifting her off her feet, spinning until he leaned against the counter again and her body rested on his. He brought his mouth down on hers and kissed her with all of the passion and love that had been bottled inside of him for too long.

She kissed him back, her hand on the back of his neck, holding him to her.

"I love you, Kirsty."

"You do?" she asked.

"Yeah. I do," he said. Those weren't words he uttered often or easily. There weren't many people he truly loved.

"Wow. I wasn't…that is… I don't know…"

He had thrown her off balance again, never seen her so flustered. He set her on her feet as she tried to process what he said and maybe what she felt for him. He wanted her to love him back, but he knew that life didn't always work out that way. She might care for him but love was different to everyone.

"It's okay. I'm not expecting you to say it back."

She worried her lower lip, eyebrows knit together. "Why is that okay?"

"I didn't say it so you'd say it back. When you feel it, it'll just feel natural to say it back."

Gia walked in. "Sorry. Didn't realize you two were…talking?"

"Yeah. What's up?" he asked her. Later he would deal with the hurt that she hadn't fallen in love with him the same way he had for her. But right now he was rolling with it. Impulsively telling a woman that he'd had a huge fight with the night before that he actually couldn't live without her might not have been his best idea.

But honestly? He couldn't have kept his feelings unsaid for another minute.

"Pete can't meet us later at the used bookstore and is coming here instead. Who has the book?"

"I left it in the living room, isn't it there?" Jasper asked her. Glad for the distraction. "I'll go look for it."

He was halfway across the kitchen before Kirsty called out to him.

Glancing over his shoulder, he immediately saw the fear in her eyes along with something he'd only caught in her expression once before. When he'd sat next to her on the floor of her room, while she tried to commune with the ghost.

"Yes?"

"I do too," she said. "I definitely do too."

He smiled at her, nodding. "We can chat more later."

"Count on it," she said.

Suddenly all that rudderless drifting that he'd done since Paul's death took a deeper meaning. What if he'd been drifting until he met her? What if it was fate, or magical coincidence, that allowed him to find what he'd been looking for all along?

Pete was a nice older man who claimed he remembered every book he'd sold, which Kirsty felt like was a stretch. But he was kind as he flipped through the old textbook. It gave her something to concentrate on so she wasn't replaying her love confession on a loop in her head.

Well her half confession. It was harder than she thought to get those words out of her mouth. She texted love ya and those funny memojis holding up heart fingers to her mom and her friends all the time, but other than that Kirsty had never told anyone she loved them.

She hadn't even experienced anything like this before. It was hard to think about anything but Jasper.

"I'm guessing this book was on a table that I kept in the front of the store. Everything for $5. I stamped them when they came in just for tracking purposes. But these books never sold. I'm guessing it was out-of-date when it came to me," he said. "Sorry I can't be of more help."

Flipping the cover open he saw the sketch of the tree and tapped it. "Wait. I think a visiting professor picked this up… can't remember his name but he stayed at the suite hotel out by the interstate for his lecture. He'd used this text as a student and wanted this as one as a refresher. Yeah. This is definitely the same one."

They were going to have to take a trip to the hotel to see if they'd kept good records. And would be willing to share the information with a couple of amateur ghost hunters. "Do you remember when that was?"

"I brought all of my ledgers with me. They are out in the car." He got up and Dan went with him to help carry them back.

Gia was on her phone, likely answering work emails. Her friend never stopped working. While Gia was distracted, Jasper came and sat on the arm of her chair. "I want to talk after this."

"I do too," he said. "But visiting professor…that might be the lead we've been waiting for."

"Yeah. Maybe. Though I'm not talking about the book."

"Oh, I know," he said, winking at her.

She punched his thigh. This was a huge deal for her. There he was all smiles and acting like a man in love. She needed to say those words to him, too. To look into his eyes and tell him how she felt.

But Dan and Pete were back before she could. Jasper got up to help them as there were three more boxes of ledgers. They were old accounting ledgers that had seen better days, full of dust. She and Gia each started going through the books while the men brought in the rest.

"Guy definitely could use some handwriting lessons," Gia said.

"Yeah, it's hard to read, but damn, it's thorough. I think we can rule out these from the '80s since the book wasn't published until the 1990s. He mentioned it was out of date when it was on the table and Professor Thompson said late '90s or he might have been wrong, could be the early 2000s so maybe start with '95?"

"Yeah. I'll do them, here's '96."

Forty minutes later Jasper found it in a ledger from 2000. The book had been purchased by Professor Hillerman. He also bought two old John le Carré novels and left his number in case Pete got a copy of *Timeline* by Michael Crichton in.

"Hillerman," Gia said, typing on her phone, no doubt doing a search to find the professor.

They thanked Pete and Kirsty carried one of the boxes back to his car with him. "Do you miss running the store?"

After looking through his journal she realized that he'd done more than just sell books. He knew his customers and their tastes. She'd read some of the notes he made of titles he thought a certain reader would like.

"Some days. I miss the people but not doing the books and dealing with the Main Street collective. They were always having meetings about theming our windows and all of that."

"I bet. That's not my kind of thing either," she said.

"The boy said you were an author."

"Yeah. Cozy mysteries. My heroine works in a bakery and talks to dead people," she said.

His grin got bigger. He took her name and she gave him a bookmark with a QR code for a free short story. After he left, Jasper came outside with Chewie. Dan and Gia were in the house and Kirsty took advantage of it.

She tried to rehearse what she'd say in her head. Things just worked better when she had a plan except this morning. He smiled at her. She just rolled her eyes and shook her head.

"I love you."

"I love you too," he said.

"I know."

"You do?"

"Yeah. You told me."

"I did. Glad you did too," he said.

There was a feeling blooming inside of her, like sunshine breaking through a cloudy sky, and she felt hot and excited and couldn't stop smiling even though nothing had changed. But everything had.

"I have my book signing," she said.

"Dan and I are going to go to the hotel and see what else we can find out about Hillerman."

Of course they were. "Tonight I'm going to try another séance and see if it's him." Maybe now that she had the right name, things would go differently.

"Good idea. I'll help you. You might think you don't have any ability. But there is something that happens when you go into the trance. I can feel it and I think Gia can as well. You have something."

"It's scary to think that I do. Almost as scary as falling in love," she said.

"That's not scary, because you're not alone," he said, leaning down and touching her cheek.

No, maybe it wasn't so scary after all.

Twenty-Three

The bookstore was decked out for Halloween with pumpkins in the window, horror and paranormal books on the tables near the front, and fake spiderwebs draping the bookcases.

Tim had space at the back of the store for her. There was a table and chair for her as well as chairs for guests. Some people were already waiting. Nervous tension made her stomach ache for a second. Then she took a deep breath as one of the readers shyly smiled at her.

"We have a few bigger book influencers driving over to see you. I'm going to ask you a few questions about your writing process and then we'll talk about your latest release," Tim said.

"Sounds good to me," she said, taking her place at the front. Her phone pinged and she glanced down to see a text from Jasper.

Jasper: Wish I was there with you. Smash your talk! Love you.

She hearted his text.

Kirsty: Any leads at the hotel?

Jasper: Yeah. Hillerman had a heart attack while staying here. I called his wife and she said he was always loaning out his books to students who forgot theirs. He'd never have gone into a textbook.

Kirsty: Shit.

Jasper: Yeah. We can talk about it more tonight. I think your séance idea is a good one.

Kirsty: Thnx. Love you.

He hearted the text and she put her phone away.

The book signing and talk went really well. She took photos with a few readers who'd come just to meet her and then took them out for coffee after to keep talking. It was fun and didn't involve the ghost-infested textbook that had been dominating her life recently.

"I saw on your socials that you're working on the next book," Jane said.

"I am, it was sort of slow going but recently I made a breakthrough and it's really flying along now," she said.

"Do you think Crispin and Eva are ever going to get together?" Lori asked.

Given the scene she'd just written and the underlying tension between the two characters... "Maybe. Neither of them really knows how to be in a relationship. So they're struggling to figure that out," she said. Thinking about herself and Jasper. They'd been struggling as well.

Her new friends left a few minutes later. Kirsty noticed

266 Ghost of a Chance

that there was a big chocolate cupcake in the pastry case. "I'll be right back."

Gia nodded without looking up from her phone where she was posting the photos from the event. The cupcake would be a nice surprise for Jasper. A way to show him she cared even if he couldn't be there today.

Being in love didn't mean their lives would magically blend together. Would she even want that?

That had never been her. She liked her silence and her space and doing things her own way. It didn't seem like Jasper's preference either.

Love wasn't the end, but the beginning of a new phase.

She had the cupcake wrapped up in a box. No one was expecting her to have a plan for the future a few hours after Jasper told her he loved her. But that part of her that had moved so much as a child, the one that craved a home, wanted it.

Wanted something more. *Star Wars* marathons, late-night writing sessions, and what if this psychic thing didn't go away after they freed the ghost from the book?

"You good?"

"Yeah. Got everything up online. Is the book really coming along?" Gia asked as they walked back to the car. "I thought you said it had stalled."

"Yeah, being here has helped me write. Also the whole haunted textbook saga gave me new ideas. Like what if Eva's powers weren't working. How would she solve the case without her ghost friends?"

"Love that. Keeps the character fresh," Gia said. "So…"

Gia was the closest friend she had but talking about being in love made her feel a little shy. "So?"

"You and Jasper?"

Her and Jasper. A little thrill went through her. They were a couple now.

She unlocked her car and Gia got into the passenger seat as Kirsty put the cupcake carefully in the back seat so it wouldn't get crushed. This was the first birthday she was spending with him and she wanted it to be special.

"Are you pretending you didn't hear me?"

"I heard you. I'm just not sure what to say."

Gia laughed, a soft tinkling sound that made Kirsty smile as she started the car. Gia wasn't going to push things. But if she wanted to talk she knew her friend was there.

"Girl."

The way Gia spoke made Kirsty blush. "I know, right? We're sort of seeing each other."

"Naked?"

"Gia!"

"So yes. Great. I like him and you two are cute together," Gia said.

They were, she thought. Jasper was a nice yin to her yang or whichever way that went. They fit together even though she wouldn't have expected it after their night at the Dead Boys' concert.

When they got back to the house there was a new car parked out front. The lights were on which did nothing to distract from the overall run-down slightly creepy vibe the house gave off.

"Who's that?" Gia asked.

"Might be Jasper's mom. It's his birthday tomorrow and she's here to celebrate," Kirsty said.

"That why you got the cupcake?"

"Yeah. Maybe we should leave them alone," Kirsty said. Loving Jasper was still too new to want to meet his mom.

268 Ghost of a Chance

That should be something that happens much later in the relationship.

"No way. I mean the way Jasper talks about her I want to meet her," Gia said. "I know you do too."

"You don't know that."

Gia wasn't wrong. Kirsty was curious about Jasper's mom. She wanted to know more about the man she loved and how he'd grown up. Of course, she would hate it if her own mom were here. Her mom never knew when to keep things to herself.

Jasper's mom and Victor were in the living room while Dan was in the dining room editing more footage. He'd captured more of the energetic figure moving around the room at 6:00 a.m.

"Why are you here?"

"On the eve of your birth, where else would I be?" his mom said. "I was in labor for six hours."

"That's not too bad, right?" Jasper said. Like he hadn't heard this story every year of his life. But he was understanding of her need to relive and reframe it. This was a hard time for his mom. She'd lost his dad at the same time he was born.

"Dude, that's not cool. Your mom went through a lot to bring you into the world," Victor said.

"I'm grateful, Mommy, you know that," he said, her resulting smile lighting up her face. She loved hearing the childish term of endearment, and it was his way of letting her know he loved her without having to say it. She blew him a kiss.

"So what's all this about a haunted textbook?" she asked.

"Victor told you?"

"It came up when I mentioned you called me. Which was a total shock to both of us," Victor said.

"It was," his mom agreed. "Are you okay?"

"Yeah, Mom. I'm fine. The book… I think it was Paul's. We were working on Dad's short story trying to finish figuring out the fictional quantum transference. Paul was doing the physics and I was working on the last few pages for you. So it would be complete."

"Ah, that's sweet," she said tears in her voice. "Dad was excited about his writing. He wanted to find a way to stop working at the hotel for extra money. Make teaching and writing his full-time gigs once he graduated. He always said…" she came over to him and touched his cheek. "That he wanted you to know making a living wasn't the only thing to life. You should go after your dreams."

Hugging his mom, he put his head on the top of hers. "I needed to hear that."

"Did Paul figure it out?" she asked.

"The theory isn't provable," Jasper said. "But since the night Paul died, actually when I got my own place in Chicago crazy stuff started happening. Lights going on and off in the kitchen and every day the TV comes on tuned to *Judge Judy*."

"Your ghost you talked about. You thought it was Paul?"

"Who else could it be?" Though he wasn't sure anymore. Professor Hillerman would have been a solid plan B but his wife was positive he wasn't hanging around.

They heard a car drive up. A zing went through him as he realized that Kirsty was back. Victor and his mom looked over at him.

"Kirsty and Gia."

Chewie got up when he heard the front door and Jasper went to the hall wanting to warn Kirsty about his mom. Not that he was embarrassed for either woman to meet the other, but his mom was his biggest fan and often talked about him in a way that was too oversharing. Plus, he didn't want her to think of her as one of those cringey "boy mom" types.

"My mom and Victor are here," he said. "What's that?"

"A treat for later. I can't wait to meet your mom."

He pulled her against his side and kissed her. Gia just smirked at them as she walked into the living room to introduce herself.

"Missed you," he said against her lips. Now that he'd told her how he felt, there was no holding back. He didn't have to pretend that he didn't want to be around her all the time.

"Me too."

Holding her hand, he led her into the living room. "Mom, this is Kirsty. Kirsty, this is Tina, my mom."

"Nice to meet you. You're the psychic helping Jaz with the book?" she asked.

"Uh, yeah. I mean I'm an author with maybe some psychic ability. He brought his book to the interview and we ended up here."

"Wow, that must have been a lot. What book is it?" his mom asked.

"Let me go and grab it. I put it upstairs hoping we could have a quiet evening," Jasper said.

Dan was in the hallway with a can of beer, looking relaxed. "What's up?"

"I'm bringing the book down for my mom."

Jasper left him to it and continued upstairs to his bedroom but the book wasn't where he'd left it. Frustrated at first then sort of relieved—maybe the book had left the house. Lights flickered on and off in Kirsty's room and he went up the stairs to the attic room.

The book was on the floor in front of the dormer window where Kirsty had done her last séance with it.

"Trying to communicate with her again?" he asked it as he picked it up.

The lights flickered. But that was it. Back downstairs he heard his mom and Kirsty laughing. Staying in the hallway he listened to the two of them. It was a nice sound. He figured his mom would like Kirsty, she liked everyone, but Kirsty was so reserved and usually kept everyone at arm's length.

Turning the corner he entered the room.

"Surprise!"

His mom had a large chocolate cake with the words *Happy 26th Birthday, Jaz* on it. Lit candles were burning and as he entered the room they all started singing "Happy Birthday."

He put the book on the coffee table, smiling. His family had always been small and he'd kept his circle of friends even tighter until this autumn in Burlington. Dan and Gia had become friends and Kirsty had become his girlfriend. Someone he loved.

"Make a wish," his mom said.

"Wish that we find out the identity of our ghost already," Kirsty said sardonically.

Winking at her, he said, "Let me find out who it is, please."

Then he blew the candles out on the cake. They were all extinguished. As bits of smoke lingered, each candle suddenly reignited.

"Mom…really? Relighters?"

"That's not me. These are the cheap ones," she said.

Dan's eyes were wide. "Yeah, there's crazy energy around your cake."

Everyone stared at it and Jasper had no idea what to do next.

"Blow them out again," Kirsty said.

He did and this time they stayed out. Everyone looked uncomfortable. Jasper had no idea how to fix that.

"What was that?"

"The ghost. Jasper's textbook ghost," Kirsty said.

"Did you get the book?"

"Yeah, here it is," he handed it to his mom.

She sank down on the couch, holding it on her lap. Her hands began to shake as she flipped it open, landing on the page with the sketch of the tree. "Where did you get this?"

"I told you it follows me. Why are you asking?"

Tears began to form in his mom's eyes. "It was your dad's. Your dad got an old physics book from a professor who was staying at the hotel. He promised it would be a good basis for your dad to use for his research. High school physics isn't as in-depth as the college level."

Everyone stared at Tina in disbelief.

"How did you not know that?" Kirsty asked Jasper.

"I never saw the book. Mom…did Dad like *Judge Judy*?" he asked her. Right now he wasn't entirely sure what to think. Could it be his dad in the book?

"Yeah. We watched it to wind down when we were cooking dinner. I used to TiVo it. That's what we had to do if we wanted to watch something before streaming," she said, wiping away her lingering tears. "Back in the old days."

Jasper walked over to his mom. "This was Dad's?"

She flipped the book open and fanned the pages, stopping to one midway through that they'd never stopped on before. There were notes in pencil.

Only geniuses understand this.

Only hot girls love geniuses.

"What is this?"

"Me and your dad flirting in class."

That was sweet. He touched the pencil marks and looked at his mom. "How did Paul get the book?"

"It must have been in the box of stuff I gave to you both. I asked Paul to help you finish Dad's story for you, not me. It was time for you to start your own life. The sci-fi short story was the last thing that your dad didn't get to do with you," she said.

She blinked a few times and he hugged her close to him. Kirsty came over and put her hand on the book. Victor did the same.

They both closed their eyes. The pages fluttered and the lights in the room flared brighter for a moment.

Gia came over next to them and Dan kept filming. Jasper felt something strong like a warmth coming into the room even though there wasn't a fire in the fireplace.

A breeze stirred around them and the pages fluttered again.

Kirsty slipped her hand in his. "Put the book on the coffee table and then everyone kneel around it."

His mom set the book down open to the page she'd shown him. His mom on one side, Kirsty on the other side, then Victor, Gia and even Dan came over. Once they were all in position Kirsty looked at him.

"What was your dad's name?" Kirsty asked.

"Jasper Marcus but everyone called him Marc," Tina said.

"Marc, we call on your spirit. You are in a safe place. Your wife and son are here with me," Kirsty said.

Sparks of light emitted from the book and started moving upward from it. They all kept holding hands and Jasper felt the energy pulling in toward the light that slowly formed into the faint outline of a body and then a face. His mom's hand tightened around his.

"Marc?"

274   Ghost of a Chance

The being was hazy and he could just make out the hair that was so like his own. His dad? Was this his dad?

"Dad?"

A hand reached toward him, he felt something cold brush his cheek. Then the ghost—*his father*—touched his mom's face.

The sparks continued moving up as another breeze swept through the room. The candles on the cake flickered back to life.

"Happy birthday, son." The voice, distant but clear, reverberated around the room. The candles went back out as wind swirled around them, and his dad disappeared.

Jasper blinked to keep his tears back but when he looked at his mom and she was crying and hugging him it was impossible. Kirsty's hand was on his back and then she was hugging them too.

He felt Gia and Victor join them and Dan awkwardly patted them all on the back. Then he pulled back.

"Let me check the playback."

As he left Kirsty pulled back. "That was the voice I heard."

"What do you mean?" his mom asked her.

"We did a couple of séances to try to talk to the ghost. He didn't speak out loud, just directly to me," Kirsty said.

Tina smiled at her. "He must have liked you."

"Well, he wasn't too pleased that I was planning to pretend to talk to him," Kirsty said wryly.

"That sounds like him. Honesty was one of his things. I wish I'd known he was in there," Tina said. "I hope I showed you everything he would have wanted."

"You did and more, Mom," Jasper said.

"My gift is going to pale in comparison to your dad showing up," his mom said with a laugh.

The playback from the cameras showed Marc's incorporeal

body disappearing. They also captured the happy birthday on the audio. They all kicked back in the living room eating cake and drinking champagne and talking about the night.

Kirsty came with him when he had to let Chewie out. "I wish I'd realized it was my dad."

"I bet," she said. "What would you have done?"

"Asked him stuff. You know, advice, things like that."

"Maybe he was giving it to you with the lights and the songs. I mean he made them explode a few times to get your attention. Even Judge Judy—her quotes seemed to be picked out for you."

"Yeah." Jasper hugged her close to him. That empty part inside of him had been filled by this woman. Getting rid of the ghost that had been following him around was just the cherry on top. Seeing his dad for that brief moment and hearing his voice.

"I'll never forget this day," he said.

"I won't either. I'm glad that voice was your dad's and not just in my head," she said.

"Afraid I wouldn't still love you if you heard voices?"

"Nah, you like that about me," she said, smacking him on the butt as Chewie came back in.

"I love everything about you," he said.

"I love everything about you too," she replied.

Epilogue

Two years later

Coming back to Burlington to get married at the Airbnb where they'd fallen in love had been Jasper's idea. He had turned out to be a big romantic at heart. They'd done the long-distance thing for a little while. Then she'd moved to Chicago to be closer to him and found a place where she fit.

Her mom had followed, buying a town house near her and Jasper which Kirsty had loved.

Her book series had skyrocketed after the *Live with Bri O'Brien* show segment had aired showing her exorcising Marc from the textbook. Media offers had come in which she'd turned down.

Occasionally she still got feelings when she was in places but she usually just walked away from them. They were married in the backyard of the house. The trees were all orange, brown and yellow. There was a tent set up for the reception.

Kirsty's dress was black because it was her. Jasper's smile

was huge when he saw her in the figure-hugging dress with the sweetheart neckline.

Their first dance was the Dead Boys' song they'd danced to the first night they met and only their close friends and family understood why there was a university physics textbook on the cake table.

Victor pulled them aside to give them a small, wrapped gift.

"What's this?"

"This was Paul's favorite book; he was rereading it when he died. I figured you'd like it since he brought the two of you together."

"Thanks," Kirsty said.

"And it was my dad not Paul," Jasper said.

The lights flickered above them and they both looked from the book back to Victor who cracked up.

"That was Gia," he said with a laugh and a wink as he walked away.

Jasper pulled her into his arms. "I don't mind being haunted now that I have my own ghost buster."

"You do have me," she promised, not sure she wanted to be called a ghost buster.

"I love you," he said.

"I love you, too."

★ ★ ★ ★ ★

Acknowledgements

This book!! Some ideas just take hold of me when I start to write them making it a total pleasure to write. This book poured out of me so fast I couldn't keep up with it at times. I'm not a particular fan of scary stuff so I knew if I wrote a ghost story it would be more spooky, cozy rather than frightening. To be honest weird cozy is sort of my happy place.

I grew up on the edge of the Green Swamp. My childhood was full of stories and places more than television or movies. So I have to thank my sisters, Donna and Linda, who were my partners in crime. We spent our days running wild through the orange groves at our house, playing in the swinging tree and making up things as we went along. That time laid the groundwork for me being a writer today.

Talking to Courtney every day gives me so many fresh ideas and a chance to express opinions. I love our debates on *The Last Jedi* and everything *Star Wars*. Also love you!

I have to thank my kids for watching so much *Scooby-Doo* and *A Pup Named Scrappy-Doo* when they were little. I've always loved mysteries and things that are a little bit odd so pitching this idea to my editor was sort of a no-brainer for me.

Luckily they liked the idea and all I had to do was start writing. I want to thank Joss and Tina for sprinting with me every day while I was working on *Ghost of a Chance*. While I was driven to get the story down on paper, it always helps to have someone to chat with while working. Our daily sprints really help me feel connected and on track.

Thank you as well for picking up this book. If this is your first book by me I hope you enjoyed it and will check out further titles. If you've been reading my books for a while: an extra special thank-you to *you*. I'm sure if we met in real life we'd have some fun conversations and laughs as we must see the world very similarly.

Until next time.
Katherine

LET'S TALK

Romance

For exclusive extracts, competitions and special offers, find us online:

f MillsandBoon

X @MillsandBoon

⬤ @MillsandBoonUK

♪ @MillsandBoonUK

Get in touch on 01413 063 232

For all the latest titles coming soon, visit
millsandboon.co.uk/nextmonth

MILLS & BOON TRUE LOVE IS HAVING A MAKEOVER!

Introducing

Love Always

Swoon-worthy romances, where love takes centre stage. Same heartwarming stories, stylish new look!

Look out for our brand new look

OUT NOW

MILLS & BOON

FOUR BRAND NEW BOOKS FROM
MILLS & BOON MODERN

Indulge in desire, drama, and breathtaking romance – where passion knows no bounds!

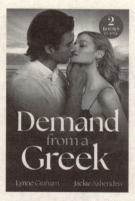
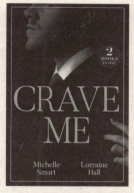
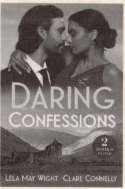

OUT NOW

Eight Modern stories published every month, find them all at:
millsandboon.co.uk

Afterglow Books is a trend-led, trope-filled list of books with diverse, authentic and relatable characters, a wide array of voices and representations, plus real world trials and tribulations. Featuring all the tropes you could possibly want (think small-town settings, fake relationships, grumpy vs sunshine, enemies to lovers) and all with a generous dose of spice in every story.

♪ @millsandboonuk
◎ @millsandboonuk
afterglowbooks.co.uk
#AfterglowBooks

For all the latest book news, exclusive content and giveaways scan the QR code below to sign up to the Afterglow newsletter:

Looking for more Afterglow Books?

Try the perfect subscription for spicy romance lovers and save 50% on your first parcel.

PLUS receive these additional benefits when you subscribe:
- **FREE** delivery direct to your door
- **EXCLUSIVE** offers every month
- **SAVE** up to 30% on pre-paid subscriptions

SUBSCRIBE AND SAVE

millsandboon.co.uk/Subscribe

MILLS & BOON
THE HEART OF ROMANCE

A ROMANCE FOR EVERY READER

MODERN — Prepare to be swept off your feet by sophisticated, sexy and seductive heroes, in some of the world's most glamourous and romantic locations, where power and passion collide.

HISTORICAL — Escape with historical heroes from time gone by. Whether your passion is for wicked Regency Rakes, muscled Vikings or rugged Highlanders, awaken the romance of the past.

MEDICAL — Set your pulse racing with dedicated, delectable doctors in the high-pressure world of medicine, where emotions run high and passion, comfort and love are the best medicine.

Love Always — Celebrate true love with tender stories of heartfelt romance, from the rush of falling in love to the joy a new baby can bring, and a focus on the emotional heart of a relationship.

HEROES — The excitement of a gripping thriller, with intense romance at its heart. Resourceful, true-to-life women and strong, fearless men face danger and desire - a killer combination!

 — From showing up to glowing up, these characters are on the path to leading their best lives and finding romance along the way – with plenty of sizzling spice!

To see which titles are coming soon, please visit

millsandboon.co.uk/nextmonth

MILLS & BOON
A ROMANCE FOR EVERY READER

- **FREE** delivery direct to your door
- **EXCLUSIVE** offers every month
- **SAVE** up to 30% on pre-paid subscriptions

 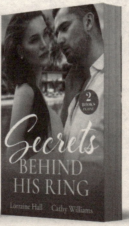 

SUBSCRIBE AND SAVE

millsandboon.co.uk/Subscribe

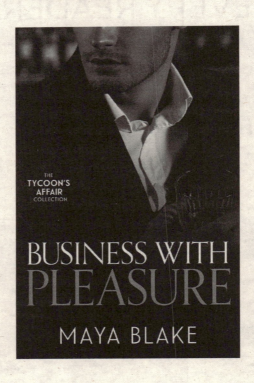